W9-CFD-738

GIRL, TAKEN

(An Ella Dark FBI Suspense Thriller —Book Two)

BLAKE PIERCE

Blake Pierce

Blake Pierce is the USA Today bestselling author of the RILEY PAGE mystery series, which includes seventeen books. Blake Pierce is also the author of the MACKENZIE WHITE mystery series, comprising fourteen books; of the AVERY BLACK mystery series, comprising six books; of the KERI LOCKE mystery series, comprising five books; of the MAKING OF RILEY PAIGE mystery series, comprising six books; of the KATE WISE mystery series, comprising seven books; of the CHLOE FINE psychological suspense mystery, comprising six books; of the JESSE HUNT psychological suspense thriller series, comprising nineteen books; of the AU PAIR psychological suspense thriller series, comprising three books; of the ZOE PRIME mystery series, comprising six books; of the ADELE SHARP mystery series, comprising thirteen books; of the EUROPEAN VOYAGE cozy mystery series, comprising six books (and counting); of the new LAURA FROST FBI suspense thriller, comprising four books (and counting); of the new ELLA DARK FBI suspense thriller, comprising six books (and counting); of the A YEAR IN EUROPE cozy mystery series, comprising nine books); of the AVA GOLD mystery series, comprising three books (and counting); and of the RACHEL GIFT mystery series, comprising three books (and counting).

An avid reader and lifelong fan of the mystery and thriller genres, Blake loves to hear from you, so please feel free to visit www.blakepierceauthor.com to learn more and stay in touch.

Copyright © 2021 by Blake Pierce. All rights reserved. Except as permitted under the U.S. Copyright Act of 1976, no part of this publication may be reproduced, distributed or transmitted in any form or by any means, or stored in a database or retrieval system, without the prior permission of the author. This ebook is licensed for your personal enjoyment only. This ebook may not be re-sold or given away to other people. If you would like to share this book with another person, please purchase an additional copy for each recipient. If you're reading this book and did not purchase it, or it was not purchased for your use only, then please return it and purchase your own copy. Thank you for respecting the hard work of this author. This is a work of fiction. Names, characters, businesses, organizations, places, events, and incidents either are the product of the author's imagination or are used fictionally. Any resemblance to actual persons, living or dead, is entirely coincidental. Jacket image Copyright spacedrone808, used under license from Shutterstock.com.
ISBN: 978-1-0943-9161-8

BOOKS BY BLAKE PIERCE

RACHEL GIFT MYSTERY SERIES
HER LAST WISH (Book #1)
HER LAST CHANCE (Book #2)
HER LAST HOPE (Book #3)

AVA GOLD MYSTERY SERIES
CITY OF PREY (Book #1)
CITY OF FEAR (Book #2)
CITY OF BONES (Book #3)

A YEAR IN EUROPE
A MURDER IN PARIS (Book #1)
DEATH IN FLORENCE (Book #2)
VENGEANCE IN VIENNA (Book #3)
A FATALITY IN SPAIN (Book #4)
SCANDAL IN LONDON (Book #5)
AN IMPOSTOR IN DUBLIN (Book #6)
SEDUCTION IN BORDEAUX (Book #7)
JEALOUSY IN SWITZERLAND (Book #8)
A DEBACLE IN PRAGUE (Book #9)

ELLA DARK FBI SUSPENSE THRILLER
GIRL, ALONE (Book #1)
GIRL, TAKEN (Book #2)
GIRL, HUNTED (Book #3)
GIRL, SILENCED (Book #4)
GIRL, VANISHED (Book 5)
GIRL ERASED (Book #6)

LAURA FROST FBI SUSPENSE THRILLER
ALREADY GONE (Book #1)
ALREADY SEEN (Book #2)
ALREADY TRAPPED (Book #3)
ALREADY MISSING (Book #4)

EUROPEAN VOYAGE COZY MYSTERY SERIES
MURDER (AND BAKLAVA) (Book #1)
DEATH (AND APPLE STRUDEL) (Book #2)
CRIME (AND LAGER) (Book #3)
MISFORTUNE (AND GOUDA) (Book #4)
CALAMITY (AND A DANISH) (Book #5)
MAYHEM (AND HERRING) (Book #6)

ADELE SHARP MYSTERY SERIES
LEFT TO DIE (Book #1)
LEFT TO RUN (Book #2)
LEFT TO HIDE (Book #3)
LEFT TO KILL (Book #4)
LEFT TO MURDER (Book #5)
LEFT TO ENVY (Book #6)
LEFT TO LAPSE (Book #7)
LEFT TO VANISH (Book #8)
LEFT TO HUNT (Book #9)
LEFT TO FEAR (Book #10)
LEFT TO PREY (Book #11)
LEFT TO LURE (Book #12)
LEFT TO CRAVE (Book #13)

THE AU PAIR SERIES
ALMOST GONE (Book#1)
ALMOST LOST (Book #2)
ALMOST DEAD (Book #3)

ZOE PRIME MYSTERY SERIES
FACE OF DEATH (Book#1)
FACE OF MURDER (Book #2)
FACE OF FEAR (Book #3)
FACE OF MADNESS (Book #4)
FACE OF FURY (Book #5)
FACE OF DARKNESS (Book #6)

A JESSIE HUNT PSYCHOLOGICAL SUSPENSE SERIES
THE PERFECT WIFE (Book #1)
THE PERFECT BLOCK (Book #2)
THE PERFECT HOUSE (Book #3)
THE PERFECT SMILE (Book #4)

RILEY PAIGE MYSTERY SERIES
ONCE GONE (Book #1)
ONCE TAKEN (Book #2)
ONCE CRAVED (Book #3)
ONCE LURED (Book #4)
ONCE HUNTED (Book #5)
ONCE PINED (Book #6)
ONCE FORSAKEN (Book #7)
ONCE COLD (Book #8)
ONCE STALKED (Book #9)
ONCE LOST (Book #10)
ONCE BURIED (Book #11)
ONCE BOUND (Book #12)
ONCE TRAPPED (Book #13)
ONCE DORMANT (Book #14)
ONCE SHUNNED (Book #15)
ONCE MISSED (Book #16)
ONCE CHOSEN (Book #17)

MACKENZIE WHITE MYSTERY SERIES
BEFORE HE KILLS (Book #1)
BEFORE HE SEES (Book #2)
BEFORE HE COVETS (Book #3)
BEFORE HE TAKES (Book #4)
BEFORE HE NEEDS (Book #5)
BEFORE HE FEELS (Book #6)
BEFORE HE SINS (Book #7)
BEFORE HE HUNTS (Book #8)
BEFORE HE PREYS (Book #9)
BEFORE HE LONGS (Book #10)
BEFORE HE LAPSES (Book #11)
BEFORE HE ENVIES (Book #12)
BEFORE HE STALKS (Book #13)
BEFORE HE HARMS (Book #14)

AVERY BLACK MYSTERY SERIES
CAUSE TO KILL (Book #1)
CAUSE TO RUN (Book #2)
CAUSE TO HIDE (Book #3)
CAUSE TO FEAR (Book #4)
CAUSE TO SAVE (Book #5)

CAUSE TO DREAD (Book #6)

KERI LOCKE MYSTERY SERIES
A TRACE OF DEATH (Book #1)
A TRACE OF MUDER (Book #2)
A TRACE OF VICE (Book #3)
A TRACE OF CRIME (Book #4)
A TRACE OF HOPE (Book #5)

PROLOGUE

Nothing but open fields, and that was how she liked it.

It was 7am, on the cusp of winter daybreak. Claire entered the park to the tapping of her running shoes. Not a soul in any direction. Just rows of trees on either side of her, and behind them a stretch of greenery which extended beyond her vision. There was nothing quite like exercise in the morning, despite the chilly weather. She had no idea how people could just up-and-go about their day without stretching their joints, pumping their blood, enlivening the endorphins. Without it, she thought, there was no enjoyment to life. Lethargy was the silent killer, and she'd make sure that it would never creep up on her like it did for so many.

Green Valley Park was so vast that one could run for two hours and not see the same area twice. Claire usually followed the same route whenever she found herself here, but today she decided to mix things up for the sake of variety.

It's Friday, she thought. *Let's celebrate.*

She jogged up the path and took a hard right past a children's play area. Like always, she kept her vision pointed straight ahead. She couldn't bear the sight of anything to do with children, not since the operation. It brought up too many alien emotions that she struggled to control. Even worse was when she saw a discarded pushchair, or a child's shoe lying in the road. There was something about these visuals that filled her with dread, heartache. A longing for something she wanted but couldn't have.

Claire thought that perhaps this new fitness kick was a result of her discovery that children were not in her future. In the three months since her finding, she'd come around to the idea. Accepted it for the truth that it was, and no amount of well-timed lovemaking or medical marvels would ever change. That was life. You could only control so much of it.

But once the energy kicked in and she felt that rush, all thoughts of work and stress and circumstances disappeared. It was just her and the open wild, and no one could take that away.

1

A curtain of mist hung above the nearby duck pond. The cold weather had banished any wildlife elsewhere. It was mid-February and winter was in full sway, but there was a hint of springtime lingering beyond the veil. A brief flash of sunshine or freshly sprung daffodil. The idea that brighter mornings and warmer weather might ease the pain of her recent troubles jumped into her mind, but she pushed them to one side to concentrate on the now. *Live in the now, not in the what-might-be,* she told herself.

These pathways had been familiar. A stray from her usual route, but not completely untouched by her pink Nike running shoes in recent weeks. She came to a cross-section with three different directions, and for the first time she continued onward along the same pathway, choosing not to veer left or right. The concrete gave way to a long strip of muddy grass, leading downward and round across a small bridge. Beneath her, a river gushed with surprising force. She briefly stopped to admire its crystal waters, then continued on until she reached the flat ground again.

Claire had never seen this part of Green Valley before. She turned back to remind herself where she'd come from but couldn't make out much since sunrise was still around thirty minutes away. A little brightness was present on this morning, but darkness had a majority seat. She still had two hours before work began, so there was time to indulge in some adventure. Besides, she was hoping that there'd be an exit back on to the road down here. Green Valley had so many ins and outs, she doubted even the rangers knew them all.

Things turned darker down here. The Ironwood trees reached higher, the shrubbery denser. Veering from the pathway onto a stretch of grass, a sense of claustrophobia began to creep in. The grass made less impact on her feet, so she was glad of the respite, but she decided that if she couldn't find an exit in this section, she'd make a return journey to familiar territory.

Something made her stop. Right there amidst a copse of trees. She stopped and listened to her own breathing for a second, then took a drink from her flask. She surveyed her surroundings, spotting some outdoor gym equipment, rusted to the point of collapse. The unfamiliar terrain jolted a sudden fight or flight response. Something told her to get the hell out of there.

It was pure intuition, the same thing that told her what the doctors were going to say before they said it. The same thing that told her that her husband still loved her despite her limitations.

The trees rustled. Not from the wind shaking their crests, but down below near the ground. Right next to her.

Then there was movement. A shadow passed beside her, rustling through leaves and stomping through the plant life at their feet. She saw a human outline, face concealed with a grey hood and no workout clothing to speak of. Whoever it was, they weren't here for the same reason as everyone else in a public park at 7am.

The figure rushed past, keeping their face down towards the ground. Claire watched them disappear down the route she came from, then quickly turned around and continued on her way. Something made her feel uneasy here. Maybe it was the unfamiliar tracks, or the way this part of the valley felt lower, more unobserved. She always trusted her gut, so she began to scout around for an exit.

But Claire caught something in her peripheral vision. Among the green and brown blurs up above, there was an unnatural sight. She stopped dead in her tracks, rubbed the sweat from her eyes and made sure that she wasn't hallucinating.

She edged closer, convincing herself that the visual in front of her was a construct of her imagination. A cluster of leaves, a few broken branches, a disturbed bird's nest – all combined to resemble the image of an outstretched human.

No. She saw the arms, legs, shoes, clothes. She saw the face, the widened eyes and the dropped jaw.

Claire dropped her flask. Her hand sprung to her mouth to conceal a scream.

There was a dead body hanging from the tree.

She didn't know how long she'd been staring in fright, but the rising sun cast new light on her discovery.

This corpse had not only been strung up but displayed. Arms and legs were extended, attached to different tree branches. The mid-section had been tied to the main trunk. Claire was sure that the dead woman's longish brown hair had been combed.

She composed herself, and as she backtracked to get a clearer view, something made her jump back in fright.

"Jesus Christ," a voice shouted.

Two people appeared beside her. Young men. They stared with the same combination of fascination and horror as Claire had. She tried to say something in response, but no words would form.

Claire scrambled for the phone in her pocket, pulled it out and dialled 911. Someone answered on the first ring.

3

"Nine-one-one, what department please?"

"P-p-police," she said, trying to catch her breath. She was patched through instantly. A man's voice now.

"Nine-one-one, what's your emergency?"

Like vultures around prey, another couple appeared beside her and stared with open jaws.

"Dead body. Green Valley Park," she stuttered. "South area."

"Stay on the line please, ma'am and we'll trace your exact location. What else can you tell me about the body?"

Claire ran over the words in her head, realizing she'd never put such a sentence together in her life. "The body has been tied to the tree."

She looked beside her and saw a man with a young child now staring up at the monstrosity too. Not surprising. Anyone passing by would surely see this.

Then she thought back to the man in the grey hoodie.

Why hadn't he stopped and gawked like everyone else?

CHAPTER ONE

Ella Dark lifted opened the steel door and walked inside the storage unit. This wasn't her ideal way of spending a Saturday morning, but it needed to be done. God knows she'd put it off long enough already.

It had been a long time since she'd last been here, and only now did she realize how much she'd missed the familiar scent of her father's old possessions. There was a part of him still attached to them, somehow. His face shone clearer when she held them. She could see the creases under her eyes and the grey patches in his hair. She could even hear that deep voice of his, full of bass, but still eloquent enough to portray worldliness. It had been 23 years since she last saw him, but she could still envision him as plain as day; the chiselled jaw, the black work-shirt, the hair that was beginning to thin but was still yet to recede. Sometimes, it was hard to believe that it had been over two decades since he'd passed away. It all felt so fresh and so recent, like her memories were carved from impenetrable stone. It was a small comfort to think that if she hadn't forgotten his face by now, she never would.

This would be her last time in this room, Ella thought to herself. The monthly payments for this lockup were significant, and while she hated the idea of discarding her father's belongings for the sake of finances, there came a time when tough decisions had to be made. She rarely had time to visit this place as it was, and while her ambition was to eventually relocate these items to her own home, reality was a different story. Her two-bedroom apartment she shared with Jenna wasn't exactly teeming with open space.

She eyeballed the dusty old container, unsure exactly where to begin the painstaking process of item categorization. One pile to keep, one pile to throw away. That was her plan, although summoning the courage to actually part with any items, no matter how minor, would be a struggle.

Her dad's old books took up most of the far wall, piled high with little grace or order. She glanced at some of the spines and saw classic literary novels, a few woodworking textbooks, a couple of leather-bound hardbacks that resembled occult tomes but were more likely just encyclopaedias and dictionaries. It was a snapshot of life before everyone had all of humankind's information stored in their pockets.

Along the walls was furniture from her childhood home: a wooden cabinet, a few drawers, a small sofa with storage space underneath. Anything that had storage capabilities was transposed from place to place, eventually finding itself in this unit. Ella had never really rummaged through everything before, only briefly looked at items when she wanted to be close to her dad.

"Let's go from left to the right," she said aloud. She was pretty sure there was no one else in the building to hear her mumblings. Aside from a hungover receptionist, she hadn't seen a soul since she parked the van outside. "Gotta be ruthless. I've lived without half of this stuff for over twenty years, so I can live without it forever. Only keep the important stuff."

She knelt down and began to pull items out of the first drawer. Batteries, a torch, a tape measure, a Swiss army knife, a pair of glasses, some tangled wires, old pens. She had to pause for a second when she found three juggling balls.

Ella laughed. "Well, I never." Everything went into the first trash bag, and Ella suddenly felt better about the whole thing. Maybe it wouldn't be such a painful process after all.

But then there was the photo frame. An old, shabby, self-standing Victorian frame, small enough to fit in her palm. Behind the dusty glass was a grainy photo of Ella and Ken, circa 1995. They were in a swimming pool, with Ken hoisting his daughter high in the air. Half of the photo was taken up by her giant yellow armbands.

Ken had always kept the photo beside his bed, and that was why the old gold frame was spattered with blood.

Before the police had arrived, Ella had taken this photo and hidden it. Five-year-old Ella had caught a scene in a soap opera where the detectives had taken a child's toy because it was evidence in a murder, and it had made the young Ella sad. She didn't want the same to happen here.

She tried not to think about it, but the images bogged her down. She saw Ken's body, limp in his bed while blood trickled from beneath the sheets onto the bedroom floor. It was a visual she'd seen a million times, usually with minor elements changing every time. The color of the bedclothes, the position Ken died in, the exact hour it happened.

The photo frame fell from her hands and clanged onto the floor. She quickly checked that it wasn't damaged. She was lucky.

"This is why I hate this," she said aloud. These relics were precious, but it sometimes felt like she was handling nightshade. Beautiful from afar, but poisonous up close.

She placed the frame to one side and moved on. Next up was a deck of playing cards, yellowed with age and missing half the contents. She flipped the tab and poured the cards out, surprised to find the cards themselves were still in decent condition. She held a Jack of Hearts between two fingers, mimed the action of throwing it across the room but held it in place between her thumb and palm so it didn't budge. It was something she did instinctively whenever she held something of equivalent size, like a business card or a credit card. Suddenly, she remembered that it was her dad who taught it to her, back when she was about 5 years old. Somehow, she'd carried the technique with her ever since. She even recalled him sitting on the lounge carpet in front of her, teaching her how to simulate the throwing actions to fool the people watching. Thinking about it, that was her first ever lesson in human psychology.

She opened up the trash bag to haul the cards inside, then stopped herself and reconsidered. "Nah, we'll keep these," she said to herself.

Piles of papers littered the base of the drawer. The first layer consisted of overdue bill payments, envelopes included. She checked some of the dates; '89, '93, '94 and was surprised to find that the whole billing system hadn't change a whole lot in 25 years. Vague threats of service removal, passive aggressive tones, industry jargon. Straight into the trash.

Below them she found writing paper, the old style, with huge gaps between the lines. She picked up a sheet and held it to the light. Something had been written in pencil but had since faded to Father Time. Fortunately, it was still readable.

Ken, you know I'm not great with words, especially in the moment. But I'm sitting here reading that book you gave me, and I got an urge to write something to you. I just wanted to say thank you for accepting me into your life. You're a strong man. A soldier. Your little girl is lucky to have you, and I'm even luckier still. Sam.

Stylish handwriting. Feminine. The letter *I* had bubbles for dots and the writing was slanted, meaning this Sam person was more likely a Samantha than a Samuel. She'd had a crash course in graphology as part of her FBI training and remembered the basics.

She side-lined the letter and continued through the pile, finding more bills, and more of the same letter paper. There it was again, the same handwriting.

Ken, in case you were wondering who this mystery gift is from, I'm afraid the truth isn't quite worthy of an Agatha Christie reveal. The video store by me had for one sale, so I thought why not surprise the most handsome gent I know? P.S., Don't let Ella get her sticky claws around this. Sam.

"My claws?" Ella asked. "Who was this woman?"

More letters revealed themselves as she emptied what remained in the drawer, along with a handful of envelopes. She checked them, finding the same writing again. She scrutinized the dates on them, finding them all through the summer of '96 into early '97. The newest one was marked the 12th March, 1997.

Only a week later, her dad had died.

Whoever this woman was, he'd been seeing her at the time of his death. And if that was the case, why didn't Ella remember her? She could remember the small moments, like her dad teaching her basic magic tricks, but couldn't remember something as important as this? Surely this would be the kind of thing that would stick in the mind of a five-year-old?

Who was this woman? Did they ever meet? What happened to her after Ken died?

Ella felt her leg vibrate. She put the papers into the *keep* pile and reached in her pocket. She had a message from Jenna.

You're coming out tonight. No excuses. If you're not back here by 6:00, I'm coming to get you.

Damn it. Ella was hoping that Jenna had forgotten that she'd agree to hit some bars with her that night. But still, it would do her good to get some new sights and scenery in her life, she thought. Since she'd arrived back from her first field case; aptly known as the Mimicker, according to the internet (although the official FBI designation was the Louisiana Copycat Murders), work had been even more strenuous than usual. Ella had gone back to the Intelligence Unit but was still in close contact with William Edis, one of the FBI Directors. Four weeks had passed without any call for her services again, and she was equal parts relieved and disappointed.

She replied to Jenna's text, piled up all of the stranger's letters and got back to clearing out the storage unit.

CHAPTER TWO

Ella was thankful that the music was low enough to still converse over, but just barely. There was nothing more irritating than pounding bass invading your senses all night. It always left her with a headache. She had no idea how anyone could enjoy their eardrums being violated like that.

She'd opted for the black dress and heels look, with her hair tied back in a loose ponytail. Glasses were foregone in favor of contact lenses. Nothing over-glamorous, but enough to fit in among the attention-seekers and the wannabe models strewn over the dance floor with their cellphones constantly pointed at themselves. Lights were low and there was enough footfall in the bar to make her uncomfortable, but she found herself in a haze, thinking about the letters. She tried to brush them to one side, but she always found it difficult to be *in the moment* in bars and clubs. Her thoughts always drifted. Maybe it was the constant humdrum of voices, music, and clinking glasses, combining to make a kind of white noise that sent her into dreamland.

Ella and twelve other people all stood crammed around a table. She recognized half of them, usually finding them passed out on her sofa on Sunday mornings. However, she barely knew their names, let alone enough about them to make conversation. They all seemed to veer off into their little subgroups, and Ella quickly found herself on the outskirts of them all. She leaned forward to listen in to one conversation but felt like her intrusion was unwanted. She looked around for Jenna, finding her talking to a guy over near the dance floor. Even in the bar's dim light, it was difficult to miss her platinum blonde locks and her bright red heels. Ella decided to back away from the social gathering and try a different approach in a few minutes. Maybe there would be a fresh conversation she could slide herself into.

She waltzed towards the bar area and rested herself against it, glad of the break from trying to keep up appearances. When the bartender finally appeared, she ordered a whiskey and Coke. She opted for Hibiki, one of the spirits Mia had made her try back in Louisiana. Ever since that week, she'd developed a taste for it.

9

In no rush to return to the group, she leaned against the bar area and observed the goings on. Her eyes rested on Jenna's new guy, watching his body language as he did his best to silently impress her with his physique. Mia had taught her the signs to look for: feet, elbows, body weight distribution. More unconsciously than anything, Ella found herself keeping a watchful eye on everyone's micro-signals now, especially the men she came across. Any one of them could harbor secrets that only their unconscious language would portray.

"Hibiki, huh?" a voice shouted beside her. "The Japanese stuff is always the best, right?"

Ella turned, startled at the sudden intrusion. She saw the side outline of a young guy, perhaps late twenties, with wavy brown hair and a pair of black-rimmed glasses. He was decked in a tight-fitting blue shirt and jeans. Few men could pull off double blue, Ella thought, but this stranger seemed to do it just fine. Maybe it was the glasses, giving off that peculiar hipster vibe that combined irony with genuine fashion awareness.

He shouted his order across the bar. Ella noted his manners. She always thought you could tell a lot about someone by the way they treated service workers. He turned back to her, and only then she realized she hadn't said anything in response.

"Yeah," she said. Then panicked, desperately trying to think of something witty to follow up with. Nothing came. "Are you having the same?"

"Oh, no. I don't drink. It's Diet Coke all the way. I'm one of those annoying tee-total types."

"Are you? How come?"

"We get tested at work every week for booze and drugs. I find it's best to stay off them. Plus, I like remembering what happened the night before."

Ella nodded in agreement. "Same. I'm an ABC drinker. Anniversaries, birthdays, and Christmas. What's your job?" She couldn't help but ask. She had a feeling he wanted her to.

"Promise not to laugh? Most women run a mile when I tell them."

"I'm intrigued."

"But you promise?"

"Sure," she smiled.

"I'm a professional wrestler."

Ella arched her eyebrows. "Like Olympic wrestling? Or like Hulk Hogan?"

"The latter. Sort of. Hogan hasn't been relevant in a while."

"That's… interesting. I've never met a wrestler before, although we had a case at work once where a wrestler killed his family and then himself."

He held his drinks to his lips and stared at her.

"I work in law enforcement," she finished, hoping it would impress him but not wanting to take the conversation purely down the work route. Although she had to admit, she was quite taken by talking to a wrestler. The people with non-conventional jobs always interested her, although she had very little idea what his job entailed. Lots of working out? Maybe he was on TV? Her curiosity was riding high.

"Wow, I mean, that's infinitely cooler than mine. You must see some action."

The DJ spun a dance track and, judging by the fact everyone but Ella shouted with joy, it was a popular one. She recognized the basic melody but had no idea who it was by. The gentleman her took his drink and turned back to her.

"You know what? This is my second favorite song," he said.

Ella smelled his cologne. Soft vanilla but with a hint of spice. As he leaned away from her, she saw him properly for the first time. He had blue eyes above a nose too small for his face. A good skincare routine, and an athletic frame, if a little wiry. "That's very specific. What's your favorite?"

"All the others are tied."

It took her a few seconds. She laughed. "Not a fan? Have you been dragged here too, then?"

"Oh yes, by that reprobate I call a best friend." He pointed to the man conversing with Jenna.

"Oh, well God help him. That's my roommate he's chatting with. She'll eat him alive."

"For real?" he asked. "Well, lucky him. Is he in for a world of hurt?"

Ella took a gulp of her drink. She felt herself loosen up a little. It had been so long since she'd had fun, she'd forgotten what it felt like. "Put it this way. If men were fruit, she'd easily get her five a day."

They both laughed. *Where did that come from?* she thought. She'd never used that line in her life, but it seemed to be a hit.

"And what about you?" he asked.

11

There it was. They always enquired about the relationship status. Although, to his credit, he'd worked his way up to it. That approach usually had more success than going full sledgehammer.

"I'm the most single girl you'll ever meet. I don't really have time for a relationship."

"But you've got time to go to bars?" He diluted the question with a smile to offset any accusatory tones. It wasn't lost on Ella.

"This is my first night out in a long time. What about you?"

"Relationships aren't for me. I'm a bay leaf," he said.

Ella stayed quiet. She knew there was a follow-up coming. She thought she had a good sense of his personality already. To her amazement, she actually felt comfortable around this stranger. He didn't overstep any physical boundaries, like putting his hand on her waist like so many club guys did. He seemed respectful, and while he was obviously trying to make a good impression, he was doing it in the most welcome way possible.

"You know how recipes always ask for bay leaves at the start?"

"A man who knows how to cook?" Ella said. "Well, I never."

"Totally. Well, *knows* is optimistic but I give it the old college try. Anyway, at the end, it always tells you to discard the bay leaves, right?"

Ella didn't really know, but she nodded along anyway.

"Well, that's me. They use me and discard me at the end. King of the ninety-day love affair."

She laughed, hoping it came off as sympathetic rather than mocking. "Sounds familiar," she said. "I think that's just how modern dating works." Every time she spoke, she had to lean in and shout down his ear, but she was welcoming toward the proximity to his admittedly appealing figure.

"I'm terrible at dating, but I can show you just how terrible if you want?" he said "Maybe over a coffee one afternoon? Maybe someplace where the music doesn't sound like a car alarm going off?"

Ella took another gulp and considered it. He seemed decent enough. He looked after himself without delving into the gym rat territory. He had a personality. He could hold a conversation. *Why not?*

"That might be nice," she said. "Do you want my number?" she asked. Maybe it was the alcohol making her more forward than usual, she thought.

"I won't say no." He pulled out his phone.

Ella did the same. "It's 2021, and we still haven't figured out an easier way to exchange numbers with other people, have we?" she said.

"We have apps that can deliver toilet paper while we're on the John, but swapping numbers is harder than a math test. Want to give me yours?"

Ella stared at her screen, only now noticing the three missed calls, all from the FBI office. Then William Edis's name popped up.

Urgent. Call me when you get this.

That rush of nervous energy. The same one she'd felt last time Edis summoned her. Was it another field job? Another serial offender? She'd heard no whispers amongst the FBI walls of new serial killers popping up, so if it was such a case, it was exclusive.

"Umm… I'm sorry," she said. "Can you wait here a second? I just have an urgent work call."

"No problem," he replied. Ella rushed outside, amongst the smokers and canoodling couples. She moved out of earshot of the rabble and dialed Edis's number. He picked up on the second ring.

"Dark." No pleasantries. "We need your services again. Up for it?"

He didn't need to ask twice.

CHAPTER THREE

"Dressed for the occasion, Dark?" said William Edis. It was nearing 11pm on Saturday night, and Ella sat in the FBI Director's office in a black dress and heels. Suddenly, the world of bars and clubs and handsome young men seemed a million lightyears away. She felt a little bad having to abandon her friends and her potential date partner with such haste. While she'd made her apologies to both them and him, she couldn't help but wonder if she'd thrown away a rare opportunity to meet someone outside of her work bubble. Was she a fool not to ask for his number? Embarrassment had prevented her from making the move. In her mind, he'd already moved on by the time she'd arrived back in the club. Did people just ask for each other's numbers outright or was there some kind of unwritten code? Maybe he was the one? She didn't know. She discarded the thought. There'd be other men, other nights out. Right now, there were more pressing matters.

"I came straight from town," Ella said. "I can go and change if you want. I've got some clothes in my locker."

"Nonsense. A little bit of elegance is always appreciated, especially under such circumstances. And I'm sorry for pulling you away from your activities." Edis said, pulling off his glasses and rubbing his eyes. He looked a lot more haggard than the last time Ella saw him, which couldn't have been more than three weeks before. He was a stocky gent, no doubt hiding good muscle tone beneath his crumpled suit and tie. But the stress of his position was evident, from his cracked skin to his receding hairline. *It must take him longer to wash his face every day,* Ella said to herself, then brushed the thought aside. Must be the alcohol in her system doing the running commentary.

The door to Edis's office burst open. Mia Ripley walked in and let the door drop shut. It had been a while since Ella had seen her, but nothing about Agent Ripley had changed. She still had that presence that drew your eyes and made you pay attention. Maybe it was that dyed red hair, pulled back to her scalp, an actress on the red carpet. It could have been the way she always held her shoulders high and took every step with an audible thud.

14

Ella sat up straight and cleared her throat. She felt her face flush red. Even in her evening dress, she felt like something was missing from her appearance. Only a few months ago, Ella and Mia had solved a serial case in record time, but even so, Ella still wasn't completely comfortable in her presence.

"Glutton for punishment, rookie?" she asked without even looking at her. Mia was dressed in a suit with her hair tied back in a tight bun. She had a bag over her shoulder, and that told Ella that they were destined for somewhere other than Washington, D.C.

"Looks that way," Ella said. "It's good to see you again, Agent Ripley."

Special Agent Mia Ripley was the FBI's most revered profiler. A 25-year veteran, with more accolades than one could count. She'd brought down some of history's most notable offenders: serial killers, mass murderers, terrorists. Most recently, the Louisiana Copycat Murderer, with Ella's assistance.

"You too, Dark. Has Edis filled you in?"

"Not yet," Edis interrupted. "I was waiting for you both. Thanks for coming at such short notice."

Mia threw down her bag and took a seat beside Ella. She shuffled up to make room. "What are we dealing with?" Mia asked. "A second body?"

"Second?" Ella asked. "I didn't know there was a first." She wondered exactly how much information passed through the FBI wasn't made known to the public, or even the staff at her level. She pondered on exactly how many fascinating cases were going cold in the FBI vaults right that very second.

"We've got a situation down in Seattle," he began. "Second body in a span of one week. This morning, a young woman was found hanging in a tree in a public park."

"Hanging?" Mia asked.

"Like a suicide?" Ella jumped in.

"No, much different. This victim was strung up by her hands and torso. This definitely isn't a suicide. Someone put that woman there."

Right away, Ella recalled at least four serial cases where the victim had been tied to tree. The most notable one was the case of the Chicago Hangman from 1967. When it came to victims being discarded at the base of trees or in parks, the list stretched into the hundreds. Was the killer trying to make these deaths look like suicides, like Hiroshi Maeue in 2005? Or could this even be a bizarre form of strappado, the ancient

15

torture technique? A British killer named Stephen Allwine had done the same 2016.

"Who called it in?" Mia asked.

"A jogger passing by. She found the body around 7:30am. Local police have interviewed her and cleared her of any suspicion. This incident echoes another body discovered three days ago, also found strung up in a public arena. We had our suspicions this would be a serial case at the time, but we couldn't intervene until it was confirmed."

"Understood," Ella nodded.

"Everything you two need to know is in these case files." Edis passed two brown folders to them. "Local police have already determined the victim's identities, so that should give you a starting point. You don't need me telling you how important it is that we make headway on this one. These aren't some murders taking place behind closed doors. These bodies are being left out for the average Joe to find. The public are on high alert. Children are being traumatized. The press are having a field day."

"Of course, Will. I understand," said Mia. She stuffed the folder in her bag. "Dark, I'm heading out there right now, and the choice is yours if you want to come with me. You don't have to. Remember what I told you last time. Don't romanticize this job. Serial killers will be here long after you and I are gone and there's nothing we can do about that. Murder is inevitable. We are Band Aids on bullet wounds, and that's not something worth dying for."

Ella was surprised at Mia's candour in the presence of the director, but she welcomed it. She let the silence settle in as she thought about the proposal for a second.

"Your assistance on the last case was the determinant," said Edis. "But I understand any reservations you might have this time around, considering what you went through. You did good out there and we want to ride that momentum."

She turned to Mia. "Do *you* want me out there with you?"

"Do you feel you learned from the last case? Do you remember the mistakes you made and how to avoid them this time around?"

I risked my life to catch the Mimicker and you're talking about mistakes, she thought. "Yes. To both."

"Then yes, I want you out there with me. What's it going to be?"

Ella already knew the answer. For six weeks, all she'd really thought about was getting back out in the field and doing it all again.

She had moments when she thought that such a life wouldn't suit her well, but her desk daydreams of chasing down real-life murderers told her otherwise. In fact, since her battle with the Louisiana Copycat Killer, everything else in her life seemed as if the volume was turned down. That had been the climax, the high which she'd chase forever, even if she had to kill for it. Admitting to her newfound lust for adventure could result in some cautious reactions from Ripley and Edis, so she knew she'd have to keep that part to herself. She'd give anything to do it all again, even if she hadn't quite fully learned from her past mistakes. All that meant was that she'd be able to make those same mistakes again.

"Let's do it."

"Good choice, rookie. Now, taxi to your place and pack your bags."

"No need," Ella said. "I've got a bag in my locker ready to go. Had it stashed there since we got back from Louisiana, just in case."

Mia leaned closer to her and sniffed the air. Ella felt slightly violated. "Well, alright. And on the subject of good choices, take your time getting ready. Wait for that Hibiki to get out of your system."

Ella turned to Edis, feeling slightly embarrassed. "It was only one shot."

"It's Saturday night, Dark. If you're not getting hammered, then you're doing something wrong. Airport, one hour, see you there."

She found herself on the other side of the office door, back out on the top floor of the FBI building. She followed the marble pathway down to the elevator and did her best to keep her wry smile concealed from the rushed midnight workers and cleaning staff.

She failed.

***

Ella got the VIP treatment from the second she stepped into Ronald Reagan Washington National Airport. A man in a high-vis jacket was waiting for her; then he led her through the security lines in a matter of seconds. Airports always seemed so vast when you were a punter, she thought, but they were actually pretty easy to get around when you removed the lines.

She'd packed lightly but resourcefully: thick socks, wellington boots, leggings, and she'd opted for simple jeans, top and jacket for the trip. After her ordeal on the last case, efficiency came first, with appearances much farther down the list. Something told her she'd be out in the Seattle wilderness at least a couple of times, and that was no place for skirts or dresses.

Gate 319 came into view. The 01:10 flight from Washington to Seattle was ten minutes away from boarding time, but her guide ushered her past the waiting line and down the tunnel without pause. Ella stepped onto the plane and had some flashbacks from the last time she did this, but was surprised that any nervousness had been replaced by excitement, determination. The first hurdle was always the hardest to jump over, and from then on it was just more of the same. She was ready for this case, ready to make it her own. On her bedroom wall she had a commendation from the Mayor of New Orleans, Louisiana, and every time she saw it, she felt like it was all worth it. Job satisfaction was one thing, but looking into the eyes of a serial killer was something else. She was part of an elite few who could claim such a feat, and she wanted to be able to claim it more. Saving lives came with the territory, but being able to actively change the course of someone's fate was a reason to live.

Down through coach and into business class, there was nothing but the gentle hum of the plane's engine to hear. She scanned the area with its leather-bound recliner chairs and small sofas and noticed Mia already sat in the far corner. She looked up and motioned to her when she heard Ella's intrusion.

"Right on time, Dark. Sobered up yet?"

Ella dropped her bags and sat opposite Mia on a white leather chair. There was a glass table between them already covered with papers. "I was never drunk," she protested. "I only had one."

"I know, I'm yanking your chain. Gotta keep you on your toes."

Ella rested her eyes on the first paper in front of her. It showed one of the victims, attached high up in a tree. Arms and legs were sprawled out with each limb attached to a different branch. She was completely naked, save for a thick piece of rope around her torso keeping her locked to the tree trunk. It was much more heart-wrenching than Ella had imagined, and seeing all of the little nuances in the display brought everything hurling into reality. This was a real woman with a family and friends, now reduced to some kind of public exhibition. Her thirst for justice grew. She needed to capture this offender, and she had to be the one to do it.

"Thoughts?" Mia asked, tapping the page Ella was staring at. "This is victim number two. This is all we have at the moment. What do you make of it?"

Ella tried to retrace the steps in her mind. She put herself in the location, imagined she was the killer. *What does this remind me of? What is this similar to?*

She scanned her memory bank and pulled out three cases in particular, the same three she'd recalled in Edis's office. Their victims had also been hung from trees but that was where the similarities ended. In two cases, the killers had tried to make it look like suicide. In the other, it was simply revenge kills. She needed to know more before she could piece things together.

"Do we know how the victim died?" Ella asked.

"Good question, but no, not right now. We're still waiting for the autopsy reports on both victims."

"Okay, well my first question is how an unsub gets someone into a tree in the first place. That must take amazing core strength, dexterity, flexibility. A dead body is going to weigh a ton, but one possibility is that one of the park rangers utilized some of the equipment in the park to do it. They must have diggers, hoists and whatever else to keep the park maintained, so we should question all of the park staff first of all. Put emphasis on the ones with access to vehicles. Yes?"

Mia nodded. "Not bad, rookie. My thoughts exactly. What else?"

Ella had to stop from impulsively congratulating herself. She relished the praise. Truthfully, she expected Ripley to rebut her comments like she usually did but none was forthcoming. A surge of confidence came. Maybe she was getting the hang of this detective lark.

Ella glued her eyes to the picture again. "He obviously put her there at some point during the night because there'd be less people around."

"What's he trying to say with this?" Mia asked. "He could have discarded this body anywhere. Rivers, mountainsides, dumpsters. Why's he placed the body here?"

Ella sat back in her chair. "Because he wants someone to find her. Wants us to find her, maybe."

The stewardess bought over a whiskey miniature and placed it in front of Mia. She nodded her thanks. "The disposal site is often one of the most revealing elements of the crime. More so than the actual murder, sometimes. It tells us the killer's perceptions of the victim. Think. What do the patterns tell you?"

Ella scrolled through a series of crime scene photos in her mind, ones which bore the same elements as the one in front of her. Chicago Hangman, 1967. Four victims, all strung up in trees by their necks but manually suffocated beforehand. Given the theatricality on display, this wasn't the same thing. Stephen Allwine, 2016, literally talked his victims into their own deaths. Hiroshi Maeue, 2005, same approach. She pictured their death sites one-by-one but the only thing that matched were the surroundings. They didn't quite fit. This killer almost seemed to be boasting, whereas the previous killers were trying to hide their activities. She changed her direction of thought.

"Bill Suff left his victims near dumpsters because he considered them trash. Albert DeSalvo pointed his victims' genitals towards the door to shock the people who found them. Danny Rolling posed his victims in sexual positions to humiliate them post-mortem."

"So, what does this disposal suggest?"

Ella let the moment hang in the air. "It's a conflict," she said. She caught Mia's eye.

"I'm intrigued by what you mean. I agree, in a way, but I'm curious to see what you come up with first."

"He's raised her high in the air, as if to emphasize her importance. It feels like he's showing her off, but at the same time he's showing no remorse for killing her. This is about more than just her death. There's something else at play here. It's like he's taunting the world, like showing off a prized possession. Some kind of performance."

The plane began to fill up. Mia took a gulp of her whiskey. "Good. You've been doing your homework."

"You know it."

"This job is a learning experience from beginning to end, Dark. The last case went well, but no two cases are the same. Some offenders go uncaptured for years, some go forever. No agent has a one hundred percent solved rate, even me. Especially me. Eventually you're gonna return to Washington, D.C., with nothing but a head full of questions."

"Okay," said Ella. "What are you trying to tell me?"

Mia looked a little offended at the comment. "I'm just trying to prepare you for the inevitable failure that comes with being a special agent. I know you've been on a high since the copycat, and that's good, but one day, the killer you're chasing is gonna go uncaught. It could be this one, it could be the next one, or it could be in ten cases time. Are you okay with that?"

"Do I have a choice?"

"No, and that's what makes it such a pain in the ass."

Ella nodded. "Do you have doubts about catching the person responsible for this?"

Mia took a deep breath. She scratched her head so hard some of her hair fell loose. "If I'm being honest, yes. Judging by what I can see here, this perp is physically capable, reasonably intelligent and mission oriented. That's a bad combination."

"So was the last guy."

"Don't get full of yourself, Dark. You were in your element in the last case. You know your history, and that guy was mimicking history. This unsub is a different beast entirely. Like I said, his psychopathology suggests he's on a mission, and once his mission is achieved, he's going to disappear into the shadows, and we'll never hear from him again. Our job is to find him before that happens. Are you ready for that? Historical knowledge won't help you here. You're going to need to put yourself in the killer's mind. See what he sees, feel what he feels. Yes?"

The plane began to move into position for take-off. Ella braced herself. She hated this part. Always had. But she showed no distress. If she'd learned anything during her time with Mia, it was that putting on a brave face was sometimes the only thing you could do.

"I'm ready, and while you might not think so, I'm confident we're going to catch him. Once we get to the crime scene, I know exactly what I'm going to look for."

CHAPTER FOUR

The plane came to a stop and the stewardess ushered them off first. Morning was breaking just as they stepped out into the cool Seattle air. A designated worker guided them from the runway through to the security gate then waved them off. In the airport foyer, a youngish gentleman in a black bomber jacket came over to them.

"Agents?" he asked. He had jet black hair, three-day stubble, sharp features. He was the athletic type, muscular, but looked like he could run a marathon without breaking a sweat.

"Correct," said Mia. "Sheriff Brooks?"

"That's me. Thank you for coming out here." He extended his hand to the women.

"I'm Special Agent Ripley and this is Agent Dark. We've been briefed on your findings, but our knowledge is still minimal at the moment."

Ella could hardly believe this man was the local Sheriff. He barely looked thirty years old. She assumed he was one of the guys from a whole law enforcement family. The son of two veteran cops, maybe.

"Of course. We're still gathering information ourselves. Where can I take you agents first? Your hotel? Precinct?"

Ella already knew exactly what Mia was going to say.

"Crime scene," Mia said, right on cue. "I want to see where the most recent victim was found."

"As you wish," Brooks said. "My cruiser's right outside."

He led them out of the airport into his vehicle. The front passenger seat was piled high with paperwork, so Mia and Ella took seats in the back. The car rumbled to life and they found themselves on the Seattle highway. They came to a red light and Brooks reached over to his passenger seat, picked up a folder and passed it behind him.

"Two victims," he said, "both found in the same sort of circumstances. Strung up in trees. One in Seattle National Park, one in Green Valley. There's around five miles between them."

Mia opened up the file and pulled out a picture of the first victim in her death pose. It was a carbon copy of the second. Outstretched arms, rope around the mid-section. The following pictures showed close ups of the ties that kept her in place, followed by pictures of the second victim. She passed the photos to Ella for her inspection.

"Forty years old," Ella said. "The second victim can't have been anywhere near that age."

"Twenty-two," Brooks said, eyeing her in his rear-view.

Mia said nothing and continued leafing through the photographs. She looked out of her passenger window. Ella thought about whether the age disparity might be significant, or whether they might simply have been victims of opportunity.

"What do you make of the age difference, Dark?"

Ella compared photos of the two victims. She scrutinized their appearances, or at least, what could be perceived of them in their post-mortem state.

"An almost twenty-year age difference, not to mention the women look nothing alike. The first victim is a middle-aged blonde, short stature, fuller figure. The second is a young brunette, tall, slim, athletic. Victimology is inconsistent."

"What does that suggest?" Mia asked, still staring at the Seattle traffic.

Ella thought on it for a second. She recalled the basics. The last case had taught her to stick to the evidence, never go too deep into unchartered territory. Most serial killers had a preferred victim type. This perpetrator didn't, or so it seemed. The only thing they had in common is that they were female.

"That victimology isn't important. It doesn't matter who he kills, as long as he's killing someone."

Mia turned back to her and took the folder from Ella. She inspected one of the photos again. "No, quite the opposite." She let the moment hang between them. Ella waited for an explanation, feeling a little embarrassed that Mia didn't agree with her, especially in front of their new colleague. Her face turned red, trying to think of a way to redeem herself. She'd done so well on the plane only to fall at the second hurdle.

"In some cases, I might agree, but there's too much theatricality on display for these to be just random victims. With such varied victimology, it suggests that these two women were purposely targeted. He's not targeting a *type* of woman, he's targeting the exact women themselves, something rarely seen in serial killers. These women aren't surrogates for the source of his frustration. They don't represent the characteristics the killer hates; they *are* the source."

Ella consumed Mia's ideas and dwelled on them for a moment. She scanned her brain for serial killers who had actually targeted the very source of their rage and came up with a disappointingly short list. Edmund Kemper, Jack the Ripper at a stretch. No others immediately came to mind.

"A personal connection between killer and victim?" Ella asked.

"Perhaps, but not always. Sometimes the killer might just perceive a certain person to have wronged them. Some might have delusions. It's not always so clear cut. But this unsub? I don't know until I've seen more. The more I think about this perpetrator, the more threatening he seems."

"How so?"

"Unsubs who target the source of their issues, whether it be rage, frustration, or sexual desire, are some of the most dangerous suspects to hunt. The stalker mentality is incredibly complex and volatile. They often appear organized, stealthy, but usually don't stop until the person they're targeting is dead or unobtainable. And sometimes, that stretches to the people hunting them. If this suspect knows of our involvement, or learns our names, then that wouldn't be good."

The cruiser turned off the freeway into a narrow country lane. Ella saw a sign saying that Green Valley Park was one mile ahead.

"It means he might come for us," Ella confirmed. But this time, the thought of such a prospect didn't scare her at all. In fact, she was determined to look into the eyes of a serial killer again.

***

Green Valley park was around 670 acres of trees and lakes with a farm located within. Ella, Mia, and Sheriff Brooks approached the crime scene area, a cluster of trees beside a gravelly pathway. This entire section had been cordoned off until forensics were able to scour the place from top to bottom. Masked technicians passed them by, and a number of uniformed officers kept guard around the perimeter, keeping curious onlookers at a distance.

Brooks handed them both a pair of gloves then stood at the foot of the tree. "Up there. She was resting just above the first branch, with her arms attached to the two branches above."

Yellow markers had been placed at the points the victim was attached. Two for the hands, one for the torso.

"He used rope to keep her in place. God knows how he managed to get up there, let alone with a body. Must have some real strength, or maybe someone gave him a hand."

Mia circled the area. Ella could see the cogs turning, trying to figure out the logistics of such an endeavor. Brooks backtracked and stood beside Ella.

"So, I hear you're new to all this," he said.

She nodded. "My second time out in the field. Agent Ripley keeps me on my toes."

"Well, I'm sorry it had to be in Seattle. Maybe next time you'll get a murder case in Hawaii."

Ella pulled out her notebook and flipped to a new page. She began writing her thoughts. "I'm never that lucky," she said. "Besides, Seattle seems alright to me. I like the mountains. Plus, you've got the whole grunge thing going for you. Kurt Cobain."

Brooks laughed, then put his hands on his hips and watched Mia go about her business, like she was in a trance. "True. My dad worked the Cobain case back in '94, actually. If that's your thing, I could show you a few choice sights. The house where Cobain lived, the apartment where he shot himself. It's all seared into my brain," Brooks laughed.

Ella suffered a wave of déjà vu. Her thoughts jumped to the guy at the bar from the previous nights. Or was it two nights ago? Time had been distorted since she hopped on the plane. She shook the thoughts off and concentrated on the now. She realized that she'd been right about Brooks being from a cop family.

"If I get a spare hour or two, I'll let you know," she said, letting him down gently. Was he hitting on her? At a murder scene? That took some gall, she thought. Or was she looking too much into it? Either way, her aunt's words rang loud and clear: never get involved with a cop or a carny, because one day they'll leave the house and never come back. She took a few steps back to get a better overview of the death site, trying her best to exit the conversation with grace. She didn't want Brooks to feel awkward, given that she'd be working with him for anywhere up to two weeks.

She thought it would be difficult to climb the tree with a corpse in tow, but not impossible. Climbing the tree itself wouldn't be too difficult, not for someone with decent core strength. The branches couldn't be gripped from the ground, but if someone could scale the trunk just a few feet, they could easily launch themselves, grab the first branch and hoist themselves up. Would such an act be possible with a

25

corpse draped over one's shoulders? She moved closer and simulated the acts, finding it more difficult than she envisioned. Mia appeared beside her and scrawled something in her notes.

"How he got her up there is anyone's guess. I can only assume it was brute strength. A theatrical killer like this wouldn't utilize a partner. This is a one-man job, I'm sure of it."

But then Ella saw something, felt something.

"Look up two branches above," Ella said, pointing. "Near the tree bark. There's a cut into the branch."

Mia followed her direction. "I think I see it. So?"

Maybe it was the mention of Kurt Cobain that did it. The act of suicide. "Looks like something has sawn through it. Like a rope."

"Could be," Mia said. "Or it could be any number of things. Don't do that theorizing thing again, Dark. You know how I feel about that."

Ella rushed past the tree, arriving at a row of large bushes, towering above head height. "Sheriff, what's on the other side of here?"

"Umm... some gym equipment, I think. Used to be some good stuff but it's rusted to hell now."

There was the spark again. Ella realized she'd seen this somewhere before. "Weight machine?" she asked.

"I guess," Brooks said.

"Can we see it?"

"Where are you going with this, Dark? What's this got to do with anything?"

Brooks led them along a pathway, away from the crime scene and round into a small, paved section. There was an elliptical machine, an exercise bike, and the item Ella wanted to see: a weight stack, with all of the weights hanging loose from the machine.

"If he wanted to get her into the tree without having to climb up, all he needed was a rope and a heavy weight." Ella moved over to the machine and pointed to the chain. It had been snapped clean, sending all of the attached weights toppling to the floor. All one-hundred and twenty kilograms of them.

Mia narrowed her eyes as she scrutinized it. Brooks's face had a similar look of apprehension.

"Explain," said Mia.

"So, he ties one end of the rope to the victim and hoists it over the tree. Then he takes the other end of the rope, feeds it through the bushes and attaches it to this machine."

"Right."

26

"Then he cuts the machine cord; easily done with cable cutters, then the weights drop and spring the victim up into the tree. Like a see-saw."

"But what about the restraints around the wrists and the mid-section?" Brooks asked. He bent down and began lifting the weights up one-by-one.

"He would still have to climb the tree to apply them, but the hard part is done."

Mia didn't look convinced, but Ella could see her dissecting the information and trying to make sense of it.

Then Brooks pulled something up out of the weights pile. The agents turned and stared.

"Rope fibers," he said. "Caught between the weights. Looks like you are on to something, Agent Dark."

Ella silently applauded herself. As she thought about it, she was slightly annoyed it took her so long to come to that conclusion. Weight down one side of the rope to elevate the other.

"Not bad, rookie. Brooks, check to see if there were any similar equipment nearby at the first crime scene too. Get forensics to check the equipment for prints and get those rope strands to the lab for testing. If it's industrial strength rope, then it can only be purchased from certain suppliers. That could help us narrow down the suspect pool."

"On it," he said, but his phone started ringing before he had the chance to make a call. "Just gotta take this," he said and moved out of earshot. Mia continued to sieve through the stack of dislodged weights. Brooks returned within ten seconds.

"Agents, that was the coroner's office. They've uncovered the cause of death for both victims."

"What is it?"

"Well, that's not all. There's something else too." He had Mia and Ella's full attention. "I think you're going to want to see this for yourselves."

CHAPTER FIVE

The County Coroner's Office was an immaculate building located in downtown Seattle. The foyer was a lavish carpeted affair, with comfortable leather chairs spaced along traditional granite walls. It had a very home-y feel, Ella thought, and the irony was not lost on her given that it was the forever home of thousands per year. She and Mia waited for their invitation to enter the autopsy room. Brooks had stayed back at the precinct to look into the victim's history.

"I considered the idea of hoisting the victim up with a rope, but I couldn't find any pressure marks in the grass," Mia said. "I'd never thought of the possibility of using something that was already nearby."

"He would still need incredible strength to do what he did, so it doesn't change much," Ella said, taking the modest route. She'd thought about her finding on the trip over to the coroner's and realized it didn't much alter the profile.

"No, it changes a lot of things," said Mia. "He'd need strength to bring the body to the park, but the apparatus did the rest of the work for him. In fact, this narrows down things quite significantly. He's nimble enough to scale trees but not so powerful to carry bodies up them. The fact he *needed* to use the gym equipment tells us even more about him. It also means he's familiar with the area and had it scouted beforehand. That shows organization, confirming what we already thought about him. It's coming together," Mia said. "What prompted the idea?" she asked.

Ella couldn't quite explain how the thought popped into her head. It was another pattern prompted by two disparate elements. "I saw familiarity," she said. "Brooks mentioned Kurt Cobain to me. You know, the singer who killed himself? That got the idea of suicide in my head. Then I remembered a different case from 2007. There was this professional wrestler who hanged himself and he did it using a weight machine. The same method we saw in the park."

She thought back to the night before, of the mysterious man in the bar. She realized she didn't even know his name. She owed him a thank you for renewing the case of the hanged athlete in her mind. If only she

28

had a way of finding him again. *Hang around the same bar every weekend waiting for him, like Madame Bijoux?*

No, that would be silly, and stalkerish.

The receptionist waved to the agents from behind her marble desk. "You can go through now," she said. "Room 221."

A glass door automatically unlocked and opened for them. They passed down a hallway with rows of steel doors on either side. The building smelled more like a show home than a medical facility, Ella thought. Mia knocked on the door to the designated room and turned the handle.

The room was heavy with the scent of fluoride, invading Ella's senses like a tidal wave. A masked technician peered up from a medical table, dressed head to toe in dirty white regalia. In front of her, the bodies she'd seen in the crime scene photographs lay on two steel slabs, filed next to each other in a neat line, barely resembling human figures anymore. Even though she'd already seen plenty, laying eyes on fresh dead bodies brought a sense of discomfort to Ella. Like she was observing something she shouldn't be. Intruding, perhaps. She couldn't deny their morbid allure, but her once-fascination with the dead was gradually diminishing.

"Welcome, agents," she said. A middle-aged brunette, late forties perhaps. A glowing smile decorated her face, despite the circumstances. Ella always found medical workers to be the most approachable people in any profession. "I'm Dr. Baker. You might want to put some surgical masks on before you head over here. These don't smell too pretty."

Mia and Ella obliged, pulling two masks and two pairs of gloves from a box on the table beside them.

"Thank you for accommodating us so suddenly," said Mia. "What do we have? Start at the most recent victim."

"As you wish." Dr. Baker took a penlight and shone it across the body closest to her. "Identity reports confirm that this is Jennifer Hoskins. Female. 22-years-old from Redmond. Cause of death was via blood loss from a laceration to the throat." Dr. Baker signaled towards the neck area. A jagged cut spread across her throat, the flesh having now scabbed over. "Ligature marks around her wrists and torso but nowhere else. There are no defensive wounds on the body. No trauma to the hands or feet or knuckles."

Mia took notes. "She was blitz-attacked, taken by surprise. The killer wasn't confident enough to subdue her beforehand. There was no

29

struggle. He snuck up on her and slit the throat. That suggests they were alone when the killing occurred. Maybe he gained her trust."

"It fits with the theory that there was a personal connection, then," Ella added.

"But there's one additional thing," Dr. Baker said. She pulled away the white sheet covering the victim from the chest down, exposing a gaping hole near her left breast. "Whoever did this also removed her heart."

Both agents fell silent for a moment. "That's surprising. I'd never expect that from an unsub like this. How accurate were the cuts?" Mia asked.

Baker shone the light near the gaping chasm on her torso. Ella looked in and saw fleshy tissue, sawn rib bones. Looking at it made her feel queasy.

"The cuts are very amateur. The attacker has cut an entire hole through the ribcage and under the tissue and muscle beneath. He didn't need to go to those lengths. Anyone with basic surgical knowledge would know the easiest route to the heart is under the breast and below the sternum."

"Tools used?" Mia asked.

"I found traces of carbon steel along the incision, and given the pattern of the cuts, I'd say he used a surgical scalpel. But don't let the word *surgical* fool you. Those things are available anywhere."

Mia nodded and scrawled on her pad. Ella did the same.

"And victim number one?" Mia asked. "I'm assuming everything is almost identical?"

"Almost, but not quite." Dr. Baker moved across to the second slab. "Victim number two is Janet Wootton, female, aged forty from Kirkland. Ligature marks are identical, but in this case, it wasn't the heart that was removed. It was the liver." She pulled back the sheet to reveal a deep wound in the stomach. Intestines and bowels were visible within. Ella winced at the sight.

"He's harvesting organs," Ella said. "Why?"

"Amateur cuts again. He more or less guessed where the liver was and dug around. Given how he mangled the intestines in the process, his estimate was quite far off."

Mia slammed her notepad shut and removed her mask. "Thank you for your time, Doctor. That'll be all for now. Let's get going, Dark. We've got something we need to do."

Ella took one last glance at the dead bodies, with their skin sucked to the bone and the holes decorating their flesh. This was the true face of death. The parents of these victims will never see their daughters again, and there was nothing to be fascinated by about that.

Back down the corridor, Ella caught up with Mia, their footsteps echoing around the empty hallway. "Does the organ harvesting not fit in with psychological profile?" Ella asked.

"I'm not sure. He might be taking them as trophies, which would fit in with the basic psychopathology. But all I know is that this unsub gets weirder by the minute."

They exited out into the Seattle afternoon. There was a hint of sun between the clouds, but the windchill still bit into her bones. "Precinct?" Ella asked.

"Let's go. We need to find everything we can about these victims. Something connects them. We just need to find out what."

***

The Seattle police precinct was teeming with moving parts, to the point that Ella began to feel like she was in a corporate office. Cops and admin staff were scattered across the ground floor office that Mia and Ella called their new workspace. The room was a giant grey square, chilled by the lifeless grey carpet and the battered wooden desks that cropped up every six feet. Fluorescent tube lights up above gave the office an alien white glow.

Brooks met them at the doorway, holding a lunchbox in one hand and a folder in the other. "It's pretty lively in here, agents, but you get used to it. There's an empty office up here you can use." He led them through the rabble, all eyes turning to them as they passed by. Mia didn't meet their glares once, but Ella couldn't help but look and nod something in way of greeting. "Don't worry about the boys," Brooks said. "I keep them in line. If anyone says anything to you, let me know and I'll sort them out."

"Nothing I haven't done myself a million times before," Mia said. Indeed, Ella had seen it first-hand. "Cops never like FBI agents, but they like a fist up the ass even less." Mia spoke loud enough for any prying cops in earshot to take note of.

"Understood. You can set up camp in here. Coffee machine is just outside. I'm just across the way. Everything satisfactory?"

"Perfect."

31

"Here." He dropped the folder on the wobbly desk in front of them. "I just put this together for you. It's all the information we have about the victims from their public files. Job history, tax returns, living arrangements, vehicles owned, spouses, family links. You name it, it's in here."

"Thank you, Sheriff. We'll call you if you need anything," Mia said.

Brooks nodded his goodbye as the agents set up inside the small glass box that was their new office. It was as barebones as workspaces come, with glass walls that peered out into the open-plan area. Privacy was not to be found here.

Ella peered around the door to make sure no one else was using the coffee machine before making a run to it. The last thing she needed was to explain her presence to one of the on-duty cops. Before she knew it, the whole precinct would be spreading rumors of their reasons for being there. As far as Ella knew, their involvement on the recent murders was still on a need-to-know basis. The Seattle press had a reputation for being particularly relentless, and if they got wind that the Feds were in town, it could derail the case something fierce.

She brought two coffees back to the office, although their color left something to be desired.

"Thanks," Mia said. "Piss water, right?"

"Looks like it."

"Some things never change." She opened the folder, pulled out the top piece of paper and scanned it top to bottom. She passed it over to Ella. It was the basic information for victim one.

"Janet Wootton. Forty years old. Married in 2014. No children. Worked as an agent for Bluegrass Entertainment."

Mia was typing away at her laptop. "Looks like Bluegrass Entertainment is a company that represents local artists. Interesting."

"Artists?" Ella asked. "Like, painters?"

"It doesn't say a whole lot. It just says it's a place that offers representation for artists. Looks like Janet was the sole member. The founder."

Ella took the initiative and picked up the folder. She scrolled through to find information on the second victim.

"Okay, victim number two. Jennifer Hoskins. Twenty-two. Unmarried. No children. Lives with parents in Redmond. Self-employed but doesn't say what industry she was in. On last year's tax return she declared $6,000, so she's either new to her industry or she's a tax dodger."

Ella pulled her laptop closer. She searched the Internet for a Jennifer Hoskins in Redmond, Washington, but found way too many results, and none which resembled the victim. "Not much online about her."

"If she runs a business, she's on there somewhere," Mia said. "Are her tax calculations in the folder? It should mention the type of work beside each deposit."

Ella rifled through the pages. "A-ha. Here. There are monthly deposits of about $550, each one labeled 'performance payment.'" Ella searched added the word *performer* to her search. She cropped up in the first result. "Holy crap. Look at this."

Mia slid over and leaned closer to Ella's screen. "Hmm. She's an artist. Apparently."

On the front page of Jennifer Hoskins' website was a banner featuring her completely naked, bleeding from various cuts onto the floor of a theatre stage. Her face was painted like a clown and her hair was dyed multicolours. Ella read her opening paragraph.

"I'm a performance artist who dies on stage every night and rebirths into something greater than before. In fluid dreams I fall. Walls made of stone are turned into water. Enlightened demons are taking me by the hand. They approach. The great eye, speaking to me."

Both agents wore the same look of confusion. "What the fuck is she talking about?" Mia asked.

Ella shook her head. "Beats me. But maybe art is the link here. Maybe Janet represented Jennifer?"

Mia moved back to her laptop. "Let me check Janet's client list." She tapped away. "No. No mention of any Jennifer on here. But you're right. This is too good a link to ignore. Our unsub could definitely be related to the art community."

Ella stood up and walked to the glass wall. She watched the officers rush between desks, make hurried phone calls, shout nothings at one another. "What if both murders have been a type of performance themselves? Look at how grandiose they were. Put on display for the world to see, like he's showing off his work. What if our killer is one of the artists in the community?"

"It's a very real possibility."

Ella felt the excitement course through her veins. She'd barely been in Seattle ten hours and she felt herself coming closer to the person responsible every minute. Maybe this could be her job, she thought. Maybe she *could* be a full-time field agent. She thought back to her desk job and felt almost sorry for the people in her department, while she'd be the one to bring down this perp with her own hands. She'd be the one to lock on the cuffs, throw him into the police cruiser and tell him he'd never see daylight again. She wouldn't trade that high for any desk job, even if it had a seven-figure salary.

"If that's the case, our pool of suspects must be tiny. How many performance artists are out here? Do you think we're getting closer to him?"

Mia took off her glasses and dropped them on the table. "Rookie, leave it. We've got a lead and that's as much as we can ask for. Don't go into your crazy theories again because it gets us nowhere. It could be another artist, yes, just as much as it could be an accountant. Stick to the facts, okay? I'm not jumping to any conclusions just yet."

Ella felt the exhilaration wane. Whenever Mia shot her down, she remembered the last case, bringing a wave of painful memories along with it. "Alright. Sorry."

"Don't be. Keep thinking, just remember that we mold theories to fit facts, not the other way around. Anyway, drink your coffee. I'm sending you out on your own."

"On my own? Where to?"

"I want you to interview Jennifer's family. They'll be more receptive to you. You're closer to their daughter's age. Take the Sheriff with you if you want but delivering bad news to grieving family members is part of the job. Maybe the worst part, and you're gonna have to get used to it. Can you do it?"

Ella panicked a little, but something about this new venture stimulated her. This part of the role had terrified her when she thought about being the angel of bad news, unsure how the recipient might react, delivering the death blow to an already-grieving family member. The physical side of the job was the easiest part, it was the emotional side that toyed with her. But if she could master this; that was one step closer to becoming a bona fide special agent.

"I can do it," she said. "I don't need Brooks with me. I'm going there right now."

CHAPTER SIX

Ella arrived at the home in Redmond just after 3pm. Tiredness was beginning to creep in now. It felt like days ago that she was out with her roommate in D.C., but less than 24 hours had passed. The passage of time seemed to speed up during these jaunts. No wonder Mia was always complaining that she felt so old.

Before leaving, she'd checked out some of Jennifer's performance videos on her website. In one, she'd painted herself as though her skin had been removed, showing all of the tendons, organs and bones beneath. In another, she'd bound herself with rope and tried to whip her own backside. Ella had no idea what their respective messages were. It just all seemed like pure eccentricity for the sake of it.

A set of luxurious stone steps led towards the front door of the Hoskins household, and beside it, a tearful woman peered her head between two grey curtains. Ella felt the air rush from her lungs, knowing that only a few feet away stood a woman going through the kind of emotional turmoil few people ever experienced. She wanted to run up to her and tell her how sorry she was that life had rained down such agony, through no fault of her own, no less. She wanted to tell her that time diminished the pain, even though it never fully healed.

But she couldn't. FBI training told her to keep the sympathies vague. Over-sympathizing sometimes came off as patronizing. It was a tough balance to master, but she was going to try her best.

The woman opened the door and left it ajar for Ella to enter. Right away, it was clear that this was a house of mourning; a place suffocated in blackness. Blinds and curtains were shut, and despite the house's generous size, an overwhelming sense of claustrophobia soon materialized. A TV talk show glared from the corner of the room, which a middle-aged couple glued their eyes to from their recliner sofa.

"Hi, I'm Agent Dark," she said. "You must be Karl and Suzanne."

"We are," the man said.

The couple struggled to even make eye-contact with her. She reminded herself that people deal with grief in different ways. It wasn't always tears and hysterics.

"Should I sit?" she asked. "Or would you prefer me to stand?"

"Do what you like," the man said. A rough voice, like his throat was infested with gravel. "We don't suspect you'll be here long."

Ella cut to the chase. Something seemed off about these two. "Is everything okay with you two? I'm sure you're aware of the circumstances around your daughter's passing by now."

Suzanne cut a glance at her. "Are we okay? Did you honestly just ask if we're okay?"

She realized how it must have sounded. "I'm sorry. I didn't mean it like that. I just expected more-"

"More crying? More despair?" Suzanne interrupted. "We lost our only daughter to some nutcase, and you're asking if we're okay? You hear that, Karl? She wants to know how we're doing."

Karl dropped his head back in his chair and put his hand on his wife's knee. Ella saw the tears begin to form. He rubbed them away with his palm. "She's just doing her job, honey."

Both parents seemed to calm. Ella waited a few moments before continuing. "Jennifer seemed like a great girl. Creative. Intelligent. What can you tell me about her?"

"Why does it matter?" Suzanne barked.

Ella took a deep breath. "Because if we can get an idea of Jennifer's lifestyle and her social circles, we can begin to pinpoint the circumstances that led to her passing. Creating a full picture of the victim allows us more visibility. I'm aware of her career as a performance artist but I'd like to know more about the other things in her life."

Karl suppressed a laugh. "Career? That weren't no career. Was a Goddamn hobby. Me and Sue hated everything about it."

Suzanne nodded beside her husband, still fixated on the TV. Something told Ella this was her way of distancing herself from the pain. Maybe she'd already done her crying throughout the past 24 hours.

"You didn't approve of her art?" Ella asked.

"Girl can do what she wants. One day, your kids have to go out and fend for themselves. We know that. We didn't exactly try to stop her."

Ella waited for Karl to continue but he turned his gaze to the ceiling, still fighting to hold back the tears. He turned to Suzanne. "Honey, how about some coffee for our guest?" Suzanne looked at him like he'd just asked her to build a ladder to the moon.

"Oh, I'm fine, thank you," said Ella. "I had one before I came out."

"For me, then?" Karl said to his wife. "I can take care of this."

Suzanne reluctantly stood up and left the room. Ella heard her run the tap in the kitchen. Karl leant forward and spoke in quieter tones.

"I didn't want to say this in front of Sue, but given the people that Jennifer hung around with, I'm..." he stopped himself, possibly to choose a better way to term things. "Not surprised," he finished. "I'm not surprised that she ended up dead."

Ella was a little shocked at his bluntness. "How do you mean? What suggested she was going to die?"

"She made some poor decisions, let's put it that way. She was naïve. Desperate for people to take her seriously. She ended up doing things for people other girls wouldn't have done. She was constantly trying to be better than the other people doing the same kind of things, you know?"

"Do you mean she prostituted herself?" Ella asked.

Karl looked to the kitchen door to make sure his wife was out of earshot. "Not quite. But she worked for pennies. People would hire her to do the crazy shit she did. Theatre managers, agents. A hundred dollars to suspend herself from hooks. Two-hundred dollars to self-harm. All in the name of art. She was exploited by those vultures."

"Do you know any reason why someone might want to harm her? While it's terrible that she was exploited, it sounds like she was more value to these people than they were to her."

Karl gritted his teeth and looked up and to the left. An indication he was trying to recall names, faces, images. "Jealousy, maybe? I mean, she wasn't getting paid much but she was still performing. That's more than what some of those other weirdo types are doing."

Suzanne returned to the lounge with a coffee in hand. She placed it beside Karl and resumed her position. "We hadn't been all that close with Jennifer over the past year," Suzanne added, much to Ella's surprise. She had a feeling Suzanne had been listening from the kitchen. "Once she found this art nonsense, she turned into a different person. Sometimes I felt like I didn't know my own little girl."

Ella felt the parents open up to her. She observed a slight change in body language, or at least she thought she did. Suzanne's feet turned towards her. Karl let his arms drape loosely over the sides of his chair. "Can you describe Jennifer's daily life? What did she do? Did she have a boyfriend?"

The question fell on Karl. "Well, she'd leave the house first thing in the morning and we wouldn't see her again until the evening. That's if she came home at all. Sometimes she'd be out all night."

"Doing what?"

"God knows. Hanging out with those imbeciles she called friends. She was seeing some guy for a little while, but she ended it. Besides, she told us that she wasn't into *conventional relationships,* whatever that meant. We didn't really ask."

"She was gay?"

Karl shrugged.

"What did you think of her performances?"

"Stupid. Weird. I don't know how she latched onto that whole scene but it's ridiculous," Suzanne said. "A bunch of freaks."

It seemed clear that Suzanne blamed Jennifer's new career direction for her death, although she didn't want to come right out and say it. "Would you mind if I took a look around Jennifer's room? Maybe to find some of her contacts in the art world? That could greatly help us with our investigation."

"Go ahead. Upstairs and first room on the right," said Karl.

Ella excused herself, leaving behind two grieving parents, lost souls who'd be filled with resentment and aggravation until their dying days.

Upstairs, Jennifer Hoskins's room was unkempt and chaotic. It had the makings of a crash pad rather than a regular residence. A single bed took up most of the room, next to it a small mahogany desk and a desktop computer. A wall-to-wall window looked out over an extensive garden with a vibrant meadow in the distance. Ella had a quick leaf through the desk drawers and under the bed, finding very little to help glimpse into Jennifer's personal life. She couldn't help but be alarmed by the Hoskins's lack of emotion regarding their dead child, especially as it took place little over a day ago. She wondered if perhaps they were relieved that they no longer had to worry about Jennifer's well-being, her hazardous stage performances, her gallivanting among unfavorable circles. Maybe death brought them peace of mind, despite the horrors she went through.

The room's centerpiece was a portrait of Jennifer. The style was abstract with an overload of vibrant colors and looking at it gave Ella a headache. There was too much going on for her eye to follow. It was like looking at a badly decorated living room. In the bottom right corner, the artist had signed it JEN. Must have been a self-portrait. Ella snapped a picture of it.

Next, she came to her desk drawers. As her gloved hands filtered through them, she stumbled upon a leather-bound notepad. She flipped through the pages, finding drawings on every one of them. They featured bizarre creatures, human-animal hybrids, schematics for devices. Ideas for her performances, Ella thought. They reminded Ella of her own diaries she kept, similarly never sharing much information or insight with the adults in her life. Would Jennifer's life have been different if her parents had nurtured her artistic desires rather than shun them?

Her thoughts turned to her own parents. Ella never really knew her mother but had enough memories of her father to last a lifetime. However, her most vivid recollection of him was the sight of his dead body, killed by someone who had never been brought to justice, at least that she knew of. The same image that had propelled her to this position, here in Seattle, hunting the people who committed the same acts that cruelly took her sole guardian from her.

Would her father have been happy at her chosen career path? Would he have pushed her to be the best federal agent she could be? Or would he have wished for something more traditional? A nurse, a teacher, a journalist?

She reached the end of the notebook, finding something lodged in the spine. Several things, in fact. They dropped to the desk in succession.

Business cards, she said to herself. *Other people's business cards.*

Different sizes, different designs. Her artistic friends, Ella assumed. She scrutinized a few of them, all of whom seemed to have pompous stage names. *Audience of One. Moment of Truth. Necrobutcher.* Were these actual people, or businesses of some kind? She didn't know, but they could provide useful. By instinct, she held one of the cards in the hand and did her magic flourish. She couldn't help herself, like her fingers had some kind of auto-response. Again, thoughts of her dad came rushing back; the person who'd taught the party trick 23 years ago. She smiled, and while she couldn't confirm it, she knew that he'd have been proud of her choices no matter what they were.

She returned the diary where she found it and headed back downstairs. She needed to get back to the precinct. There was a killer to find, and that killer's business card could be in her hands right now.

CHAPTER SEVEN

Mia Ripley took the Sheriff's car to Kirkland. She hated having to rely on taxis to get around, so she did everything she could to avoid them. Besides, she'd been to Seattle so many times, she pretty much knew the city like the back of her hand. The GPS told her she was two miles from her destination – the home of Janet Wootton's husband.

Although they'd only been on the case for a day, Mia was happy with their progress already. Ella had been much more reigned-in this time around, much more level-headed. It meant that she'd taken her lessons from last time on board and applied them where she needed to. The sign of a good rookie, a good learner, and perhaps a suitable replacement for herself one day. She tended to get ahead of herself at times. Over-thinking and hastiness were her biggest downfalls. She sometimes needed to step back and see the forest through the trees, and if she could master that, there was nothing stopping Ella achieving the same accolades she had.

Not only that, but Ella had been correct about the recent murders. There was a good chance they were a sort of performance, a showcase of artistic merit. But on the flip side of the coin, there was a chance they weren't. It was still important to explore every avenue and not get blindsided by a singular theory. That was how mistakes were made. That was how killers went free.

Mia turned into a row of new-build homes, somewhere in the $300,000 bracket, she imagined. They were all identical in structure and brickwork, the only difference being the vehicles parked outside each one. She scouted the numbers until she found the residence she needed.

Stone steps led up to a porch area. A welcome mat declared NEVER MIND THE DOG, BEWARE OF THE WIFE. She looked out into the trash cans sitting beside porch and saw a mass grave of empty liquor bottles. Someone had been finding comfort in alcohol.

She knocked on the door.

"Go away," a voice boomed immediately.

"Mr. Wootton, my name's Agent Ripley. I'm with the FBI. I know you're not expecting me, but I'd like to ask you some questions about your wife."

Mia heard someone shuffling on the other side, frantically pulling away locks. The door opened and a face appeared, red-eyed and flushed. "I'm sorry, miss," the man said. "I thought you were a cold caller or a dodgy journalist or something."

He was a stocky gentleman, bearded, with curly black hair reaching down to his eyes. He wore a long-sleeved black t-shirt that Mia could see was tear-stained. "Understandable. We tried to call but couldn't reach you. Sorry for the abrupt approach."

"Turned my phone off," the man said. "Had nothing but empty well-wishes since yesterday. Sick of it."

"May I come in?"

"Yes, my apologies." He moved out of the way and held his arm out for Mia to come inside. "I'm Stephen. Please take a seat in the front room. Sorry, it's a mess."

Mia entered into a small but striking lounge and sat herself on a single chair. The interior had no doubt been designed by someone with artistic intent. She'd never seen room decked entirely in yellow carpet before. "Your wife had colorful tastes," Mia said.

Stephen looked to the floor and nodded. "Oh yes. Color influences the soul. That's what she'd say." He sat opposite her on a two-seater sofa, its bright orange fabric contrasting against the blue wallpaper behind it.

"I'm sure you're already aware of what happened to Janet," Mia began. "What can you tell me about her? What was her day-to-day routine?"

Stephen pulled up a bottle of cheap wine from beside the sofa. He unscrewed the cap. "She lived for her job," he said. "Always hustling. Always on the lookout for young blood. Her words."

"Young blood?"

"The hottest new thing. The modern-day Yoko Ono. She was just looking for that one client she could hit the big time with, but instead she mostly ended up with duds."

"What kind of artists caught her attention?"

"The freaks and geeks. The outsider artists. The more outlandish, the better."

Mia had an idea of the type of artists that Janet represented since her client list was already known to the police. However, she wanted to ascertain how familiar Stephen was with his wife's work. With the creative types, relationships went one of two ways. They either shared everything or nothing.

"And what did *you* make of this scene, Mr. Wootton?"

"Why? You don't think I was involved, do you?"

"No. I understand the police have already confirmed your alibi. I'm just trying to get a feel for Janet's personality, and her marriage is an important component."

Stephen swigged from the wine bottle then wiped his mouth with his sleeve. Maybe it wasn't tears Mia had noticed after all. "Some of it was intriguing. Thought-provoking. A lot of it wasn't."

"Not a fan?"

"I love art, don't get me wrong. I'm actually an artist myself. I paint landscapes. But that's my kind of art, beautiful scenery. Watching a girl push out menstrual blood on stage isn't for me."

Mia pictured the scene then did her best to vanquish it. "I see your point. Now, this may seem an insensitive question, but was there anyone who might want to hurt Janet? Whether for business or personal reasons? Anyone she didn't see eye-to-eye with?"

Stephen looked lost in thought for a moment. His leg began to quiver nervously. "Jan had her ups and downs with her clients. She sometimes had disputes about pay or their performance levels. But nothing that would warrant murder. She was always good to them. Took them out for drinks and meals. Boy, did she like a drink. She was known for it," he said, his eyes lowering to the floor.

Mia took some notes but decided to leave the question hanging. People didn't like silence and would usually say anything to fill the gaps. Quite often it could turn out to be useful information.

"But thinking about, there was one thing," Stephen continued.

There it was.

"Any information you can share could be useful," said Mia, "no matter how minor."

"There was this *other* agent on the scene. A newbie. Some scumbag named..." Stephen rubbed his forehead with his fingertips. "Lee something. I can't remember. Jan had a run-in with him recently because she poached one of his clients."

"Is that a big deal in the artist community?"

Stephen shrugged. "I mean, not really. People find new agents all the time, and it's not like these artists are bringing in the millions. But I remember her mentioning that he'd made a vague threat to her. She thought nothing of it, though. Said it was part of the job."

"Do you remember exactly what the threat was?"

"Lee said he was going to *bury* her. I remember it because it seemed like a weird term to use."

"It certainly is." Mia shut her notebook, eager to run her new findings by Ella. "I'll look into this person. You don't remember his full name?"

"No, sorry. Jan used to call him Shitstain, so I'm lucky I remember his first name at all."

Mia saw a smile creep up on Stephen's face as he remembered his wife's words, which then turned to despair when he realized he'd never hear them spoken aloud again. Even after thirty years of interviewing the bereaved, it never got any easier.

***

Back at the precinct, Ella showed Mia her findings while she'd been gone. It was closing in on 6pm and the new wave of night shift officers was peering at the out-of-towners taking up residence in their office.

Ella was thankful she hadn't been present at the Wootton household. One bereaved family was enough, but at least the Hoskins had each other to get them through the grief. The thought of Janet's husband sitting alone wondering about the hell his wife went through filled her with great sorrow. Even though she didn't know these people, they shared a common pain. She'd lost someone close and didn't quite understand the hows or whys, even after years of replaying the events in her mind. She'd likely never see these people in person, but just knowing their pain existed in the world they shared was enough to spike her anxiety. She quenched her blues with coffee, half for the taste, half for the caffeine injection.

"Bury?" she said. "That's a pretty damning statement."

"It is. We need to find this guy, but I'm not having much luck tracking him down. It doesn't help I only know his first name. There's a shit-ton of Lees in this town. The internet's bringing up a whole load of nothing too."

Ella slumped into her chair. Something jumped into her mind. "Hold on, did you say Lee?"

Mia turned to her. "Yeah. What are you thinking?"

Ella reached into her pocket and pulled out a pile of business cards. "Here. I took these from Jennifer's bedroom. Her dad gave me permission." She flicked through them. She looked up for Mia's approval, but her eyes were fixed on the cards. "And look who we have here."

She pulled out a black-and-red business card with the words LEIGH NEVILLE, AGENT, in block letters imprinted. She pushed it across the desk to Mia.

"Well, wouldn't you know who won the pony? This could be our guy." Mia typed something into her computer, leaned closer to the screen and adjusted her glasses. "Dark, look."

Ella read the webpage in front of them. The main page featured a picture of the man she presumed to be Leigh Neville, posing in a suit with slicked-back hair like an eighties greaseball. Mia hit the news section of the site, and the first post caught their attention right away.

Jennifer Hoskins is no longer represented by Leigh Neville's Agency.

They exchanged a look of shock. Neither of them needed to say it. This man had a link to both the victims.

"Grab your things. We need to pay this guy a visit."

CHAPTER EIGHT

Away from the suburbs and into the slums, Ella and Mia approached the house of Leigh Neville. It was a petite townhouse nestled away in a Bell Town backstreet. A crumbling wall gave way to an uneven pathway, weeds sprouting between the cracks.

"Not exactly the Hollywood Hills, is it? I expected more from an agent to the stars," Mia said. She banged on the front door.

Ella saw a face peer from the window. Whoever the person was, it took them a long time to get from their window to the front door, almost like he was keeping them waiting on purpose. After what seemed like minutes, the door opened. The man standing there was tall, skinny, wearing a button-down shirt and shorts. A strange combination, Ella thought. He had slicked hair, jet black, and tiny weasel eyes.

"Yes?" he said. His voice was weak and nasally with no bass to it at all. "The fuck are you?"

"Mr. Neville, I'm Special Agent Ripley and this is Agent Dark. We're investigating a string of recent homicides and we believe you may have connections to the victims. May we talk for a moment?"

He looked both agents up and down before responding. "No. Get off my property." He went to shut the door, but Mia slammed her forearm against it. The impact made Leigh jump back. Mia stepped into his house and stared him in the eye, inches away from his face.

"Buddy, we have it on good authority that you recently threatened a woman who's now dead. We also found your business card in the home of another dead girl. So, you can either start talking or we can haul you down to the police station by that greasy hair and embarrass you in front of everyone."

"Is that a threat?" he asked, peering between the door and door frame.

"Yes, it's a threat. And let me tell you, you'll have a lot *more* clients leave you when they find out you've been humiliated by two women. So, what's it gonna be?"

The door opened up. "Okay, but we talk here. Not inside."

"Something to hide?" Ella jumped in.

"No. I'll explain in a second. What do you want from me?"

45

Mia and Ella swapped a look. This would have to do. "We want to know why you threatened to *bury* Janet Wootton? A harsh response, wouldn't you say? And pretty coincidental that she winds up dead not long afterward?" asked Mia.

Leigh began to laugh. The sound irritated Ella. "Janet got what was coming to her. She wants to hang in this world she needs to thicken that skin up. Well, more like *needed* now, right? She won't be poaching any more newbies of mine. Not after her... unfortunate accident."

His tone annoyed her. She wanted to reach up and punch him square in his face. "You're glad about what happened?" Ella asked.

"Oh, no. Not at all," Leigh winked. "I have her crime scene photo saved as my screensaver because I miss her so much."

"Mr. Neville, you're making a very good case for murder here, especially after your threat to the victim. Mind telling us why you're being so abrasive?"

"Ladies, listen here. *Burying* someone doesn't mean killing them, you fools. It has a distinct meaning in the creative world. Do some research, will you?"

Mia pushed her glasses up and composed herself. Ella could see his tone was taking its toll on her too. "And what's your connection with Jennifer Hoskins? We found your business card among her possessions. Was she the client that Janet poached?"

"God no. Janet would have been welcome to that skank. I represented her for a while, but she was..." he pursed his lips. "A bit trashy for my tastes. A bit too desperate. She's what we in the performance community call a Grenade. Limited shelf life. Good for one explosion. I want longevity, so I sacked her."

Ella eyed his body language. He continually shifted his weight between his legs but maintained eye-contact with both her and Mia. He didn't show any signs of nervousness, and surely someone with a genuine reason to fear the police would.

"She got what was coming to her too. Looks like that grenade finally went off," he laughed.

Ella saw Mia compress her rage. She obviously wanted to hit him too, and worst of all, Leigh knew it.

"Where were you on the nights of the 15th and 19th of February?" Mia asked.

Leigh turned and looked back into his house. He turned around, stepped past Mia and gently shut the door behind him. "On the 15th I was at home all night, with my girlfriend. She's in there and you she'll corroborate my claims. On the 19th I was... with someone else."

"We need names, Leigh. We will be following up everything you tell us."

"There's no way this info will leak to my girlfriend, right? It's not gonna be on some TV show or podcast, is it?"

Mia sighed. "No."

"The client I took from Janet. Roxy Barker. I was with her. All night until the next morning."

"Sleeping with a client?" Mia said with a patronizing smile. "That's why she left Janet and came to you, correct?"

"Keep your voice down," he hissed, waving his hands near Mia's face. "If she hears anything, I'm fucked."

Ella had to fight to conceal a smirk. She knew damn well that once the journalists and the reporters got intel from the police, this little tidbit would be broadcast to the world.

"We'll be following up on your alibis, Mr. Neville. Tell both of your girlfriends to expect a visit from local officers."

Leigh narrowed his eyes at Mia in a silent rage. He withdrew into his house. "One last thing, Leigh. Do you know of anyone who might want to hurt either of these two women? Anyone in this art community you're so in touch with?" Mia asked.

"No. Absolutely no one. And even if I did, I wouldn't tell you. The world is better off without those two wasters, and that's all I've got to say on the matter."

Leigh slammed the door and Ella was glad to see the back of him. But she couldn't help feeling a little defeated that Leigh might not be their guy.

"What a piece of shit," Mia said, walking back to their vehicle. Ella followed.

"Something doesn't add up with him. He was way too brash. Even if his alibis check out, we should still look into him. Those girls could be accomplices."

Mia started the engine and took one last look at Leigh Neville's derelict property. "No, these murders are a one-man operation. I'm sure of that part. And our little friend in there doesn't have the mental cunning to pull off something like this. I can see it. And if he was our man, he'd have been much coyer about it. He's being arrogant because he knows his alibis are solid."

"So, dead end," Ella said. She dropped her head into her headrest and blinked away the tiredness. Exhaustion was starting to take over now. "So, what next?"

"He's not our guy, but it's not a dead end. Buckle up. We've got somewhere very important to be."

CHAPTER NINE

He concealed himself in the shadows, watching the rabble disperse from the theatre out into the streets. He'd seen her enter in a bright yellow jacket, so that's what he'd be looking for on the return journey. Something noticeable. Something visually striking.

Amongst the mass, he looked just like one of the punters. Jacket zipped up all the way. Hat and scarf to cover his face. His style was classic, timeless. Not like these new wave artists with their ridiculous dresses and needless accessories and neon hair colors. That was all just a substitute for real talent. People playing the part of artists in lieu of possessing actual artistic ability. He understood them, in a way. If you couldn't be something, the next best thing was just to look like it. It would fool most people, especially these talentless drones, but not him. He saw them for who they really were. Vultures, hacks, throwaways. None of them were capable of creating the masterpieces that he did.

He lingered among a few gatherings, hoping to hear whispers of the recent events. But it was the end of the night, and surely such vital conversation topics had long been depleted by now. Or maybe people still didn't know? Under other circumstances, both Janet and Jennifer would have been at this very event, so surely their absences weren't unnoticed?

The sight of her interrupted his train of thought. She was walking beside a group of hip young things, with their oversized bags and their flowery shirts. They all seemed much younger than she was, but he'd heard that she had a thing for youth.

He moved closer to learn their conversation topics. The man among them mentioned a local bar, and he felt the dread begin to grow.

Don't go to the bar. Go home, he said to himself.

For a moment it seemed that hope was lost, but he heard the woman say that no, she had to get home.

He moved away and lingered beside a streetlamp. He lit a cigarette, blew out smoke then pretended to check his watch. He stalled until the group parted ways. She kissed the man on the cheek then walked the opposite direction to her friends.

I told you, the voice said. *If you anticipate the human mind, it leaves nothing to chance.*

Oh, her voice. Soothing the dread and bringing an ounce of comfort to these beautiful but horrific proceedings. Even though he couldn't see the source of the sound, her voice alone was maddeningly erotic, especially when she spoke words of encouragement.

Now follow her.

He did as the voice instructed. She walked down the main street, past the midnight bars and the takeaway restaurants. He kept a good distance, continually checking his watch or phone or something to indicate he was busy. But really, his eyes never left her.

Down through an underpass and through Seattle's attempt at China Town. She walked at a hurried pace, perhaps familiar with Seattle's crime rate. These weren't the best places to be walking alone at night, but his nearby presence kept her safe from any would-be muggers or attackers. They'd be much more likely to attack someone who was completely alone with no passers-by in the area. He snorted at the irony.

They left the city behind and entered into a residential area. Rows of apartments came first, followed by a street of townhouses. He wasn't familiar with the area, so he made notes of the street names as the signs came into view.

And then she was home. Barely a mile out of the city, he thought. Close enough to visit performances whenever she wanted but without having to swallow the extortionate rent prices of inner-city apartments. Skimping on money again. He expected nothing less from old Katherine.

She put the key in the door and fussed at a yapping dog at her feet. The door closed, providing her the sanctuary of four walls and a roof, and leaving him stranded in the evening streets. Wind blew trash to his feet. He surveyed the area, planning his next move.

Get in there and do what you have to do. Don't let her get away with what she's done. She owes you. Make the slimy bitch pay.

Yes, he was going to do just that. He'd developed a taste for it now.

She was going to be a great canvas for his next masterpiece.

CHAPTER TEN

Ella sat opposite Mia in the Spread Eagle bar. It was half lit with subdued orange lamps, shielded behind scallop shades, tinting the entire space a homely shade of ginger. On the panelled walls, sports pennants and photographs fought for space with hockey and baseball memorabilia. A jukebox flashed. Strip lights hovered over a pool table behind them.

Mia returned from the bar and planted two beers on the table. The last thing Ella wanted right now was booze, but she liked to spend time with Mia outside the precincts and the crime scenes too. Mia Ripley appeared to be a different person outside the spotlight of her job.

"Beer?" Ella asked. "That's not you."

"I like to change things up now and again. Don't tell me you're not a fan, Dark."

"I don't mind it."

"Beer's unique. It's the cause of life's problems, but it's the solution to them as well."

Ella laughed and took a quick glance at the punters. The Spread Eagle wasn't one of those trendy city bars. Not by a long shot. Mia had a tendency to choose the more hardened places, she'd found. Local taverns, family-run joints. Places that served real ale and mead. The Spread Eagle was one such hotspot.

She sipped the beer and was suddenly reminded of the previous night, drinking in a D.C. bar worlds apart from this one. That guy popped into her head, probably for the fifth time that day. His voice rang clear, she could even recall the smell of his cologne. And his terrible jokes. What was his name? Did she even ask? How could she leave so suddenly without getting his number? She cursed herself, wishing she'd pay more attention to the little things. Sure, they probably wouldn't have gotten married, but she could have enjoyed his company once or twice. She'd be lying if she said she hadn't thought of ways to track him down again, but none seemed very effective. He said he was a professional wrestler? Maybe she could scour through wrestling rosters to find him. Although she had no idea where to start.

"Does the WWF still exist?" Ella asked.

Mia had already gulped down half the glass. "The what? The World Wildlife Foundation?"

"No. The wrestling company. Remember them?"

"Vaguely. Why'd you ask?"

Ella thought it best not to go into too much detail. "No reason, really. It just popped into my head."

"Invasive thoughts. We all get them. How have things been since you went back to Intelligence?"

Ella shrugged. "Mostly the same, except people are more scared to ask me for favors now. It's like some of them think I'm too important for the basic stuff, which I guess helps a little."

"Are you okay with everything that happened? Have you come to terms with it? Did you ever see one of the counselors?"

Ella had been offered the opportunity to see a therapist following the incidents on the last case. Apparently, it was something all agents had access to if they needed it. A perk of the job, if it could be termed such a thing.

"No, I never saw any of the counselors. I didn't feel the need to. I understand that I put my life in danger and that's all on me. I made some mistakes, but it worked out for the best. It was a learning experience." Ella let Mia digest the information. "Have you ever used the counseling services?"

Mia took a long drink, leaving only an inch of beer in the bottom. She held up her glass to the bartender and nodded the *another one please* look. "Yes, actually. Once. I had a case that messed with me."

Ella hoped Mia was in the mood to share. Her past fascinated Ella for some reason. "What happened?"

"Tobias Campbell." She spat the words, like her lips were trying to prevent her from saying them.

"Campbell?" Ella asked, wide-eyed. "No way. You worked on his case?"

"Are you familiar with him?"

"Of course. The Executioner. He killed five women in Chicago in the early noughties. He imprisoned them and made them hang themselves."

Mia nodded reluctantly. "Yes, but there's something else. I was the one to apprehend him in his little shack in the middle of butt-fuck nowhere. I broke into his house, and I found... everything."

"All the evidence?"

"I found about twenty pairs of women's shoes. Some were small, like children's. I found piles of I.D. cards. I found bloody nooses and locks of hair. I found things that could incriminate him in around thirty murders, maybe more."

"Holy shit."

"Then Tobias attacked me. He restrained me and dragged me into the woods. Stupidly, I told him backup was coming, and that just made everything worse."

"He tried to kill you?"

"Not quite. He beat me, gave me head trauma. He doused his shack in gasoline and made *me* throw the match inside. I had to watch all the evidence inside burn to a crisp. Completely destroyed. He knew exactly what he was doing. He was giving me a punishment worse than death, because he'd predicted exactly what would happen afterward."

Ella saw where this was going. "He made you look crazy. He made you doubt yourself."

Mia blinked rapidly. "Luckily, my partner at the time arrived and took Tobias down. He went willingly. There was no wild shootout or dramatic showdown. He just surrendered because he knew he'd prolonged his game-playing by doing what he did."

"What about the evidence?" Ella asked.

"Forensics found no traces of shoes. No I.D. cards. No nooses. Nothing. They said I was traumatized and that I hallucinated it all. Blamed the head trauma. That's when they sent me to therapy. I'm certain I saw it, but professionals have told me otherwise. No modern serial killer could be responsible for thirty-plus deaths, not in this era of surveillance and DNA testing. That's what they said. They had the nerve to say this to *me*."

It all felt eerily familiar to Ella. Every time she recalled her father's death, it was different. In some imaginings, she locked eyes with the killer and he knowingly spared her. Sometimes, she found her father dead the next morning. It was all a blur. She didn't know what was real and what wasn't, and the only person who could possibly know the answer is the person who killed him.

"But that's not all. Every year on my birthday, I get a pair of shoes delivered to my house."

"Oh my God. He taunts you?"

"Every year, without fail. I've moved houses four times since it happened, and he always manages to find me."

"Have you ever spoken to him?" Ella asked.

"Never. He's in supermax and I have no intention of seeing his face ever again."

Ella didn't really know what to say. She couldn't imagine what it must be like to be taunted by someone capable of such horrors. While she'd seen the unsub she apprehended in the news, she was yet to make personal contact with him, and would avoid doing so at all costs.

"Shit. I'm sorry for bringing it up."

A barman dropped two more beers on the table. Ella was barely a quarter of the way through her first one. She said thank you anyway.

"It's fine. Like I told you last time, we can't save everyone. I'm under no illusions about that. It's just that I was so close to finding a treasure trove of evidence, to give around twenty families closure. And the children's shoes. I couldn't believe it. We'd profiled that Tobias might have experimented with kids but could never prove it."

A song she recognized came on the jukebox. Def Leppard. One of her dad's favorites. One of the things she'd found in storage, among the letters, was a whole host of classic rock cassettes. She had no way of playing them. "I found some strange letters addressed to my dad," she said. "From some woman back in the early nineties."

"You did? What was strange about them?" Mia seemed glad of the subject change.

"First of all, who sends letters? I just want to know who this woman was. I never saw my dad with another woman."

Mia stifled a grin. "Everyone sent letters back in the day. If someone didn't have a landline phone, the only way to communicate was through the mail. It's not that strange."

"It's just odd. Having a conversation must have taken weeks."

"A lot of people sent them as keepsakes. If your dad kept them, they must have meant something to him. I still have some old love letters locked away somewhere. Old friends, boyfriends, that sort of thing. Did the woman leave her name? Or her signature?"

"Just a first name, but yeah she signed it."

"Run the signature through the graphology software at HQ. I'll hook you up with one of my guys in there. If her signature is anywhere else in the world; legal documents, census forms, medical notes, they'll find it."

Ella hadn't thought of that approach, but the writing was from twenty-plus years ago. There was a chance the woman's signature had changed in that time. "Good idea. Why didn't I think of that?"

54

"Because you're on case number two and I'm on case number two-hundred. Spend enough time hunting people down and you learn a trick or two. Anyway, let's get back. Tomorrow's a new day, with new fun to be had."

**

Their taxi dropped them at the Montanari Hotel in Redmond, a stone's throw away from the Hoskins's family home. Ella glanced at the house as Mia grabbed her things from the trunk. Under the cover of nightfall, the house looked even more tragic. Inside there were two parents, spending their second night in the knowledge that their daughter's corpse had been strung up in a tree. The thought gave Ella a strong awareness of her own mortality, maybe because Jennifer wasn't all that different from herself.

It wasn't a luxury hotel, but it was enough. It had a nice marble floor and an abundance of plants in the foyer, all of which had been gently tended to. Mia checked them in, picking up two keycards. They made their way to the elevator and ascended to the third floor.

"You're in 334, I'm in 340," she said, handing Ella her key.

"What time in the morning?" she asked.

"Taxi at 8. Be ready."

"Always." Ella glanced at her phone and saw it was after midnight. Still, if she fell asleep within the next hour that would mean around seven hours of sleep. Not as much as she'd like, but enough to function on. Ella liked a lot about Mia, but her sleeping habits needed some serious work.

Room 334 was the first one on the row. Ella held the key to the electronic lock and opened the door. Mia followed her in with her bags and dropped them on the floor.

"Right. Looks like I'm at the end of row, down the hall."

Ella moved to the window and looked out on the town beneath. She saw the Hoskins household crystal clear. There seemed to be a light over it, singling it out from the rest of the street.

"Everything okay?" Mia asked.

Ella turned to her. "This might sound like a weird request, but could we switch rooms?" Ella asked. She saw Mia pondering why she might ask such a thing.

"Sure. They're all the same anyway. Is this because you can see the victim's house from here?"

55

Ella complied. "Yes. How'd you know?"

"You've been staring at it since we got out the taxi. Once a profiler, always a profiler." Mia threw her key at her. "Go on. Get to sleep."

"Thank you." Ella took a last glance at the Hoskins home and ruminated on what might be going on inside. She couldn't seem to take her eyes off it. There was a frustration there, directed at the grieving family members for not being as heartbroken as she imagined they should be. Maybe they were still in shock and the real distress was still to come? Memories of her own past came hurtling back, the trauma still as fresh today as it was 23 years ago. She knew what it was like, so she couldn't be mad at Jennifer's parents. Bringing this killer to justice was the only salvation she could offer, and the more she stared at the house, the more she was determined to bring about justice. Ella never made promises to herself for fear she couldn't keep them, but she knew that she wasn't going to leave this city until the creep who did all this was locked in a jail cell.

CHAPTER ELEVEN

Katherine Adams dropped onto her sofa and hit the vape. Greg hated it when she did it in the house, but from what she could tell, he was already asleep. Time for a green tea, a vape, and a late-night film. Maybe there'd be a classic on TNT.

The performance tonight had been below average. Awful, in fact. There was no subtext, just pure hit-you-over-the-head bluntness. If it had been better, she might have hit the bars with her friends, but she had a sour taste in her mouth that she couldn't shake. Was this what the punters wanted now? She remembered when Shakespeare retellings were all the rage, then it was classic novels adapted for the stage. Now it's just... whatever the hell that was.

She thought about reviewing it for one of the publications but decided that no review would be worse than a bad review. Before the show, she had ideas of bringing the performance to her own theatre. But no, that possibility was dead in the water. She wanted classy acts, performance art that had a message beneath the hideous exterior. Finding it was like trying to find Sasquatch.

Katherine flicked through the channels top to bottom and back again. For a Saturday night, pickings were slim. Trashy infomercials, celebrity panel shows, a comedy film about unwanted pregnancies. Hilarious, she thought. Just what kids should be taught. Maybe this was the world now. Maybe she'd been left behind, still clambering for something with meaning behind it.

She went to the kitchen and flicked on the kettle but switched it off again when she heard a sound outside. She looked out the window at her tiny backyard. There was no place for anything to hide out there. It was barely big enough to fit her two trash cans. She returned to the kettle, brushing the sound off as her imagination working overtime. God knows she had a busy one.

The kettle roared to life. She moved to the cupboard and picked up a cup, then almost dropped it smashing to the ground when she saw a blur in her vision. Outside again. Something rushed past. She turned off the kitchen light to get a better view of the exterior, seeing nothing but small pavement, a fence, and a few bins.

She thought about waking Greg up, but he'd just tell her she was being hysterical. It would be the spider-in-the-bathroom incident all over again. Screw it, she'd take matters into her own hands for once.

Katherine pulled open the back door with force. A feeble attempt to scare off intruders. She peered over the fences into the neighbor's gardens and the adjacent alleyway but saw no signs of life. Over to her trash cans, she saw that the lids were off center. She'd never leave them like that. Her OCD wouldn't let her. She edged over, pulled off the lids.

Her hand jumped to her throat. She concealed a scream.

"Jesus H.," she said.

Staring back at her was a tiny little creature. Beady eyes, long grey whiskers, sniffing the air. He seemed to be smiling at her. Relief set in. "You raccoon bastard," she said. "You scared the shit out of me."

Her new little friend gripped a chocolate wrapper between his paws and scurried away, sniggering as he made his escape. If he wasn't so cute, Katherine would have been madder. She went back inside and cursed herself for being so stupid. Thank God she didn't wake her husband up. He'd never have let her live it down.

She returned to the kitchen and locked the door behind her for peace of mind. She went back to the kettle, poured her tea, then heard something else from the living room. She peered around the door, finding the TV blaring loudly with static.

She was sure she left it playing that awful comedy film. Had the aerial fallen out? No, it couldn't have. It was HDMI. Not to mention that the volume had been turned up much higher than she'd left it. OCD meant the volume was either on eight or ten, nothing more or less.

Katherine began to feel like she wasn't alone. Maybe tonight's show had imbued her with some unnatural, negative energy that would haunt her for the rest of her days. She felt watched, exposed, like maybe Greg was messing with her for being out so late. Had those passive-aggressive comments he always made whenever she got back later than planned finally made him retaliate? Whatever it was, it wasn't funny.

She leaned behind the TV to check the aerial and found nothing unusual. Before rationale could take over, she felt the pressure mounting against her neck. Her first instinct was to scream, but any chance of exclamation had been silenced. Her blurry vision made out the sight of gleaming steel, a sharp blade, and before she had time to react, a gush of warm blood. The visual came first, then the sensation of her skin being slit open. She toppled backward in shock, hands clutching her neck in a futile attempt to stop the tsunami of blood escaping from her throat. The world went blurry, she lost all function; paralyzed, unable to do nothing but stare at the person standing over her.

He bent down and covered her mouth to keep her mute. Her convulsions gradually came to a stop as death began to take hold. She thought of Greg, upstairs, unaware. She thought of her business, now left without an owner. Suddenly, she regretted ever doing what she did. Such a hasty move, and it had brought her to the end of life.

He removed his hand and caressed her face with the tip of his knife. With her dying breath, she tried to scream his name.

CHAPTER TWELVE

"Okay, so let's go over everything we know," Ella said. She stood before the whiteboard in their office at the precinct. It was a new day and sleep had rejuvenated her. She was ready to bust this case open, find some connection they hadn't made the day before.

"Start at the beginning," Mia said, scanning through some paper documents. She turned her attention to the whiteboard.

"Janet Wootton, victim number one, was abducted on the night of the 15th. The killer blitz-attacked her, slit her throat and then extracted her liver. She was on her way home from work when the abduction took place, putting it around 7pm."

"The organ extraction means he took her somewhere private. He couldn't have removed her liver at the scene, or in the back of his vehicle. This unsub has his own space, probably lives alone. That means he's capable enough of looking after himself, maybe a professional."

"Right. Then he took her to the disposal site and put her up on display. Officers checked the scene and found weights similar to the one we found at the second victim's disposal site. We can safely say that's how he's erecting these victims in trees."

"He found a process that works for him and he stuck to it," said Mia. "The complex nature of it could mean he's creative or he works in an industry that familiarizes him with hoists, pulleys, installations."

Ella began drawing up a timeline on the whiteboard. "Three days later, he abducts Jennifer Hoskins as she's heading from a night out. That puts her abduction around 11pm. He attacks her and displays her in an almost identical way to the first victim, but this time he removes her heart."

"The organ removal is what throws me," Mia said. "It's at odds with everything else about his modus operandi. Everything he does is for aesthetic purposes, theatricality. That could be why he kills with a single laceration to the throat because it results in less trauma to the body. No one is going to see a removed organ, so why do it?"

"Signature?" Ella asked.

"No, signature is the component of the crime that doesn't need to be included but has to be to appease his fantasies. His signature is that he displays his victims in trees. He could have disposed them anywhere, especially in a mountainous area like Seattle, but he chose to string them up in parks. That part of the crime is the most important to him."

"If we go with my artist theory, maybe the organs are just a keepsake for him. Apparently, Picasso kept every stub of chalk that he used."

"No, we can't focus solely on this artist theory you have. I see where you're coming from but it's not conducive to a successful investigation. It just blindsides us and makes us less open to alternative theories. We need to keep an open mind and focus on the facts. It's even possible that the unsub has no links to the artistry world at all and knows these women through other avenues."

Ella sighed internally. She thought otherwise, but it was best to follow Mia's guidance regardless.

"Okay. As far as we know, there's no connection between the two victims outside of their links to the art world. Janet never represented Jennifer."

"The tech department is looking into their digital footprints and as of this morning, the two never crossed paths. We can safely say the two weren't aware of each other. The only link is Leigh Neville, who knew both, but his alibis are solid."

"Damn it. We're still waiting on the full forensic reports from the crime scenes. Sheriff Brooks should have them." Ella looked towards his office. Empty, lights out. Mia's buzzing phone interrupted them.

"Speak of the Devil," she said. She answered the call.

Ella saw the look on her face sharpen. She knew what it meant. Mia exposed that bad news smile. "Okay. Text me the location." She hung up.

Ella threw down her whiteboard marker and grabbed her jacket.

"We need to meet Brooks at High Memorial Park. They found another body."

***

Ella had seen photos of the first two victims but seeing a strung-up corpse in the flesh was a different experience entirely. Ella, Mia, Brooks, and a few local officers stood at the foot of a large Redwood in High Memorial Park. Rain trickled from the overcast skies, muddy

61

grass dogged their steps. Ella pulled off her glasses and wiped away the residue.

The victim was an older woman. Blonde, slim, but weathered by age. Her hair was thinning, skin was cracked, fingertips were yellowed. A smoker, Ella thought, and one who'd been doing it a while. She'd been displayed in an identical manner to the others, bound by the wrists and torso and displayed around fifteen feet in the air. Two ladders were perched up against the tree so forensic officers could closer inspect the body.

"A dog walker found her this morning. Barely thirty minutes ago. Everything is the same as the other victims," said Brooks. "We're just waiting to play the organ lottery. My guess is on the kidneys."

Neither of the agents laughed. "A single laceration to the neck again, it seems," said Mia. "And we can assume he used the same approach to elevate her up there."

"No, actually. There's no gym equipment in this park at all. He must have used a different technique."

"A serial killer altering his M.O. at only the third kill? That's unlikely. If everything else is consistent, then the signature process would be too."

Ella looked around. The area was a dense cluster of trees, far away from the public park area and war memorial the place was known for. During the early hours of the morning, someone could move through here relatively unobserved.

She walked in the opposite direction and landed on a dirt path. She checked the distance between the path and the disposal site, determining it to be less than thirty feet. When they arrived, the cruiser had dropped them a further fifty feet away.

The ideas began to form. Ella envisioned how such a process might play out, wondering if it was feasible for an organized offender to pull off. A flurry of past crime scenes manifested in her mind, quickly recalling several that involved dirt tracks in wooded areas. There was Peter Sutcliffe, killer of thirteen women who brushed away his tire tracks after stalking his victims. There was the Hillside Strangler, Edmund Kemper, the Forest Park Killer, William Bonin, Randy Kraft. They all used the same technique, so there was no reason this killer couldn't do the same. She ran through it in a linear fashion, finding it was more than feasible, it was obvious.

Ella bent down to inspect the dirt trail. She ran her fingers through a small puddle, then followed the track along back to the body. There was more water here than there was everywhere else, as though this particular track attracted rainfall more than the surrounding areas.

Then there were the swirls. The circular motions on the dirt, something which nature couldn't create. They had to be put there by a human.

Mia and Brooks seemed to be arguing about something. She heard raised voices, but she kept her mind on the emerging theory. She thought that Mia would probably shoot her down, but she was in the company of everyone who needed to hear it.

"He used a car this time," Ella said. Mia and Brooks closed their mouths and turned to her.

"I checked. No tire tracks," said Brooks.

"Because he's removed them. He drove his vehicle through here. That's probably how he hoisted her up there. Tied the rope to her body, threw the rope over the tree and then attached it to his car. Agent Ripley, come and see this."

Mia appeared beside her. Ella bent down and ran her fingers along the dirt.

"This whole dirt track seems to be waterlogged, like he's tried to erase them by throwing water on them. Then he's brushed through them in a circular motion, maybe with a trowel or a brush." Ella decided to hit her with it. "You know who uses circular motions? Artists, when they paint."

Ella waited for a rebuttal. Mia scrutinized the dirt track leading away from the disposal site. She followed it along, finding the same small ditches and clumps of mud that Ella had.

"But our victims aren't artists as such," Mia said. "There's a difference between regular art and performance art."

"Most performance artists dabble in regular painting too," said Ella. She recalled the painting in Jennifer Hoskins's room. Jennifer considered herself a performance artist but had tried her hand at portraits too. "That's how a lot of them start out."

Ella saw it all as clear as day. This unsub saw himself as an artist and these were his unique pieces. These parks were his backgrounds, the bodies were his canvases, and their mutilations were his brushstrokes. He targeted these women because they represented something he either loved or hated, the same way a painter might use their favorite acrylics or their favorite canvases.

Then she thought of the liver removal, the heart extraction. Mia thought these didn't classify as his signature, but Ella thought she was wrong. It was rare, but it wasn't unheard of, especially after what she'd learned during their last stint together. This was his way of signing his work, the way most artists literally put their names in the corner of their prints. He was taking credit for the work in the most deranged way he could.

Then it hit her.

"Ripley, I've got it. I know why he's taking organs."

"I'm all ears."

"He's watermarking his work. He's putting his stamp on his masterpiece so he can be the one to take credit for it. Outside of law enforcement, he's the only person who knows about the organ removal. So, when the time comes, he can prove that he was the killer."

Mia stood up from inspecting the tracks and exhaled deeply. She looked up at the dead body in the tree, now being unhooked by forensics and lowered to the ground. Brooks stood by directing traffic.

"We got something else," Brooks shouted, commanding their attention. "Get a load of this."

Mia and Ella approached the corpse, now lying in an unzipped body bag. Ella saw it was a fresh death with barely any signs of rigor mortis setting in. She still looked like a human being, except for one thing.

"What's wrong with her eyes?" Brooks said, directing his question to the two forensic technicians inspecting her. Ella was wondering the same. They looked cloudy, a strange greenish shade that she'd never seen in any eye color before.

"Sheriff, this woman is blind," the technician said. "That's your simple answer. Look at this, though." He then held a gloved fingertip to something on the side of her head.

"That's new. He tried to cut into her skull."

"Brain removal?" Ella asked.

"Why go through the temples?" said Brooks. They both directed their questions to Mia.

She rubbed the rainwater from her face and scratched her neck in one swift motion. "I don't know about that. Get her to the coroner's and fast track the report. But you know, Dark, you might be onto something with this artist theory of yours."

Finally. Acceptance. She revelled in the dopamine hit.

A ping sounded from Mia's phone. She stared at the new message.

"What's the news?" Ella asked.

"Come on. We have some alibis to check out," Mia said.

"Great. Who are we meeting?"

"I'm going to meet a couple of local artists. You're going to meet Roxy Barker, the client Janet poached off Leigh Neville. She seems like a firecracker, so keep your wits about you."

"Don't worry about that," Ella said. "I'm ready."

CHAPTER THIRTEEN

Roxy Barker's studio was a modern-day sideshow. It was a one-room affair located on the outskirts of Seattle, and no doubt the rent was extortionate, but she must have covered it several times over given the price of admission. Thankfully, Ella was awarded entrance for free.

Ella and Mia had each gone to separate appointments. They'd contacted a number of major artists in the area and requested their services with the investigation. It seems they were all as eager as each other to gossip about the so-called art community. Ella's first stop had been with self-proclaimed *Nymphetamine* Roxy Barker.

She browsed the pieces on display, most of which were just pictures from Roxy's old performances. Each piece seemed to have overtly sexual overtones. In one, she was dressed as a giant vulva. In another, she was giving birth to a pig. There were some props on display too. Ella had no idea the kind of people who'd pay to see this stuff, but she'd love to know.

Roxy arrived from a back room. She was a striking figure, annoyingly attractive. She had an athletic body, toned in all the right places. Long purple hair that framed her naturally appealing features. She even had bronzed skin all over, possibly through use of a tanning bed given the season. "Agent Dark, yes?" she said, extending her hand. "Ha, like the old Nintendo game. Perfect Dark. The girl on that was named Agent Dark."

"Oh, I didn't know. Never had video games in our house. Thanks for agreeing to meet me."

"No worries, hun. Come and sit in the back. It's warmer in here."

Ella followed, surprised by Roxy's bubbly demeanor. She hadn't expected someone so lively. Judging by her art, she expected a somber, introspective type. They took a seat on a pair of stools in a small kitchen area.

"So, two murders, huh? That's crazy. It wasn't me, if that's what you're thinking," she laughed.

"Three, actually. There was another one this morning. We don't have an ID on the victim yet, though." As she finished her sentence,

Ella wondered whether or not she was supposed to tell anyone about the new finding. She cursed herself.

"Holy moly. That's horrible. Another artist?"

"Possibly. We don't know yet. We're just trying to gather some intel on the kinds of people involved in this community. Maybe find someone who links the two victims together. Your insight would be greatly appreciated."

"Well, Janet was my agent for a while, but we didn't really see eye-to-eye. She wanted me to tone down the visceral nature of my work. She wanted political statements, gender statements, but I'm more interested in exploration of the human condition. My whole ethos is sex and how it defines us. Jan wasn't a believer in that. She wanted me to jump on the feminist bandwagon and that's not my style."

"What about Jennifer?"

"Never met her. My new agent used to represent her, but he sacked her. That's all I know."

Ella resisted the temptation to spill the beans about Leigh's relationship status. Maybe Roxy already knew. It wasn't her place to judge.

"Is there anyone in the community who might want to hurt either of those people? Someone with an unsavory reputation, perhaps?"

Roxy bit her nails and lost herself for a second. She tapped her fingers against her teeth. "Well, there is one person. I probably shouldn't tell you this, but…"

"What is it? Anything you say will be dealt with in confidence."

"He'll never know it was me who told you about him, right? You'll never mention my name to him?"

"Never. We won't say a thing."

"Dax Matheson. A real… piece of work. Lives in Capitol Hill but that's all I know."

Ella wrote his name and location in her notebook. "Who is this fellow?"

"I take my art seriously, as you can probably see. But if I had to give it all up tomorrow, I would. Some people wouldn't be so willing. Some people live for this stuff. There are some very intense individuals in this scene. Total crazies. Borderline psychopaths."

"And Dax is one of these people?"

"Very much so. He has an obsession with blood. That's his medium."

It took Ella a few seconds to connect the dots. "He paints with blood?"

"Exactly. I've met him a few times and I always found him very unsettling. He offered me an extortionate sum for a vial of my blood. I had to decline."

"And you think he could be responsible for the recent killings?"

"It's hard to say. I mean, he's always pushing the envelope. He's been known to paint on some strange canvases. He's been arrested for painting on public walls, shop windows, things like that. He once made a piece of out of blood and human bones. Most people stay away from him, but obviously he attracts the outsider crowd."

Sounded like someone Ella needed to speak to. He seemed like a fascinating person, if a little intimidating. She'd need Mia by her side when she visited him. "Do you know if Dax had any connection to the Janet or Jennifer?"

"I don't know much about him, but he ran in the same circles as those two. Pretty much everyone in the scene knows Janet Wootton, and Jennifer was the hottest new piece of ass, so it's not a stretch to think he knew them. You can probably Google him and find out all about him." Roxy picked up her phone beside her and tapped in her pin code. "It was only a few months ago he was in the news for painting something on a butchers' window. I think he painted a human heart."

Ella froze. Her fingertips lost all feeling for a second. Something icy ran down her back. "A heart?" she asked.

"Yup. Does that mean anything to you?"

She considered it. "No, it just seems odd," she lied. "Thank you very much for your time. You've been a great help."

"No worries, just... hold up," Roxy stopped herself. "Dax has a gallery tonight at the Woodward Centre. It's all over his socials."

Her curiosity peaked. "Will he be there?" she asked. "I've never been to a gallery before."

"Absolutely he will. He'll be the center of attention, like he always has to be."

Ella thanked Roxy took her leave, eager to share her findings with Mia. One thing was for sure, they'd be seeing Dax Matheson in the flesh tonight.

***

Ella and Mia reconvened at Laiho's Bar in downtown Seattle for lunch. The city's finest club sandwich, it said, but Ella wasn't convinced. The place stank of cigarettes and spilled liquor, and their strip lights were nothing short of blinding. A waitress in a tartan skirt pirouetted from table to table, enticing each customer to buy another coffee, another beer, a dessert to compliment that fine steak dinner. It was the classic American diner turned up to eleven.

"You're not going to believe this," Ella said with half a mouthful of bread. She chewed and swallowed quickly. The bread was harder than she'd like, and the lettuce was too leafy. "There's this local artist who paints in blood. A real freak, apparently. A shock artist, I'd guess was the term. He's doing an event tonight. Maybe we should pay him a visit?"

Mia sipped an Irish coffee. Now that Ella thought about it, she didn't think she'd ever seen Mia eat anything. It explained how she kept her figure, at least.

"Dax Matheson," Mia said, like she was reading Ella's mind. "His name cropped up in my research too. Two ladies I spoke with said he propositioned them. He wanted vials of their blood."

"Really? So he's a well-known deviant around the community. That sounds like a solid hit to me."

Mia checked her phone. She squinted to read something on the screen. "I'm just not sure he's capable of something like this. Have you seen him?"

"You mean what he looks like? No."

"He's a giant. Absolutely huge. Wider than a London bus and twice as tall. Whoever committed these crimes can climb trees without using ladders."

"Big guys can be flexible too. If he's got core strength, he's more likely to be able to pull himself up."

"Maybe, we'll see. I've got Brooks pulling his file for me. He's been arrested before, so we know everything about him."

Ella finished her sandwich and turned to her Coke. "He has a criminal record?" she asked excitedly, gripping her glass with trembling fingers. Dax seemed to fit the profile almost perfectly. Everything was falling into place.

"He does. Vandalism, reckless behaviour. And what's the next step in that pattern?"

"Aggravated assault, maybe homicide. Do we have a name on victim number three yet?"

Mia smirked. "You're getting pretty astute, Dark. You might need to slow down before you end up wanting to do this full time."

A waitress appeared offering additions. Both agents declined. "Give me a few weeks on this case and let me see. I'm still in two minds about the whole thing. Sitting behind a desk is comfortable but being out here gives me that *job satisfaction* thing everyone raves about."

"Consider it wisely. Thanks to this job, I've been to this bar more times than I can count. I'll let you decide whether that's a good or bad thing. But to answer your question, yes, we do. Victim number three is Katherine Adams. Forty-four years old. And guess what."

"Artist?"

"No. Venue owner. A small indie theatre in the city, but most of the performers there are artists of some kind. Gallery showings, the crazy shit that Jennifer Hoskins got up to."

"Another link."

"Yes, and it's starting to look like you were right. The murders, the artistic touches, the victims. Everything suggests this is an artist. Just so you know, I sometimes oppose your theories to give you motivation to prove them. So far, it's worked. It makes you refine them. If I don't agree with something you put forward, it doesn't mean I'm completely against it."

Ella smiled. She thought Mia was maybe trying to convince herself of her statement rather than her. "I know," she said. "Keep doing it."

A buzzing on the table distracted them both. "Be good news, please," Mia said. She browsed her phone with that curious look on her face. Eyes narrowed, lips pursed. Ella used the moment to take in her surroundings. Sometimes, she struggled to believe this was her life. It still felt like a dream and that, any second, she'd wake up at age 21 still working for the Virginia police.

An older waitress passed by and collected her empty glass. Ella noticed her nametag. SAMANTHA. What were the odds this was the same Samantha from her dad's letters? Almost zero, but it was an interesting thought experiment. She tried to imagine them together, frolicking in her childhood garden while Ella jumped through sprinklers as an innocent five-year-old. While it certainly wasn't the woman in front of her who'd sent them, there was a woman out there who had. Was she still alive? Would she even remember her dad if she was? Impossible to know, but she needed to try. She'd never met anyone else who knew her father, and she had a longing to talk to someone about him, to say his name aloud and bring him back to life for the briefest of conversations. Maybe this woman had more pictures of her dad? Maybe she had her own fond memories she wanted to share?

"Well, here's something," Mia said. "Stop eyeing up waitresses for a second and listen up."

Ella returned to the room. "Ha. Sorry. What is it?"

"Brooks got the lowdown on this Dax asshole. So, guess who his former agent was."

"Janet Wootton?"

"Correct. A few weeks ago, he had a private showing at a venue in the city. Guess who that venue belonged to."

"Victim number three." Ella decided to be honest. "I've forgotten her name."

"Yes, Katherine Adams."

"Damn. What are we waiting for? Let's go."

"Hold your horses. Brooks is sending me another file. It's a big one so it's taking a while to come through."

Ella cleaned her glasses and then pulled on her jacket. She could taste the cheap lettuce still teasing the back of her throat. She jokingly thought maybe they'd have free coffee at the gallery, then genuinely hoped it would be a reality. Bag a suspect, grab a drink. That would be the exclamation point on a successful day.

Ella watched Mia's face go from technology-induced annoyance to shock and awe. Ella tried to sneak a glance at her phone but just saw the blur of text running across her screen as she swiped.

"Well, fuck me running, looks like we've got ourselves a red-hot suspect."

"Something else?"

"Looks like our man is more than just a deranged artist. He's a sex pest too. Let's go meet this piece of shit for ourselves."

CHAPTER FOURTEEN

The Woodward Centre in downtown Seattle wouldn't open to the public for another four hours, but Ella wasn't going to let that stop them. Mia assumed driving duties after they left the bar. It was a Sunday afternoon and it seemed most of the city had opted to stay indoors.

"The tech department got a hit. They found a bunch of emails exchanged between Jennifer Hoskins and Dax Matheson. Well, I say exchanged, but they were mostly one-sided."

"Dax harassed her?"

"Yeah. Grab my phone. Take a look. Password is Alfie."

Ella found Mia's phone in the cup holder. She picked it up and unlocked it. It opened up to a long PDF file with screen grabs from an email client.

I was thinking about you last night. Your body would make a great canvas. I'd like to paint it white. What do you say?

Jenny, you know I can just take whatever I want from you, don't you?

A private showing of my work is just what you need.

There was very little in way of response from Jennifer. Ella had seen this approach from plenty of men over the years. Aggressive pursuing, a misplaced romantic gesture. The idea was to weaken the target until they gave in; until adhering to their requests was less hassle than ignoring them. For a lot of men, it worked.

"She ignored him and he just kept contacting her."

"Exactly. Until it all got too much for him. Check the very last message."

Ella scrolled down. "Oh, shit."

I'm coming for you. You can't hide from me anymore. I've had enough, Jenny. Sent the night before Jennifer died.

"He was obsessed with her."

"Here, grab the cuffs. We're bringing this guy in. We're not a believer in coincidences."

They came to an alleyway barely wide enough to fit a single vehicle. On either side, two rotten buildings competed to be which could be the most repulsive. The alley appeared to be a dumping ground for trash bags and beer cans. Ella jumped out the car, noticing a rat scurrying beneath the building to her left. Her eyes towards the tiny black door below a sign. WOODWARD STAGE DOOR.

"We've arrived at the back exit."

"I don't care," Mia said, charging towards the entryway. "Since you don't have a gun, follow my lead."

Ella did, entering into a dim foyer with gig posters covering every inch of the walls. The only route was up a flight of stairs. At the top, Ella heard voices.

A figure appeared as they reached the pinnacle. They found themselves staring at the palm of a hand. "Woah, excuse me. Who are you?" the man shouted. He was wearing a black work-shirt with WOODWARD embroidered on the breast.

Mia flashed her badge. "FBI. We're looking for a Dax Matheson. Is he here?"

The guard slowly withdrew his hand. It seems he wasn't used to be people being above him in the authoritarian hierarchy. "Yes, he is. Can I ask what this is about?" A desperate attempt to claw back some dominance in the situation.

"No." Mia pushed him to the side and stormed past. Ella followed, flashing the guard a look that subtly apologized for Mia's cavalry approach. Beyond a door, they found themselves in a tiny concert venue of some kind. A very small stage with amps on either side. A DJ booth across the room. There was a bar, stools and some deflated sofas lined up along the walls. Not at all what Ella expected.

More concerning was the bizarre artwork and sculptures perched on display stands, creating a curved path around the room. Each piece was behind protective glass, emitting a strange specimen-in-a-jar look. Every one, it seemed, featured human blood as part of its design. The first one Ella came to was a simple painting; a human spine that morphed into a giant insect. Next was a portrait of a man, tearing his head in half by the ears.

Ella heard footsteps approaching from afar. Beside the stage, a curtain swayed. There was no doubt that the man who emerged from within was Dax Matheson.

He had to duck his head to fit through. He was monstrously tall, with large hands that promised reckoning to anyone who might cross him. His shaven head gleamed in the spotlights overhead, accentuating the pulsing veins within. He wore a tight black t-shirt, exposing his

73

incredibly muscular arms and chest. Below his right eye was a teardrop tattoo. He carried a glass cabinet with a single hand.

"Who might you two be?" he asked, stopping where he stood.

Mia flashed her badge again. "FBI. We want to speak with you."

The breaking of glass, the blur of a giant on the run. Dax dropped the cabinet, smashing it to a thousand pieces and disappeared behind the curtain. Instinctively, both agents hurried after him. Mia went first, jumping over the glass and running into the private area. Ella followed close behind, thinking that the backstage room couldn't be very big considering the size of the venue.

But she found out she was wrong. It was a long stone corridor with a number of doors on either side. "Dark, check all these rooms, I'm going up ahead. I'm guessing this building is much more than just that shitty venue."

"On it," Ella said. Mia scrambled down the corridor and out of sight. Ella pulled open the first door and peered inside. Just a toilet and sink. She moved to the next one. Surely there weren't many places for a giant to hide.

The next room seemed to store more of Dax's bizarre creations. Glass boxes with freakish designs inside them. Ella struggled to stop staring at one; a weird snake structure made from bones. Something made her want to smash it to bits.

She turned and continued, finding a row of heads having popped out from one of the doors. Staff, maybe, or other artists. Ella didn't know nor care. "Dax. Where did he go?" she shouted.

The people looked at each other, then all seemed to shake their heads in unison. Ella ran past them, finding the last door on the row. She tugged at the handle and found it rigid. It moved slightly, but not enough. She realized someone was holding it from the other side.

"Dax, you have nowhere to go. Come on out."

A sudden force sent her flying back against the wall behind her. Her spine cracked against it, the pain drawing all the air from her lungs. Dax emerged from the door and sped back the way he came, his thunderous footsteps echoing throughout the passageway. Ella jumped to her feet in pursuit, ignoring the agony running up and down her back. "Stop him!" she screamed at the gawking onlookers.

One of them attempted to block Dax's path, but Dax grabbed the nameless person by the throat and threw him back into the fray of people. He disappeared back into the main area with Ella not far behind.

Suddenly, an idea came to her. Surely, Mia would hear the commotion and return. Ella just needed to stall until Dax found a gun barrel pointing at him. Although, given his inhuman look, she doubted even that would be enough to take him down.

She reached the stage area just in time to see Dax scrambling towards the flight of stairs leading outside. She thought back to what Roxy had told her about the man in front of her. Ella screamed as loudly as her vocal cords allowed.

"I'm going to smash every piece of shit in here,"

And he stopped. Turned around. Realizing that his life's work was at the mercy of others.

"I'm going to rip up every stupid painting. Smash your sculptures. It'd be a fitting end to your legacy, wouldn't it?"

"You wouldn't dare."

"Want to try me?"

"Touch anything and I'll tear your head off."

Ella could see the conflict on his face. He hovered between the foyer leading downstairs and the stage room. She watched his body language. His anchor points seem to be pointed towards the exit, suggesting he was going to bail at any second. Could she reach him in time? Probably not. Even if she did, he was much more physically capable than her. She couldn't take him down. She noticed that the security guard had made himself scarce too.

There was only one way to keep him here. Ella looked beside her and saw a clay sculpture. It was a bust of a man vomiting up tentacles. Only the tentacles had been painted red. She rocked its glass box on its base, then turned back to see Dax's face burning bright red.

"I'll fucking kill you right here," he screamed, a thick vein popping in his forehead.

She grabbed the glass cabinet and tipped it on its side, keeping her gaze locked on Dax.

He began moving closer, seemingly unable to leave his work behind.

The glass began to slide between her fingers. It was dense, fragile, much heavier than she thought. She adjusted her grip to keep it firm. She had no intentions of letting it go. It was just a ruse.

But just the sight of his sculpture in the throes of falling propelled Dax towards her. In a matter of milliseconds, his hands were around her neck, squeezing the life from her. She dropped the cabinet and to her fortune, it fell in an upright position. She instinctively grabbed

Dax's hands to relieve the pressure, but it did nothing. She kicked out, connecting with his thighs, but it was like colliding with solid steel. The man was seven feet of muscle and rage.

Ella felt her feet leave the ground. Dax picked her up by her neck and held her in the air. Her vision blurred but she continued to kick maniacally, eventually catching him in the groin. Dax loosened his grip and keeled over, dropping Ella to the sticky venue floor.

He was on her again immediately, but she rammed the clay statuette straight into his face, knocking him back and sending a gush of blood onto the stage. She saw around five people watching the battle from the corridor, all with jaws dropped and teeth clenched. Ella decided to capitalize on the momentum by grabbing Dax's arm and twisting it into a submission, but the pain seemed to fuel him. He slammed her spine-first into the ground, held her by the neck and raised his fist in the air. Blood dripped from his nose onto her face and in her mouth.

"You broke my masterpiece," he screamed. "I'm going to make you suffer."

"Don't move an inch. Stay right the fuck there."

Mia's voice. Finally. Ella would have breathed a sigh of relief if Dax's hand wasn't crushing her windpipe. When he realized there was a Glock 22 in his face, Ella felt his grip lessen. He stood himself upright.

"And if I don't."

"Listen here, Steroids. I'd love nothing more than for you to haul ass so I've got an excuse to shoot you. Be my guest."

Ella scrambled to her feet and positioned herself near the exit. This man wasn't going anywhere. "Cuff him," Mia said. She turned to the onlookers lingering behind her. "Thanks for helping out, you lousy fucks."

Ella slowly edged towards Dax and locked the cuffs on him. There was barely enough room to fit them around his iron wrists.

"Sorry for taking so long," Mia said. "It's a maze down there. I came back as soon as I could."

Ella looked at the destruction. Blood, glass, shattered icons. Crystal shards lodged in her arm. A hulking giant in handcuffs. She felt like her spine was on the verge of collapse. "I was Van Gogh there for a second," she said.

Mia checked Dax's restraints, then slapped him on the back in a *let's get out of here* gesture.

"Excuse me?"

"I was Van Gogh. Left ear, all alone."

It was the first time Ella saw Mia laugh.

"Come on. Mr. Matheson here has got some explaining to do."

CHAPTER FIFTEEN

Ella felt all eyes turn to her. Walking into the precinct with Dax in cuffs caused an abrupt end to everyone's activities, at least for a minute or two. The entire workforce stopped and stared at the human giant being directed by two women half his size. Dax maintained his broad-shouldered posture the entire time, never once reducing himself to a defeated slump. Ella knew that he loved the attention regardless of the circumstance.

She felt calmer now that Dax was surrounded by capable police officers. The whole journey back from the venue she'd had invasive thoughts of him brute-forcing his way through the restraints, hijacking the vehicle, snapping her neck. It was surprising how the threat of a bullet could reduce someone to such submission.

They passed Brooks's office. Ella spotted him through the blinds talking on the phone. He promptly hung up and exited when he saw the agents arrive. His door burst open, and his eyes locked on the suspect.

"Fuck me."

"Exactly what we said."

It must have been quite a sight, this hulking monster decked in gashes, his nose dislodged from its regular position. Dax didn't even look at Brooks, keeping himself in stern refusal mode. "Welcome back, Mr. Matheson." Brooks called for the assistance of two officers. "Take him to the holding cell."

Ella watched him disappear from view. It was clear he wasn't going to talk, least of all be honest with them. Extracting the truth from him was going to be a difficult process.

"He didn't want to come quietly, then?" Brooks asked.

"Not quite," Mia said, "but he's here and he's not leaving until he either confesses or we find something that incriminates him. I'm ninety-nine percent sure he's our guy."

"What's your strategy?" Brooks asked. "Out here we wear them down until they give in. How do the FBI do things?"

"Dark here is going to do the talking."

Ella snapped her head around. "What? Me?"

"You're the one who kicked his ass. He'll be more responsive to you than anyone else."

"Kicked his ass? He nearly murdered me. If you hadn't have shown up, I'd be dead."

"By the way, Sheriff, what's the charge for vandalism in this town? Rookie here smashed a few valuables."

"Depends. Get a confession out of him and I'll waive any criminal charges. How does that sound?"

"Corrupt, but a deal. What do you say, Dark? We'll be watching from the outside. I can keep a good eye on his body language from there. I can look for any significant tells."

Ella thought back to the incident in the seventies involving Edmund Kemper and famed FBI profiler Robert Ressler. For a short while, the two were left alone in a holding cell, and Edmund jokingly threatened to kill him. It left Ressler mentally scarred.

"What am I going to say? Interviews aren't my strong point. You saw that last time."

"Present him with the evidence and watch him squirm. Nothing more," Mia said. Something told Ella that Dax didn't often do much squirming, but he might be different when faced with a possible murder charge. Coppery blood teased the back of her throat. Her body was still reeling from her war. Maybe it would give her the adrenaline she needed to look this son of a bitch in the eye and demand answers.

"You want to be the cream of the FBI then you need to master it all, and there's no better teacher than experience."

Ella pushed her hair off her face, finding it damper than she expected. She didn't know if it was blood or rainwater. "Alright, but keep a close eye on him. Something tells me he isn't going to be very friendly."

***

The holding cell was a small box room with two chairs, a steel table and anchor points attached to the floor. When Ella walked in, she found Dax Matheson leaning back with hands behind his head. His massive frame barely fit in the wooden chair.

Ella trembled with anticipation. Being locked alone with a potential serial killer was something she'd had both dreams and nightmares about, especially one as imposing as the giant sitting in front of her. But she had to keep her cool and stay focused. If there was any hesitation in her voice or body language, she had a feeling Dax would pick up on it. Despite their size difference, she was the one in charge. That's what she told herself as she looked into his eyes.

"Mr. Matheson, I'm Agent Dark. We need to talk."

Dax wiped a smear of blood off his lip and rubbed it into his arm. "You're lucky I didn't kill you."

Before she brought up the incident, there were some other things on Ella's mind. For all his brashness, Dax seemed a bizarre individual. Ella decided to use the moment to satisfy her curiosity.

"Why blood?" she asked. "What's the deal? A gimmick?"

Dax shook his head in a patronizing manner. "Blood is the life force. I feel a deeper connection to my work. My paintings are meditations on the canvas. I wouldn't expect someone like you to understand."

She quickly decided she wasn't going to give him a platform to boast. "Given your reaction to our intrusion, I suggest you know why you're here."

He breathed deeply and kept his stare locked on her. He had that penetrating look, desperate for dominance, always needing to be the alpha. Ella saw it all the time, and she liked to think she knew how to combat it. But still, his stare shook her. If not for Mia, Dax could have easily killed her.

"No. Why don't you tell me?" he asked. His voice had a slight European twang. Romanian, maybe, but raised in America.

"If you don't know, then why did you flee when we announced ourselves as FBI? Innocent people don't do that."

"Panic. Anxiety. I lost control."

"You don't strike me as someone who panics or gets anxious often, Mr. Matheson. And you appeared to be in complete control of your faculties when you had your hands around my throat. Why don't you just drop the act and tell us the truth? We have a mountain of evidence against you." It felt good to present him with the facts, but if she was being truthful to herself, she feared this guy. She was as safe as chains and onlookers could keep her, but that didn't mean there wasn't a chance something could go wrong.

Dax dropped his hands to the table. The handcuffs clanked with a raucous clang. Ella felt the table bounce.

There was a moment of silence. Ella saw the consideration on his face, the conflict. He was weighing up his options. She just needed to break him down further.

80

"So, he ratted me out, did he? I knew I couldn't trust him."

And there it was. The confession she needed. Ella felt the high, the dopamine. *Goddamn, you've done it again. Two serial killers in as many months.* She naturally looked towards the two-way mirror. *I hope Mia is getting this.*

"Who are you talking about?" she asked.

"I'm not telling you his name, but he helped me with everything. He set everything up, but that's all I'm telling you."

"You had an accomplice help you with your *art?*" She emphasized the word.

"I had to. It was the only way I could take my work to the next level. Achieve greatness. Go beyond the mundane and live alongside the greats. Even a corporate servant like you should understand that."

"That's why you *killed?*" Ella said. "For art? You took the lives of three people so you could become famous?"

Dax sat upright in haste, like someone had poured ice down his spine. He held up his palms, exposing giant hands that blocked Ella's view of his face. "What the fuck? Killed?"

"Yes, genius. Killed."

"Woah. What in God's name are you talking about? I haven't killed anyone. Murder is unspeakably ugly to me."

And the relief washed away. Ella looked for any signs that he might be lying and saw very little. He stared deadpan at her, never looking away, keeping his entire torso still as the mountains. "Then what do you think I'm talking about?"

"The blood. My art. One of the pieces at my gallery had real human blood in it."

"Whose blood?" she asked. The questions were mounting in Ella's head. She didn't know which to ask first.

"No idea. I utilized the services of someone in a blood bank. Said he could get me real blood if I paid him. I don't outright say it, but all of my other work uses animal blood. I let people's imaginations fill in the rest. Perception is reality."

Ella rubbed her forehead with her fingertips. She pulled off her glasses and dropped them on the table. "You think we busted you because you're using smuggled human blood to make paintings? That's all?"

"Umm... yes. Is it not? I don't know anything about any killings."

Ella wasn't buying it. There was something else at play here. This didn't make sense. She began to worry. It felt like things were slipping. She began to panic.

"Janet Wootton. Does the name ring a bell?" she asked, quickly trying to get things back on track.

"Yes, my old agent. I have no issues with her."

"She was found dead five days ago, strung up in a tree. Throat slashed."

Ella saw Dax's posture weaken. He slumped down. His face dropped. Water began to encircle his eyes. "What the hell? Janet's dead?"

"Don't play games. What about Katherine Adams? Venue owner who displayed some of your work. Killed last night in the same way."

His giant hands moved to his mouth as he mumbled something. "Katherine? She was an exceptional promoter. She takes this industry very seriously, unlike a lot of so-called artists. She's dead?"

Ella ignored his question. "And then there's Jennifer Hoskins. You're very familiar with her, aren't you?"

"Jenny? What about her? Please don't say…"

Ella panicked as she saw genuine fear in Dax's eyes. Either the news of these murders was a genuine surprise or he was an Oscar-worthy actor. "She was found dead Saturday morning. Same method. Same everything. But…"

The giant broke down, collapsing into the table and putting a sudden end to Ella's dialogue. She saw the inhuman veins decorating his skull, throbbing like unearthed worms. *What the hell is going on?* she asked herself. *This isn't right.* She looked to the two-way mirror with a look of puzzlement. Almost on cue, Mia broke through the door and stood beside Ella.

"Buddy, cut the horseshit. We have incriminating emails sent from you to Jennifer Hoskins the night before she died. Save the crocodile tears for the jury. We don't have time for them."

Dax slowly rose up back to a sitting position and took a second to compose himself. He wiped his eyes clean with the back of his hand. "Me and Jenny have a… relationship," he said between sobs. "A mutual relationship. Pure fantasy. Nothing on those emails is genuine."

"How convenient," Mia said. "Mind explaining how *I'm coming for you* is fantasy?"

"Did you know Jenny at all?" Dax said, staccato in his voice.

"No, but we saw her corpse in a tree. The corpse you put there."

82

Dax shook himself back to full self-possession. He regulated his breathing and steadied his shaking hands. "Firstly, agents, I was away all last week. In France. I was working a tattoo convention – my day job. Okay? I got back on Friday afternoon, and it was that morning I sent your so-called incriminating text message to Jenny."

Ella and Mia exchanged a glance. Their faces said the same thing. Dax had an alibi that excluded him from at least one murder, something they couldn't deny no matter how much manipulation he might throw at them. Ella felt nauseous. The ironclad case they had was rapidly dissolving.

"Why send a threatening message like that?" Mia asked.

"Role play. Fantasy. Not fuckin' real. Understand?"

Ella weighed up the possibility that Dax was telling the truth, and suddenly, a realization hit her like a lead weight. Yes, there was sense to what he was saying. Karl Hoskins had mentioned that Jennifer claimed not to enjoy conventional relationships. She saw Dax Matheson, the power-hungry alpha, the most dominant man in any room. She recalled Jennifer Hoskins, the submissive, the masochist. She thought back to the performance video she'd watched where Jennifer spanked herself.

"You had a dominant-submissive relationship, didn't you?"

"Yes," Dax said. "Exactly." He seemed relieved that one of the agents understood where he was coming from.

Mia held her palms up as if to say *what*. The gesture was directed at Ella, but Dax spoke first.

"I chase her. She's a submissive. It's all one long role play. We very rarely actually meet up and do anything. In the past six months, I've only met her in person a handful of times."

"Your relationship wasn't romantic?" Mia asked.

"No."

"It seems strange you'd email each other. Pretty impersonal, no?"

"We couldn't text because Jenny was seeing someone. She was worried he'd see our messages. He didn't understand our deal."

"Name?" Mia asked.

"Not sure. They might not have even been together. James. Joe Jay. Something like that."

"But you have ties to all of these victims," Ella said, still hanging on for life. Dax was everything she wanted from a suspect, but he was slipping through her grip at a pace she couldn't hold on to. She felt so close to the end, only for the finish line to be pushed back another mile.

"So do a lot of people. I could name about ten people right now who are familiar with Janet, Jennifer and Katherine. Artists, professionals, venue staff, agents, fans, groupies."

Dax covered his face with his forearm to conceal fresh tears. It seems the reality was hitting him. Ella knew that once Dax was alone, he'd break down into an emotional wreck.

She let Dax cry it out before resuming, suddenly feeling an intense wave of guilt for all that she'd done in the past hour. Destroyed this man's art, broke his nose, accused him of murder - all for nothing. The successes felt good, but the failures felt ten times worse.

She felt a hard tap against her shoulder.

"Get the names of anyone who might be linked to all three victims," Mia said.

Ella turned to her, both sporting the same look of deflation.

"Then get him out of here. He's not our guy."

CHAPTER SIXTEEN

Ella watched two officers escort Dax Matheson past her office and out to freedom. She wondered if she should apologize to him before he left. She turned back to the whiteboard where Mia was drawing up a new timeline. She turned around and threw the marker pen at her.

"Rookie, I know that look. Drop it."

She picked the pen off the floor and spun it between her fingers. "What look?"

"The *woe is me* look. Shit happens, alright? Sometimes you get cockteased by a red-hot suspect only to end up blue balled. It's happened before and it'll happen again. Get used to it."

She conceded, tried to focus on the positives. Dax had given them the names of twelve people in total, all of whom had some, if tangible, connections to the three victims. "Alright. Where to start with the next step?" she asked.

"We've got an agent, an artist and a venue owner. The chances that our killer has a personal link to all three of them is almost certain. Your artist theory is still rocky for me, but we'll keep it in mind. It might be best if we start with the most recent victim and work backwards. What if we look through the performances which took place at Katherine's venue and see if any of the names match up with Dax's list. If we get a hit, we can see if that person has history with the other victims, see if there's any bad blood and so forth."

Ella nodded. "Okay, I'll put up the list of performances in the past month."

"Past year," Mia said. "This could go way back. This unsub is organized and capable of channelling his emotions over a long period of time. These murders weren't impulsive. He'll have been planning this for a while. Leave no stone unturned."

Ella pulled up her laptop and searched the venue website. She searched the venue's show history and cross-referenced them with the names. Mia continued jotting her thoughts on the whiteboard. Ella had no problem finding the first name on the list, who'd done a show there six months before. Then the second, eight months before. Then the third.

"Uh, well, the good news is that they're all on here. The bad news is that we've got a lot of people to look into."

"Better than nothing," Mia said.

"Of the twelve people Dax gave us, eight of them are artists. They all played at this venue."

"All of them?"

"Looks like it," said Ella. "Well, except one."

A knock on the door interrupted them. Brooks stood there with a file in his hand. "Agents, here's the file on the latest victim, including autopsy results. There's also the contact details for her husband in there if you need to speak to him. I haven't had chance to look through it myself."

"Leave it with us, Sheriff," Mia said. Brooks dropped it on the table and returned to his office.

Ella scrambled for it and scanned the first few pages, quickly landing on something useful.

"Says here that Katherine and her husband ran their venue together. I'll give him a call and see if he recognizes any of these people. Maybe he'll remember if Katherine didn't get along with anyone."

She decided to use the opportunity to get some air, clear her head and get a new perspective. The office felt stuffy and the humidity was making it difficult to think. The interrogation had taken it out of her. Ella stood up and pulled on her jacket.

"Where you going?" Mia piped up.

"Outside. I just need a quick break."

Ella walked away from the precinct into the Seattle streets. It was early afternoon and the clouds had rolled back to allow a trickle of sunshine through, but the wind blew heavy still. The cool breeze felt good against her wounds. She dialed the number for Katherine's husband on her mobile. He answered on the third ring.

"Mr. Adams, my name's Agent Dark and I'm with the FBI. Please forgive my abrupt call. I'm sure you have other things on your mind right now."

"I do, but I'll do anything to help catch the sicko who killed Kath. Some cops have been out to see me this morning and they said they'd pass my number onto you."

Ella was relieved. She couldn't imagine what it must be like to get an intrusive phone call within hours of losing a loved one. Greg seemed more angry than upset, and that was understandable. "That's good, thank you. I was just wondering if you could help me. We have a short list of people who were familiar with all of our victims, several of whom played shows at your theatre. I was wondering if you could pinpoint any who might have held a vendetta against Katherine for whatever reason."

"A vendetta? I don't know anyone who'd hold anything against Katherine or me. We hired, we paid well, we had good relations with every artist we worked with."

Ella surveyed the distant traffic. There was something calming about the continuous flow of life, especially after the sights she'd seen the past few days. "No disputes? Nothing like that?" She could sense Greg was wracking his brains. She gave him all the time he needed.

"I mean, we've canceled a couple of shows in the past. But it was always for good reason."

"What kind of reason?"

"If the performance is too grotesque, or if we're losing money. One usually leads to the other."

Then Ella realized something. As she stood using the humdrum of life as her background noise, she wondered why they'd been so focused on people inside the art community when there could equally viable artists who were still on the outside. She'd been so busy thinking of people who *had* performed shows that she'd overlooked people who hadn't. The fringe wannabes, the peripheral aspirants. Every scene had an inner circle, an outer circle, and stragglers trying to break in.

"Did you cancel any shows in the past year?" Ella asked.

"I think so. Let me check."

She heard a thud, then Greg shuffling around in the distance. He picked up the phone again. "One. A fellow named James E. Newark. A painter and performance artist. He was booked in for a week but we canceled after two days. Strange stuff and barely anyone showed up."

"How did he take the news of being canceled?"

"Not too happy. He said we couldn't see artistic talent if it shot us in the foot. After that he just disappeared. This would have been about six months ago though."

Ella began to make her way back to the precinct, but something along the main street caught her attention. "Thank you, Mr. Adams. If you think of any other artists who might hold grudges against you or Katherine, just call me on this number."

They said goodbye and hung up. Ella made her way along the road to a wooden bench on the sidewalk. Sitting there was Dax Matheson, leaning forward with a cigarette in his hand. The guilt came hard and heavy. A few hours previously, Ella was certain he was a murderer, but the evidence said otherwise. How could things change so suddenly? Thinking back, she felt a fool for being so certain of herself. She'd fought with this man and broken his nose – for what? She'd subjected an innocent man to unnecessary suffering. Even with all the professionalism in the world, she wanted to apologize.

She took a seat next to him. Dax kept his focus on the traffic up ahead. He exhaled a plume of smoke. Ella waited for him to calm to her presence, not wanting to risk any more altercations.

"I'm sorry," she said.

After a few seconds, he laughed, much to Ella's surprise. She expected aggression and frustration, especially from a man of his demeanor.

"Me too," Dax said. "You put up quite a fight for someone who's five-foot-nothing."

Ella wasn't sure how best to respond. Keep it professional? Be a little more light-hearted?

"Nah, you're just weak," she said. Dax smiled. "What are you still doing here?"

"Waiting for a cab. I can't drive," he said, looking down at the ground. Ella thought back to the third crime scene with the washed-out tire tracks. "I can't believe she's gone."

"Off the record," Ella said. "Did you really only just find out about her death when we told you? She's been dead two days."

Dax nodded. "My agent runs my social medias. I don't read news. Life is pain enough without consuming all that stuff." He pulled his phone out and opened up his pictures. Ella saw his camera roll in her peripheral vision, which mostly consisted of his paintings. Dax tapped and showed Ella the screen. "Look at her. I took this during her last performance. Look how happy she is to be on stage."

Ella saw a picture of Jennifer Hoskins covered in paint, contorting herself into an unnatural position. He minimized the photo and scrolled more, showing more pictures of her eccentric art, her smiling face.

"You really liked her."

"She took this industry seriously. She bled for it. She wasn't here for the money or the fame."

"A good painter, too," Ella said. "I saw a self-portrait in her room."

"Jenny? A painter?" he laughed. "She sucked. I tried to teach her, but it wasn't really in her."

Ella pulled a face. She took out her phone and showed Dax the photo she'd taken of Jennifer's wall art. "Looks pretty good to me."

Dax leaned closer. "Abstract, broad brush strokes, acrylics, color theory is completely out of whack. Jenny didn't do that."

"It's got her name on it." Ella zoomed in to see the word JEN messily scrawled in the corner.

Then she stopped. The spark hit her like an explosion of dynamite. *Holy shit.*

She quickly said bye, jumped off the bench and ran back into the precinct. Something finally made sense.

CHAPTER SEVENTEEN

Ella ran back to her office without ever stopping for breath. She found Mia scrawling away on the board. "Ripley, do we have access to Janet Wootton's client list?"

"Yeah, why?" Mia looked at her like she'd never seen before. "What are you thinking?"

"Throw them here."

Mia handled a pile of brown folders, pulled out the second one from top and found the necessary papers. She passed them along.

Ella scanned them in record time, absently reminding herself of the days she'd speed-read books for fun. She devoured the contents from top to bottom and back again, then slammed her palm against her forehead. She couldn't find the name she wanted.

"Shit. He's not in here."

"Who?"

Ella was too far gone to acknowledge Mia's comment, too frenzied. Another idea quickly sprung to mind. "Emails," she said. "Do we have Janet's emails?"

"Yes, tech have given us access to search them. I can pull them up." Mia took a seat, pulled her laptop close and hammered at the keyboard. "What do you want me to search for?"

"James Newark," Ella said. "See if Janet corresponded with him."

Mia scrunched her face, silently telling Ella that that was a completely new name to her. She watched Mia lean closer to the laptop and scrolled through her search results. Ella saw a few red blocks spring up on the screen, suggesting Mia had a hit.

"Yeah, there's a James Newark in here. Looks like he conversed with Janet quite a bit."

Ella clenched her fists so hard her fingernails almost cut her palm. Victory could be on the horizon. It was a feeling unlike any other. When the stars aligned, it was like a drug hit. Or at least what she imagined a drug hit to feel like. "What about?" she asked, taking a closer look at Mia's screen. Mia opened up a long email thread with the subject *REPRESENTATION*.

"This James guy wanted Janet to rep for him," Mia said. She continued down the conversation. Ella quickly noticed a pattern. James's emails were huge blocks of lengthy paragraphs whereas Janet's were one-line responses.

"Janet didn't seem interested. He practically begged her, and she brushed him off every time. What's the very last message say?"

Mia jumped to the bottom of the thread. She read out Janet's final email. *Sorry, you're not what I'm looking for. Good luck in your search.*"

Ella didn't have to look below Janet's message to know there'd be a rebuttal. There always was.

"Then James responded by calling her a *haggard old drunk*. That's one way to ruin a professional relationship." Mia clicked out of the conversation and checked the email client for any more mentions of him. "You think this is our guy?" she asked.

"Yes I do. He has links to every victim." Ella focussed herself. The excitement sometimes made it hard to focus, especially when her head was full of possibilities. She had to stop herself imagining what the capture scene would look like when they apprehended this guy.

"Wait a second, I have something else. Check this," said Mia. "Janet Wootton emailed Greg Adams, Katherine's husband."

Another connection. This had to be the unsub. Ella was rapidly becoming sure of it. "What about?"

"This James fellow. Janet asked Greg why they canceled his shows." Mia clicked around a little more.

"And?"

"Greg says it was because James's shows were outlandish, and his venue was losing money. Looks like Janet was doing a little research on James before making a decision about representing him."

"So, James is mad at Janet for overlooking him."

"Back up a second, Dark. How did you find this guy? What relations does he have to the other victims?"

Ella took a deep breath and tried to picture the events chronologically. She condensed everything as best she could in her mind. She grabbed a chair and pulled her laptop close then searched for James Newark's website. There was one thing she had to check before confirming her theory.

"James Newark is a painter and performance artist, one that was shunned by all of our victims. He has a vendetta against all of them."

"I'm listening," Mia said.

"According to Katherine's husband, James was booked for a series of shows at Katherine's theatre, but they pulled him because they didn't like his work. They lost too much money, so they sacked him off. That would have left a very sour taste in his mouth. He was one of the few artists to ever have their shows canceled at their theatre."

"Right. That would have embarrassed him pretty badly."

"Exactly. As those emails show, he tried to get Janet Wootton to represent him, but she turned him down. Again, that would have upset him, infuriated him."

"Makes sense. And what about Jennifer?"

Ella found James Newark's website. It was a stony black-and-grey page with his name in block letters at the top. Below that were amateur shots of James posing against various backgrounds: concrete walls, forests, freeway bridges. This was her first time seeing this man's image. He had scraggly blonde hair reaching his chin, thinned from extensive dye jobs. He was small in stature, weedy, with almost nothing to his shoulders and upper body. The pictures didn't blend in well with the site's theme at all.

Ella showed Mia the photograph she took in Jennifer Hoskins's bedroom. "See that? It's a portrait of Jennifer. I thought it was a self-portrait because look at this." She zoomed in to the bottom right corner. "It says JEN. I thought it was just Jennifer signing it in shorthand but it's not. It's this guy's initials. James E. Newark. He painted this for her because they were lovers."

Mia's lips twitched but nothing came out. Ella saw she was digesting the information and that she couldn't deny they had something.

"How do you know he painted that?" Mia asked.

"Look at his style," Ella said as she navigated his webpage. She went to the *Paintings* section. "It matches perfectly. Abstract, broad brush strokes." Dax's words, but Mia would never know.

"Shit the bed. They were dating?" Mia asked.

"Uh huh. Jennifer's father told me she was seeing someone but recently broke it off."

"Maybe James found out about Jennifer's relationship to Dax? That could have been the stressor that led to all this."

"This has to be him. He's an artist with ties to every victim. These murders are his way of exacting revenge *and* showcasing some kind of pretentious artistry. It's a middle finger to the people who overlooked…" Ella's eyes turned around and rested on the whiteboard.

She saw Mia had added some new information. "What's that?" she asked.

"Coroner's report came back from the third victim," Mia said.

In the midst of her revelation, Ella had completely forgotten about the organ extractions. "Liver, heart and…."

"He took her optic nerve."

Overlooked, Ella said to herself again.

"Oh my God. That's it. Of course. The organ removals. I know what they all mean."

As the words escaped her throat, Sheriff Brooks passed by the open door. He peered his head through.

"Woah, what was I heard?" he asked.

"Sheriff, first of all, we've got a hit. A gentleman named James Newark. Ever heard of him?"

"Doesn't ring a bell. What makes you so sure? And what about the organs?"

Ella walked Brooks through the timeline using the information on the whiteboard. "James is a local performance artist with ties to the deceased. Janet declined to represent him, Jennifer broke up with him, and Katherine canceled his run of shows at her theatre."

Brooks nodded as Ella gave him the rundown. "Gotchya. Is that his only link to the victims?"

"Not quite," Ella said. "Look at this. He extracted Janet's liver. This wasn't just a power move or some kind of experimentation, it was symbolic."

"How so?" Brooks asked.

Mia jumped in. "Janet was known for taking her clients out for lavish meals and cocktails. She was a heavy drinker. When I visited her home, I saw a mountain of liquor bottles in her trash. I thought her husband had been drinking to cope, but they were more than likely Janet's from the previous week. In an email to Janet, James called her a *haggard drunk.*"

Ella picked up. "Next, he extracted Jennifer's heart. Another symbolic gesture because they're former lovers. Jennifer broke his heart, so he literally removed hers."

"Jesus wept," said Brooks. "And the most recent victim?"

"He's gone a little further this time," Ella said. "He removed her optic nerve."

"Her what?"

93

"The nerve that sits behind the eye. It transmits visual information from the retina to the brain. Another symbolic gesture. He told Katherine Adams she couldn't *see* artistic talent. It's an insult to her attentiveness," Ella said.

Brooks looked confused. "Odd. Wouldn't he just remove her eyeballs if that was the case?"

"No," said Mia. "For several reasons. Number one, he's evolving. His art is evolving. At the crime scene, forensics told us that Katherine Adams was blind, but that was a misjudgment. When the optic nerve is removed, the eyeballs become visually distorted. Glazed over, cloudy. But the brain has to be functioning for that to be the case. Which means-,"

"He removed the nerve while she was still alive," Brooks said.

"Yes. Something which we haven't seen him do before. All the other victims were mutilated post-mortem. The second reason is that he tries to keep the corpses as pristine as possible. We know his cuts are amateur and he knows this too. If he'd have cut her eyes out, he'd have left a huge mess. He didn't want that."

"Sheriff, can you get us this guy's address? We need to bring him in right away. His website says he lives somewhere in Bainbridge," Ella said.

"I'll get everything I can. Start heading there and I'll text it over to you. What about backup?"

"One cruiser but stay back," Mia said. "We don't want to spook him. Someone like this will have an escape plan in place in case he suspects anything. If he spots a squad car, he'll get the hell out of there." She turned to Ella. "Grab your things, rookie. I've got a feeling this is our guy."

Suddenly, the exhaustion disappeared, replaced by exhilaration. This new suspect had secrets and she was going to be the person to unearth them, be it through persuasion or brute force. In just a few minutes, there was every chance she'd be eye-to-eye with a serial killer, and that was the reason she came here. She downed her coffee for a quick buzz, but it would be nothing compared to the high of capturing Seattle's newest boogeyman.

CHAPTER EIGHTEEN

On either side was a row of ground-floor apartments, small and inexpensive by Ella's quick calculations. She had an idea of what James might be like as a person, but if experience had taught her anything it was that you could never fully realize someone on presentation alone. She expected a creep, a fiend, but predators often knew how to blend in with the crowd. Mia drove them the four miles from the precinct to Bainbridge in less than ten minutes. Dusk began to set in as they turned the corner into the street James Newark called home.

They parked at the bottom of the road as not to raise suspicion or to scare the suspect into running. The agents stepped out and headed towards the end of the street, slowly and casually. To any prying neighbours they could just be insurance sellers. At the end of the row, they stood in front of the suspect's residence.

"Here. Fifty-seven," Mia said.

There was a small driveway missing a vehicle. The small patch of garden beside it was immaculately presented with trimmed plants and fancy brickwork. Mia knocked on the door while Ella stood beside her and discreetly peered into the curtainless window. She couldn't make out much in the darkness other than a couple of blinking lights.

They waited but no response came. Mia knocked again, this time with force.

No answer.

"He's not home. Son of a bitch." Mia pulled out her phone, but Ella held up her palm. She moved closer to the window and peered inside without caution.

"Ripley, there's something in here."

"What?"

"Movement. I saw it in the back." Ella could see through the lounge into a small kitchen area at the rear. Amidst the shadows, something shifted, black on black.

"You sure?"

"Positive. Listen. Did you hear that?"

95

They froze. From the rear of the house, something shuffled, like the brush of overgrown grass against feet.

"Come on," she shouted, hurrying towards the rear gate. Her heart began to pound. She'd seen something and that thing had fled, fuelling her belief that this was their man. Ella shouldered the gate with a raucous thud, shaking it on its hinges. She tried again and again, rocking it in place but not breaking it down.

Too sturdy, she thought. Too many deadbolts on the other side, perhaps. "Forget it," she said, jumping up and grabbing the ledge above. Ella hoisted herself up using the side wall as leverage, stepped on top of the gate and dropped down onto the other side. It was a lofty drop, landing onto a concrete pathway. Her ankles absorbed the impact, but she had too much adrenaline in her system to feel pain. Behind her, Mia did the same.

Ella ran along the side of the house into a tiny back garden. There was a 10-foot-high perimeter fence on every side. "He can't have jumped over that," Ella shouted, hoping Mia had caught up. She appeared beside her.

"He definitely could," Mia said. "This guy is a nimble motherfucker. He can climb trees like a pro. Scaling that would be easy for him."

"Shit," Ella said. "He could have gone in any direction."

Mia called her backup and told them to be on the lookout for anyone in the adjacent streets. "Let's try the next best thing," Mia said. She grabbed the back door and shook the handle. Locked.

"Window," Ella said. "It's open." Beside the door, the kitchen window sat slightly ajar. Ella reached her hand inside. "It's on the latch."

"Get those skinny fingers in there," Mia said.

Ella did, managing to touch the latch hook with her fingertips. The window frame dug into her shoulder to the point of drawing blood, but she maneuvered the hook from its position. The window flung open. "I'm in." She pulled herself up on the windowsill, lowered her head through and found herself perched on the kitchen worksurface. She jumped onto a tiled floor and checked her danger areas for any signs of life. When she saw it was clear, she unlocked the back door.

"He can't have escaped through here," Ella said as Mia entered the house. "It was locked from the inside. I doubt he would have got through the small gap in the window too."

Mia ran her hands along the wall until she found a light switch. She flicked it, illuminating the room a deep orange. Suddenly, something hurried past them. Ella jumped back and had to steady herself against a kitchen unit.

It was a small black blur. It traveled along the ground and up onto the kitchen worktop before escaping through the open window. It was a small black cat.

Ella and Mia exchanged a glance. Ella realized that the movement she'd seen through the window was probably the animal, not the suspect. "Is a cat probable cause?" she asked.

"Doubt it, but we're in here now. We'll worry about the legalities later."

Ella stepped through into the adjoining lounge, finding it to be pleasantly designed and decorated. A single white sofa sat in the center facing a large wall-mounted TV. There were signs of life dotted around in the form of empty soda cans and a half-finished meal. A painting of his hung on the wall beside the TV, an abstract piece dripping with greens and purples. Ella scrutinized it, seeing a human eyeball lost within the shapes and designs but unsure if it was just her imagination. "What are we looking for?" she asked.

"Anything that connects him to our victims. They were all found naked, so there's a chance he stole some of their belongings. I.D. cards, purses, keys, phones."

Ella moved into the bedroom, finding an unmade bed and the aroma of sweat. It was a tiny box room with a wardrobe along the right-hand wall. Ella pulled it open and rifled through his clothes, finding a pretty plain selection of apparel, especially for someone who considered themselves an artist. She checked some drawers, looked under the bed but found very little incriminating material. She found a small calendar resting on the bedside table. She grabbed it and quickly scanned James's schedule.

"Dark, get in here," Mia shouted from another room. "Bathroom."

Ella rushed out and found the small, tiled room. Bright white from every angle. Her eyes jumped to what was laying in the bathtub. "Goddamn. Is that…?"

"Looks like we've got what we need."

Inside was a pile of bloody clothes folded in plastic wrapping. Some of the blood had seeped into the tub and dried a deep crimson. Mia reached down and pulled up the pile to inspect them. "Shit me.

There's more. Look. Scalpels, caked with blood. And an icepick. This must be what he used to remove the optic nerve."

The surgical tools gleamed in the orange light. Ella suddenly felt sick as she imagined their razor-sharp blades cutting through human flesh. But even so, triumph soon overtook it. This was more than enough to arrest and hold the suspect on, maybe even enough to charge him. It was nothing short of a smoking gun.

"We just need to track this son of a bitch down and he's as good as done for. Great work, Dark."

"What should we do? Wait here and see if he comes back?"

"No. Too much of a risk. If he gets a sniff that we're onto him then he'll flee. We'll keep an officer on watch, but we need to hunt this guy down. We can't let him get a head start."

Ella only now realized she was still clutching the calendar in her hand. She eyeballed today's date and found a smudge of black text in the small square. She had to squint to translate it.

"Ripley, look." She tapped the calendar. "I think I know where we can find him."

CHAPTER NINETEEN

The Saint Luca Centre for Performing Arts was a constrained building, despite its grandiose name. Ella expected a majestic affair, but the downtown Seattle venue was what casual conversationalists might term a dive. According to James Newark's calendar, this is where he'd be tonight, although exactly what was taking place inside was unknown. Ella had checked the venue listings and found no show scheduled for the evening.

The entryway was a small black door nestled between two takeaway restaurants. Ella and Mia entered into a tiny little foyer and descended a flight of stairs. At the base, two security guards halted them.

"Private showing tonight, ladies. Do you have an invitation?" one of them said.

"A private showing of what?" Ella asked.

"I'll take that as a *no,*" the guard said. "Sorry. You can't come in."

Mia held up her badge and thrust it inches from the guard's face. "FBI. We have reason to believe that someone in here is responsible for a recent string of murders."

"Murders? The park murders?" asked the other guard.

"We can't reveal any information," Mia said as she pushed her way past. The guards exchanged a look of powerlessness. Ella followed and they entered into the venue area.

Inside was a little more luxurious, spacious. Around fifty people stood huddled in their circles, sipping wine or coffee or some colorful concoction. Some were dressed in typical avant-garde artist getup, others looked like they'd just walked in from the slums. Ella, in her black top and jeans, immediately felt like an outcast. She didn't have time to bask in the irony.

"See him?" Mia asked.

"Nothing."

"Same. Their stupid clothes don't help. Keep an eye out. He might not be here yet."

"I still don't know what's happening here," Ella said. "Is this just a regular bar?"

"No idea, but I'm sure…"

Before Mia could finish, the house lights switched off and a yellow light appeared on the stage. Ella expected applause but none came. Instead, everything fell silent.

Then a figure walked into view onstage. Small, scrawny, luminous blonde hair. He wore drainpipe trousers and a plain black t-shirt. Ella recognized him immediately. "Looks like we found him," she said.

She scanned the audience to gauge their reaction to the performer. The majority of them appeared indifferent, many sporting a look that said *impress me*. James Newark didn't address his audience. Beneath the spotlight he dropped to his knees, held back his head.

"Should we?" Ella whispered to her partner.

"No. Wait. Look at what he's doing."

Ella never really *got* performance art. It was all too abstract, too pompously exaggerated. However, it was quite clear exactly what James Newark was trying to say with his piece.

He ran his thumb along his neck. Suddenly, liquid began to spurt from it, creating a morbid silhouette on the venue wall behind him. Even in the dimness Ella could see the falseness of it all.

"Is he… recreating the murder scenes?"

Mia didn't respond. From the look on her face, Ella saw that she was ready to intervene.

James dropped into the pool of fake blood and writhed like some kind of dying animal. It was a bizarre sight, as puzzling as it was pathetic.

"He's insulting his victims," Mia said. "This is basically a confession. Come on. I've seen enough of this shit."

Ella barely had time to register their next move before Mia darted towards the stage, pushing past the front-row gawkers. "FBI," Mia screamed. "Don't you dare move."

Everything stopped. James froze onstage, a look of despair overcoming him. Ella saw his hands begin to shake, his legs tremble. He knew what was going on. Mia stepped up onto the stage and withdrew her pistol. She pointed it at the suspect.

"James Newark?" she said. "Are you him?"

James nodded like a child who'd been busted stealing. Ella glanced at the faces around the room, some still sipping and conversing nonchalantly. Maybe they thought this was part of the show.

"We're arresting you on suspicion of murder. Please, come with us. You're surrounded, so don't even think of trying to run."

100

The house lights came on. Ella saw that James was brandishing something gleaming in one hand. He began to back up against the rear wall, hesitant to say a single word. The audience began to realize that this wasn't part of the show. They moved away from the stage towards the exit door.

Ella, remembering the incident with Dax, moved towards the small curtain that led to the backstage area. If he tried to flee, there'd be nowhere for him to run.

"I'm not coming with you," James said, his voice absent of any confidence or assurance.

Ella's mind turned to other mission-oriented killers from the past, ones who'd been cornered in the same way. Was James's mission over? Was this performance his coup de grace? A kind of exclamation point on the atrocities he'd committed? If so, was there anywhere left to go?

She thought of Harold Shipman, Fred West, Jack Unterweger, Israel Keyes, Richard Chase. Deluded, mission-oriented offenders. Suddenly, she realized they all had something else in common. And she saw a look on James's face that told her he had something similar in mind.

"I don't want to shoot you, James, but I will if I have to. Now, drop the weapon and surrender yourself."

Back against the wall, the suspect cast a pitiable shadow, like a small creature caught in the crosshairs of a much larger beast. Ella saw Mia edge her way towards him.

But then James gripped the blade with both hands

And turned it on himself.

"No!" Ella screamed.

***

Ella, Mia, and Sheriff Brooks stood outside the interrogation room with James Newark locked inside. In just a few short days, they'd gone from unwelcome newbies to heroes among the officers in the precinct. Word had traveled around about the new suspect already, the bloody evidence, the scalpels, the weird performance. It seemed the case was all but closed.

All that remained was a confession, and Ella was damn sure one was coming.

"He hasn't said a word?" Brooks asked.

"Not a thing," Mia said. "The silent treatment since we locked the cuffs on."

"What's the approach, then?" Brooks asked.

"Present him with the evidence and watch his reactions. If he's not talking, that's all we can do."

"Okay. You want me in there?"

"No, me and Agent Dark will do this."

Ella breathed a sigh of relief. She didn't want to do another interrogation alone.

"Let's go, rookie. Be stern with this guy. He thinks he's some kind of genius but he's really just a weasel. Look at how he reacted to us. He was one comment away from pissing himself. Keep him rooted in reality and don't pander to his fantasies."

"Understood."

"And one last thing, *don't* mention the organs. That information hasn't been revealed to the public. The only people who know about them are us and the killer. If we can get him to somehow acknowledge them, that's as good as a confession."

Ella took the lead. "Let's go." They entered into the interrogation room where James Newark sat at the steel table. They had uncuffed him at Mia's request. A kind of power play, Ella assumed.

"Hello, James," Mia said. "I'm Agent Ripley and this is Agent Dark. Not a very good day for you is it, son?"

James kept his gaze fixated on the table. Ella saw the anxiety spread throughout his body. A definite good sign. "James, we know who you are. We know everything about you. We know you consider yourself a performance artist, but you've been shunned by everyone in the community. Is that correct?"

James shook his head.

"People consider your stuff too morbid, too extreme, is that right?"

He shrugged.

"One person who didn't like your work was Janet Wootton, correct? Do you know her?"

James just stared down, into the abyss.

"We're sure you do," Mia added. "We've seen emails between you two. And what about Katherine Adams? Does her name ring a bell? She canceled some of your shows because she thought you sucked."

James twitched a little. Ella knew that Mia was upping the ante to get a response of any kind.

"No? Well, what about Jennifer Hoskins? Your ex-girlfriend." Mia reached down under the table and pulled out a folder. She rifled through, selected a photo and threw it on the table. She pushed it over to James. "There she is. Hanging from a tree. Whoever did that to such a pretty girl must be really screwed up in the head. Don't you think, James?"

Nothing. James glanced at the photograph and quickly averted his eyes back. There was no remorse there, but no look of triumph either.

"What do you think, Agent Dark?" Mia asked.

"I think you're exactly right. I think Jennifer moved on, and her incel ex-boyfriend didn't like it. I think she broke his heart and he lashed out like a child."

No response. James tapped his fingers on the table but showed no signs of concern. Ella could sense the frustration on Mia's part.

"Or, maybe she left him for a real man. A real artist."

Finally, James looked up and made eye-contact. There was frustration on his face. A red overlay. But still he remained silent.

"Look, James, we've been to your house. We found your bloody clothes in your bathtub. We found the scalpels. We saw your weird little performance piece earlier," said Mia. You were re-enacting those murder scenes, weren't you? Some kind of artistic gesture?"

James smiled. It was a smug look. Ella wanted to punch it off.

"Well, I hate to tell you but there's a saying in showbusiness. People only ever remember the finish. Everyone remembers Ali standing triumphantly over Frazier, but they don't remember Ali spending ten rounds on his back. No one's going to remember your little show tonight. All they're going to remember is you being hauled away by police. How do you feel about that?"

It was no use. He wasn't going to cooperate.

"We have everything we need to charge you," Ella said. "All the evidence, all your emails, some very clear motivations, even a suicide attempt. Your guilt is obvious. You're looking at life in prison without parole."

"A young guy like you," Mia said. "They'll eat you alive in general pop. Or, you could cooperate with us and I can negotiate to get you a nicer prison, a bigger cell, maybe some privacy. How about it?"

James went back to staring downward. He shook his head again.

"Oh well," Mia said, grabbing the photo and placing it back in the folder. "We tried. You'll be held in custody until you're officially charged with multiple accounts of homicide. I don't suspect it will take long. Once forensics have confirmed the blood stains belong to the known victims, it will be game over. When you're ready to talk, and you will be, we'll be waiting."

Mia stood up and Ella followed. James didn't even glance up as they left the room. Ella wasn't sure if he was just scared or whether he knew exactly what he was doing. He didn't look like a killer at all, but they rarely did. Mia slammed the interrogation door shut and returned to Brooks.

"The silent ones are always the worst," Brooks said.

"Tell me about it. But from the small body language samples I could get, he's responsible for these murders. If he wasn't, he'd have protested. He wants us to think we've missed something. He's trying to make us second guess ourselves, but the fact he stayed quiet is another nail in the coffin for him."

Ella felt the high, the buzz, the electricity. She wanted to climb to the top of the building and shout that she'd just caught her second serial killer within the span of a few months. She wanted to call the victim's families and tell them the news right away. She wanted to tell them how the killer of their loved one was sitting in a freezing interrogation room awaiting transportation to a jail cell.

"We've enough evidence to charge him. Case closed," Mia said. She slapped Ella so hard on the back it caused her back injury from the day before to erupt again. She didn't mention it though. "Three days and we're done. That's what I'm talking about, rookie."

"I can't believe it. Just like that, it's over."

"Not all serial killers evade us for years. Only the good ones do that. This guy clearly isn't one of them," said Mia. "Come on, it's time to celebrate."

CHAPTER TWENTY

The rookie had requested they hit a restaurant instead of a bar and Mia had happily obliged. It was her who pieced the case together, so it was only fair she got to choose the celebratory reward. Mia was gagging for an Irish coffee to take the edge off and felt a pang of frustration when it wasn't listed on the menu perched in the window. It would have to be beer instead. A small sacrifice. The next flight back to D.C. was at 8am the following morning, so it would be a hearty meal, a few drinks and bed before midnight. The Seattle police would do the follow-ups with James Newark, but Mia was fully convinced he was the person responsible for these murders.

"This place takes me back," Mia said as a waitress led them to a table. The Keymaster was a family-owned restaurant tucked away in the Seattle backstreets, far away from the city slickers abusing their expense accounts. Old fashioned furniture, drapes instead of blinds. A real homely feel. "Last time I was here was in twenty-ten. I was working on a terrorism case. It didn't end quite as well as this one, though."

The waitress showed them to a booth somewhere near the back. Mia found that groups of women were alwayst given the best seats in the house. She dropped onto the padded bench and shook off the tension in her legs. It felt good to just sit down without having to worry about murders or suspects or autopsy reports. Moments like this were rare, she thought, so best enjoy it before the next case reared its head and consumed all her thoughts.

"You didn't work on terrorism cases very often, did you?" Ella asked from across the table. She was already poring over the menu. Poor girl must have been starving. It was expected given that they'd mostly been living on motel food and supermarket sandwiches since they got there. Mia sometimes forgot that not everyone shared her lack of appetite.

"No, they're the cases I hate the most. I requested to be taken off them that same year."

"How come?"

"Too much teamwork. Terrorism cases involve whole networks of people. Specialist consultants, negotiators, your Intelligence department. Lots of liaising with the CIA and the military. I can't be fucked with it all."

Ella closed her menu and stared out the window beside them. She turned back to Mia. "You prefer to work alone, then."

"Most of the time. It's just easier."

The waitress came over and took their drink orders. She opted for a lemon and lime beer and the rookie had Coke. Mia could hardly imagine being Ella's age and choosing soda over party juice. It didn't seem right. Maybe it was a sign of the times. The youngsters were more health-conscious, maybe. Less likely to give in under societal pressure to conform. She began to wonder about Ella's life outside of work, only now realizing that she didn't know a whole lot about what that entailed. Mia had her predictions, but she always found the younger generation always had a weird hobby or a special interest that she could never have guessed.

"Cheers," Mia said and clinked Ella's glass.

"To a case well solved," Ella added.

"Forget that for tonight," Mia said. "We'll be talking about it for the next few weeks back in D.C. anyway. No work talk. Tell me something about you."

"About me?" Ella looked surprised.

"Yeah. When Edis called you into his office the other day you were in a snazzy dress. Were you on a date?"

Ella hesitated a little. Lying? No, Mia doubted it. She had no reason to lie. Unless she was ashamed of something. Lesbian? Again, doubtful. Mia had caught Ella stealing glances at some of the handsome gents they'd met on the road.

"Not really. I was out with a few friends, but I did meet someone."

"Did you? What was he like?"

"Bit scrawny. Hipster. Smelt like vanilla and coconut. I liked that."

"Hmm. I always say that if you can smell a man's cologne then he's wearing too much. The only exception is when he's on top of you. What else? Did you get his number?"

Ella laughed. "Not quite. I got the call and ran away like a scalded dog."

"What? Why?"

"I got scared. Like, I probably could have summoned the courage to ask him if we hadn't been interrupted. But just going back in there and asking felt… I don't know… a bit brash. I said bye to him, but I didn't ask for anything else. He probably got talking to some other girl within five minutes of me leaving, anyway."

"You can't think like that! He might have been the one."

"Maybe. I guess I just struggle to let people in, you know? Like, I'm always left wondering if I'm good enough for them. Or if they're just using me for something. Or laughing at me. I don't know. It's hard to describe."

The waitress dropped two drinks on the table. Mia gulped down a third of hers immediately. It wasn't an Irish coffee, but it did the job just as well. "I get that. I think we all feel it sometimes. Well, the intelligent people anyway. Stupid people are full of confidence and smart people are full of doubt."

"Bukowski," Ella said. "He said that."

"He did. When you get back home you should look this guy up. I bet you a steak dinner he'll welcome your call."

Ella went quiet for a moment and re-tied her hair into a tighter ponytail. "I might, if I can find him. Who's Alfie, by the way?" she asked.

The question took Mia by surprise. How did Ella know? Had she mentioned him? She thought back to their previous conversations then the realization hit her.

"Oh, my password," Mia said.

Ella nodded.

"Alfie was my first husband. The father to my boys. He passed away in ninety-five. You're wondering why I still use his name as my pass, aren't you?"

"No. I totally understand. He was important to you."

"He got taken from me at our peak. That's why I still think about him. It's not like the relationship went sour or anything. After that, I didn't want to meet a man ever again, despite all the chances I had."

Should she be telling Ella this? Was this too much information? No, surely, it was good for her. The rookie might be wise to the history of serial murderers, but she seemed to be inexperienced in personal areas, especially matters of the heart. If they were partners, and Mia hoped they would be again, then it would be good to share some of that worldly advice she'd accumulated over her fifty-five years. Besides, in this game, you needed a level-head to get by. You needed to know how the world worked and how it sometimes didn't.

"I can't imagine how hard it must be," Ella said.

"Ready to order?" a soft voice interrupted. The waitress appeared beside them with a notepad in hand. Mia motioned for Ella to go first. This was her night. She'd earned it.

The rookie opted for chicken and salad. Once upon a time, Mia might have done the same, gone the healthy route, although those days were long past. She wondered at what point the rookie might succumb to the harsh realities of this job. Endless traveling, stress like no other, the lives of other people constantly in your hands. Even if she couldn't teach Ella about the logistics of relationships, she felt a responsibility to ensure that the rookie didn't end up as messed up as the haggard old veteran opposite her. Suddenly, retirement – that old escape plan that reared its head every time a case came to a conclusion – felt like a world away. For the first time in a long time, Mia felt like there was a reason to carry on. Some people said the purpose of life was to plant trees whose shades you'd never sit in, and that was something she'd always disputed. Until now.

CHAPTER TWENTY ONE

The young woman was arched over the sink, vomiting and spitting up phlegm. She looked up into the broken mirror, cracked down the middle from the force of her fist. Tears stained her face, smearing her eyeshadow and transforming her into a weeping clown. She fell down onto the bathroom floor; the only space in her apartment not decorated by debris of her own making. She clutched James's scarf in her hand and inhaled his musty scent, inadvertently staining the item from her bloody knuckles.

This wasn't how it was supposed to end. There was supposed to be much more. But now it was all over.

She'd been there when the agents stormed James's performance. She'd watched it all with her heart in her mouth. How could they know it was him, and worse still, how could they interrupt such a moving showpiece? Those bitches, how dare they do what they did? They were clueless corporate servants who would be better off six feet under. Like everyone else, they couldn't appreciate what James was doing. He was cleaning up the streets, removing the parasites, creating a more beautiful world in his vision.

Nearing midnight now, the world outside felt silent, like there was nothing left out there for her. Her love was gone and all that was left was pain and heartache. Is this how it would be from here on out? Would she feel like this for the rest of time? Pain and heartbreak until the stillness of death put an end to it all?

She crawled along the floor into her bedroom and clambered on top of the bed. A mannequin lay beside her, dressed in clothes that James had left there during his overnight stays. It was her substitute during the times she couldn't see him.

What next? What could she do? She was the only one who could help him now. The thoughts overwhelmed her to the point of a skull-shattering migraine, conjuring new idea after new idea but then discarding them when she realized how insane they sounded. Maybe they'd post bail for James and she could be the one to free him? Then they could escape to rural Iowa and no one would ever find them again. She could assume a new identity, work the streets to provide for her man. James could get reconstructive surgery so no one would recognize him. They'd be outlaws. Outsider artists in every sense.

But what if he'd already confessed? Those snakes had ways of rattling suspects. James promised her he'd never tell anyone the truth, but what if they tortured him? Waterboarded, flogged, pulled apart by horses. Anything to get the answer they wanted. Maybe James had enjoyed confessing to everything. He might have even mentioned her name to them. She saw the look on his face when the bitch pointed her pistol at him. He had a weak side to him, despite how hard she tried to help him shed it.

She pulled the mannequin closed and rested her forehead on his. "What the fuck do I do now?" she screamed. "You have to tell me." She closed her eyes and let the exhaustion settle, drifting into something between awareness and hallucination.

Then an idea formed.

James was locked up.

The FBI thought they had their man.

But what if they didn't?

**

Closing in on 1am, she found the streets deserted. She waited at the park entrance just behind the entrance gate. Few cars went past, and each time they did she pulled up her hood and retreated into the shadows.

Her hands shook with nervous energy. Could she actually do this? Did she have the skills, the courage? The others had been messy affairs, and luck had been on their side every time. There was a lot that could go wrong, but if she wanted to see James again, at least outside of prison, it had to be done.

Where the hell was this guy? Punctuality was never his strong point. On the one date they'd been on, he'd been thirty minutes late then too. If she remembered rightly, he told her she was creepy and weird and that he wasn't interested in her. However, he'd jumped at the chance to sell her drugs again.

Then she saw a silhouette in the distance. It drew closer, but rather than stare, she waited back just in case.

Eventually, his footsteps came within earshot.

"Becca?" the voice asked. It was him. She turned around and pulled down her hood. She didn't walk any closer to him, suggesting that he should venture inside the park gates away from prying eyes.

"Stephen, thank you so much," she said, adding some insincere bounce to her voice. "Thank God you were available."

"No worries. You... err... live 'round here now?"

He was still a looker, with his short curly hair and tight cheekbones. She suddenly remembered how often she used to think of him, announcing his name every night when she was alone under the covers. Time had squashed that infatuation, but she recalled the feelings with great clarity.

"Close enough. What about you?"

"Same place. A couple of streets away. So, you back on the nose candy?"

She already knew where he lived. That's why she made the trip down here; because she knew he'd walk and leave the car at home. "Never stopped. I just started using someone else since you ditched me."

The memories of Stephen dissolved to rage. She'd found someone better now, but still, there were unresolved feelings there. Those feelings would be addressed within the next few minutes, she thought.

"Well, that's in the past now. So, it's sixty dollars per gram. How much you want?"

He was eager to get the ball rolling. It seemed he wanted to be in and out. All this time since they'd seen each other, and he couldn't even do her the courtesy of small talk. Typical Stephen.

"Can we go into the park?" she asked. "I'm worried we're being watched. Can we make it look like we're just friends meeting up?"

"In a park in the middle of the night?" he asked. "Bec, it's pretty obvious what we're..." he trailed off. "Oh, wait a minute. Is this a ruse?"

"Huh?"

"Do you want a hook up? Is all this just a way of getting me alone?"

Sort of, she thought. "No, not at all. I have a new boyfriend now. In fact, this coke is for him."

Stephen's face scrunched up. "But you just said you never stopped using?"

Shit, I'm lying and he knows it. She began to panic. Despite the cool breeze, sweat developed on her forehead. She felt her face flush red. "I do, but I have some at home. My boyfriend wants his own stash."

"Couldn't you just give him some from your own, then?"

"No, it's not like that, it's…"

"Sorry Bec, I don't trust you. I was right about you. I'm out of here. Thanks for wasting my time."

She felt the walls close in. This was her opportunity, and it was escaping. If she didn't do something, James would be behind bars forever. Stephen backed up out of the park entrance and onto the main road. It was now or never.

She gripped the handle on the blade in her back pocket and took five huge steps towards Stephen. She quickly checked both directions and saw no signs of life, no cars, no midnight runners. Stephen turned around just as she was within touching distance.

The momentum took her completely off the ground as she aimed the blade at Stephen's neck.

CHAPTER TWENTY TWO

It was 6am and despite several hours sleep, Ella still felt exhausted. She stared out the motel window and took in the city to try and wake herself up a little. There was an overbearing greyness on the Seattle skyline, muting the vitality of early spring. By now, there was usually a hint of sun during these early hours, but today showed nothing of the sort.

At times like this, Ella was thankful she packed light. She shoveled her clothes into her bag and tidied up her motel bed in preparation to leave. Home was only a short plane ride away and she was looking forward to sharing her findings with the FBI higher-ups. A part of her wanted to visit the families again and tell them the good news, but that was in the hands of the Sheriff's team now. The fact that she was happy to leave the grandstanding to others reinforced to her that she was doing this job for the right reasons, not for the fame or the accolades.

Mia told Ella she'd be knocking on her door at 6am sharp and she was never late. The clock turned to 6:05 and there was no sight or sound of her coming down the corridor. Maybe she was human after all, Ella chuckled. She used the moment to reflect on the past few days. Three dead bodies, two altercations and more suspects than she could recall off the top of her head. Some missteps along the way, but like Mia said, people only ever remember the finish. All that mattered was that there was a suspect in a holding cell a few miles away, and the evidence to land him a life sentence was rock solid.

Would he become a well-known serial killer, or would he fade to obscurity? If Ella had to guess, she'd pick the latter. The media would run with it for a few months, probably embellishing the details to the point of ridiculousness. Then he would disappear from the public eye, banished to a jail cell and left to rot. His name would crop up in late-night documentaries, small-time podcasts and the odd newspaper article on the anniversary of the murders. Other than that, the name James Newark would be said for the final time within the next fifty years. He wouldn't be placed alongside the Bundys and the Dahmers of the world. He was missing that spark, that edge. Newark was a petty little coward fuelled by jealousy and rage, a school shooter in a serial killer's body.

A knock at the door startled her, even though she was expecting it. Why was Mia so heavy-handed all the time?

Ella hoisted her bag over her shoulder and opened the door. Mia's face was different. Her bags were nowhere to be seen.

A little light flicked on in Ella's mind. She'd never seen Mia look so downtrodden, so filled with disappointment.

She knew what Mia was about to say before she said it. The term *kuuki wo yomu* sprung to mind. The art of reading the situation without the need for words.

"I'm sorry, Dark. We need to stay here a little longer."

The frustration almost drove her to tears.

***

Mia parked the car around fifty yards from the park entrance. They walked the rest of the way. The overcast sky hung low above them. It was 6:30am.

"We had him dead to rights," Ella said. "Everything matched up. How is this possible?"

"Relax, Dark," Mia said. "We don't know anything yet. Newark could have killed this guy before we took him in. Secluded area like this? It could have easily bypassed everyone."

Ella prayed that Mia's assumptions were on the ball, and if she was thinking logically, it was the only possible conclusion. But there was that niggling uncertainty, that seed of doubt that seemed to be a constant in the back of her mind.

Sheriff Brooks stood at the park gates. Black bomber jacket, hands in pockets. He looked like he hadn't been to sleep since the day before. He nodded his greeting to the agents.

"Sorry for keeping you in Seattle." He directed the comment at Ella.

"Understandable. What have we got?" asked Mia. Brooks lifted up the yellow tape obstructing the scene and ducked underneath. The agents followed. A long pathway with rows of trees on either side came into view. The greenery on either side ran around fifty feet deep, with tree clusters becoming denser the further back they went. Two masked technicians stood at the foot of the tree nearest the pathway.

114

Then she saw the body. Strung up like the others but not quite. There was something off about it. It was the remains of a young man, hanging from the lowest branch by his neck. He was fully clothed, although blood decorated his brown jacket and white t-shirt. All of the others had been found naked and attached to trees in different ways.

They'd taken James Newark into custody the previous evening around 6pm, and even if he'd committed this murder within an hour of him being arrested, that meant this corpse had been strung up here for 12 hours. There was no way that was the case. More likely, this body had been placed here within the past few hours, while their number one suspect was stuck in a holding cell.

"Some kids found this here last night at about two in the morning. Forensics have already done the preliminary swabs, but they haven't found anything we can't see on the surface."

"Male, thirties, throat slashed. Do we know his name?"

"Stephen Treen," said Brooks. "Local fellow. One of the kids who found him recognized him. Said he was a local dealer. It checks out since we found some cocaine in his pocket. One of the officers at the precinct confirmed his identity."

"Was he in the artist community?" Mia asked the Sheriff.

"No, it doesn't look like it. I've got some officers doing some digging back at the precinct but from what we've found, no links to the art world. He's an I.T. technician, lives with his sister about five minutes from here."

Mia positioned herself below the victim and eyed her surroundings. Ella brought it upon herself to say the obvious.

"Are we sure this isn't a suicide?" she asked. "He's hanging by his neck. All the others were attached by the wrists and waist."

"I'm thinking the same," Mia called back. They both turned to Brooks.

"Afraid not. See the blood on his clothing?"

"Maybe stabbing himself failed so he resorted to hanging?"

Brooks shook his head. He motioned to one of the forensic officers nearby. "Show the agents, please," said Brooks. The officer approached the tree and climbed up the ladder which had been placed against the trunk. He lifted up the victim's shirt with his gloved hands.

"Organ extraction," Mia said.

"Not quite. He cut around the heart but didn't take it. Maybe he couldn't."

"He was interrupted," Mia said. "There's no way a methodical killer like this wouldn't have completed his work. Something stopped him from finishing it."

"Do you think we have the wrong guy?" Brooks asked.

Mia stopped and stared at the fresh victim. She sighed loudly. "I really don't know."

Those words were hard to hear. When the best profiler in the FBI didn't know what to think, what chance did Ella have?

"Ripley, isn't the fact that this is nowhere near as refined as the other murders a good thing?"

Mia slowly turned to her. "Why?"

"It suggests it's not the same perpetrator. Everything is different. It's a male victim. He's fully clothed. He's not in the art community. The presentation is all wrong. There's no organ extraction, despite the attempt. Could it be that someone has heard about these murders in the press and decided to copy them?"

"No, and that's a dangerous route to go down," Mia snapped. "If we assume that this *isn't* the same unsub then that could bite us in the ass. We might overlook vital circumstantial evidence. Our profile might be completely wrong. The circumstances are too similar to ignore. Right now, we have to assume it's the same person responsible for all four murders."

Ella had questions but didn't want to push. The copycat angle was best left unsaid, despite in being a possibility in Ella's mind. "Is it possible for an offender to change their M.O. this drastically?"

"There's no change in M.O., at least from what I can see. He slashed the neck to subdue the victim, hauled them to the tree and strung them up. In my book, that's pretty identical to the others, no? Victimology is different, but like I said the other day, this unsub doesn't have a type. He targets the individuals themselves. Somewhere along the line, this Stephen gentleman has wronged our killer."

Ella wasn't buying it, but she had no cause to speak up. She had theories but no evidence to prove it.

"And the bloody clothes found at James Newark's house? The scalpels? The connections to all the victims?" asked Brooks. Ella was thankful that he did. She could tell Mia was beyond frustrated with this new advancement and she didn't want to risk irritating her.

"This doesn't mean James is in the clear, not by a long shot. But there's something else to all this. Something we need to find out. Sheriff, keep digging for info about this new victim. Get him to the

116

coroner and see if there's anything we've missed. You said this guy has a sister, yes?"

Brooks nodded. "We've already told her the situation. She's shook up, as you can expect."

"Come on, Dark, we're going to pay her a visit."

She should be in a departure lounge right now, Ella thought. En route to D.C. to go home and catch some needed rest. But now there was another dead body, another traumatized family member. Suddenly, home felt further away than ever before.

CHAPTER TWENTY THREE

Ella didn't think that the West Garden apartment building was much to look at, and was even less to be in. Chipped blue paintwork decked the exterior of the three-floor building while a heavy scent of grime fragranced the rough hallways. The main door had been lodged open, so they'd just walked straight inside. Stephen's flat was on the middle floor. The agents ascended the stairs.

"Why the heart again?" Ella asked.

"He didn't take the heart," Mia said. "For all we know, they could be frenzied stab wounds. Or he might have taken a different organ and the chest wounds could be a swerve to detract from the real extraction. We need to wait for the coroner's report."

Ella struggled to piece things together. He'd taken the second victim's heart because she was his lover, but this new victim was a male. Was her theory about the organs completely incorrect? Were they not significant at all?

They arrived at the apartment they needed. Mia knocked on the door. It only took a few seconds for the door to swing open. Standing before them was a young girl, around mid-twenties, wearing smeared make-up and a dressing gown.

"What?" she said.

"Miss Abigail Treen, my name's Agent Ripley and this is Agent Dark. We're with the FBI. Do you mind if we speak to you for a couple of minutes?"

Abigail looked at them like they were speaking a different language. "Yes, I do mind. My brother died a few hours ago and you're here knocking at my door."

"We understand, but we believe that your brother was purposely targeted by whoever did this. With your help, we can uncover the person responsible. We assure you we'll only be a few minutes."

Abigail turned and surveyed her apartment, still holding the door a few inches above open. "Now's not a good time."

"Miss Treen, we know Stephen had a drug dependency and that's not why we're here. We don't care if you're sleeping on a bed of cocaine. We just want to talk about your brother."

Abigail rubbed her eyes, bringing a smudge of make-up out onto her fingers. "Look, I don't know anything, okay? Me and Stephen were roommates more than we were brother and sister. We lived separate lives."

Ella assumed they were doing this interview from the door. She found it interesting how people reacted so differently to grief. Some were happy to reveal everything to the authorities, some didn't want to say a thing.

"Do you know of anyone who might want to hurt Stephen?" Ella asked.

Abigail shifted her weight against the doorframe. "Absolutely no one. Stephen is a saint. He deals a bit of drugs now and then, but he keeps out of trouble. He doesn't get involved with the wrong types."

"We believe you," Mia said.

"Does Stephen have any connection to the world of artistry?" Ella asked. "Either painting or performance art?"

Abigail shook her head. "No. That's not his style at all. He works with computers. He's a logical kind of person. Stephen has no interest in art whatsoever."

"Do you have any idea where Stephen was headed last night?" asked Mia

Abigail shook her head then pressed her fingertips to her eyes. "Look, I can't do this. Leave me alone." She turned away, leaving the agents staring at a navy-blue door.

"Should we?" asked Ella.

"No, leave it. She's no use to us in that state," Mia said and motioned for them to leave. They began to walk back towards the staircase.

Ella wasn't convinced by Abigail. A drug dealer with no enemies? A victim with no links to the others? It seemed too disconnected, too purposeful. Like the murder was *meant* to be different to throw them off. The swerve, as Mia might say.

Behind them, a click. A latch unlocking. "Wait," a voice called. They turned around to see Abigail peering out of the doorway, reluctant to overstep the threshold. "There is one thing."

"Yes?" Mia said, walking back to the young girl. Ella followed.

Abigail held out a mobile phone. "This is Stephen's. He left it here last night."

"Is that unlike him to do so?"

"No, but it means he was on a drug run. He never takes his phone with him when he's meeting someone in case he runs into trouble. He's been ambushed and had his stuff stolen before, so he doesn't take anything with him."

"Thank you," Mia said. "We can get this checked out and see who he last had contact with. I'm guessing you tried to look yourself but don't know his passcode?"

Abigail nodded. Mia took the phone from her. "You're gonna catch whoever did this, right?"

Ella noticed that almost every family member asked this question, but Mia never directly answered it. She didn't want to make promises she couldn't always deliver on.

"We're going to do everything we can."

There it was. Vague and discouraging. The last thing anyone wanted to hear. Ella saw Abigail was holding back tears. She didn't want to leave Abigail here like this. She wanted to reach out and comfort her, tell her that it would get better one day. She remembered the pain of losing her dad, back when she was barely old enough to tell the time. Now here was a fully grown adult going through the same hellish trauma that circumstance had bestowed on her. This poor girl, left alone. Ella made a mental note to send a welfare check later in the day. In a few days, maybe she'd return herself, or send some flowers. Just something to let her know she wasn't alone.

"We're going to check up on you, Miss Treen," Ella said. "Make sure you're doing okay."

Abigail made a mumbling sound and shut the door, leaving the agents out in the dank hallway. Ella sighed, but didn't want to push her anymore. Let her deal with the grief in her own way, then offer her sympathies.

The agents returned to the stairs and walked down. "So, Stephen was lured to the park under the pretense of selling drugs, then ambushed?" Ella asked.

"Impossible to say right now. He could have been abducted while en route. A killer this organized contacting a potential victim to arrange a meet-up? I don't see it. He's been very good at covering his tracks so far."

"But his technological skills have been sub-par. He's left email trails to two victims already."

"True, but again, we can't assume anything. We need to get this phone checked out and see who he's been communicating with."

There was a small glimpse of hope that the phone could yield a new lead, but despite Ella's misplaced optimism, she believed there'd be nothing on the phone worth a damn. Could it be an accomplice responsible for all this? Maybe James Newark had made arrangements for this to happen prior to being arrested. Perhaps someone had been helping him all along and they were now taking matters in their own hands?

No, that was farfetched. The kind of baseless theory was Mia would have scoffed at. Besides, this victim was messier than the first three. Haphazard, amateur. If it was the work of an accomplice, then they would have ensured that the murder followed the same pattern as the others.

The dreaded copycat word circled around her head too. But a copycat so soon? Even if they were judging by the first murder, that was less than two weeks ago. The possibility of someone mimicking a crime so soon seemed completely implausible.

And then there was James. A mound of evidence against him. A perfect fit for the profile. Even with this new turn in the case, could they still pin the first three murders on him? It would be a victory, albeit a small one.

But there'd always be that doubt in the back of her mind. Something left unfinished. An itch she could never scratch. They arrived back at their car.

"Speaking of phones, the tech team are working their way through James's phone right now. Go and see what they have."

"Alright," Ella said. "What are you going to do?"

"I'm going to have a word with James back at the holding cells. There's something I want to talk to him about."

CHAPTER TWENTY FOUR

The uniformed officer buzzed Mia Ripley into the holding cells attached to Seattle Police Department Headquarters. It seemed that this was one area of the precinct that was yet to be modernized. The cells were the old style eight-by-six cages with metal bars as opposed to full walls. The first three were empty. In the fourth, she found James Newark curled up on his mattress.

"Enjoy your first night in captivity?" Mia asked. Next-day interrogations always went one of two ways. Either the suspect had come to terms that they'd be imprisoned and so confessed all, or the uncomfortable night's sleep made them even less willing to comply.

James roused from his slumber and sat up. Noticing Mia, he dropped back down again without saying a word. It seemed to Mia that he was still going the silent route. "Do you want the good news or the bad news?" she asked.

This caught James's attention slightly, but still not as much as she'd hoped. In truth, she'd considered the idea of keeping James in the dark and not revealing the new developments to him. However, it was a chance to gauge his reaction. If James thought that the FBI might be hunting someone else for these murders, it might get him to open up a little more. It might give him a reason to talk. In his mind, freedom was a possibility again. Hope was the catalyst to a confession, she believed.

James sat up and perched himself on the edge of his bed. He clasped his hands together and stared the floor.

"There's been a fourth victim. Slashed and strung up in a tree, just like the others."

Then his reaction changed. A brief look of confusion spread across his face. Mia saw it, if only for a millisecond or two. James must have realized and dropped it. He was playing a game. Mia knew that for sure.

James shrugged.

"So, that means one of two things," Mia continued. "Either you're not responsible for these murders or you have someone helping you. Care to tell me which one it is?"

James shook his head. *Goddamn, I'm giving him a chance to declare his innocence and he's not taking it.* The frustration made her want to slam her hand against the metal bars. What the hell was going on with this guy?

"If I was a betting woman, I'd guess it was the latter," Mia said. "I believe you've got someone else working with you. Someone like you couldn't do all this alone so you had to commandeer the assistance of someone more capable than you. Am I right?"

James sat back against the far wall and pulled a sheet around his shoulders. He stared up at the tiny window which was now letting in a beam of light.

"Either way, James, any scenario is good for you. Yesterday, you were looking at life imprisonment. But now, you could be looking at a reduced sentence if you testify against this accomplice of yours. Twenty-eight years, maybe less. What about that?"

It was no use. James wasn't going to say a word. They'd have to do this without his conformity. She decided to try one last approach.

"Or we can do this the hard way. When we find this accomplice of yours, and judging by what we've found on your phone, we will, we'll put you both behind bars until the day you die. Does that sound more appealing?"

A smile spread across his face. Mia recognized it. It was the manipulation smile. The pretend smile. He was trying to give the impression they were missing a crucial part of the puzzle, but in most cases, they weren't. It was often a last-ditch effort to send investigators down the wrong path.

"Fine. We'll do this your way. Know anyone named Stephen Treen?"

James looked at her and narrowed his eyes. Once again, he looked confused. Mia read the micro-signals. The curvature beneath the eyes, the pursed lips, the flared nostrils, the furrowed brow.

Mia didn't like what she saw.

"How about Abigail Treen? Ring any bells?"

The same look, interspersed with a look of indifference. Mia had stood opposite countless manipulators in her time, and even the best ones always gave something away. That was the beauty of body language. It could scarcely be controlled by the conscious mind. There was always a glimmer of truth hiding amid the performance.

But there was none of that with James.

Mia banged the bars to signify her exit. She returned the way she came and left James as she'd found him. Cold, silent, and unwilling to share even the slightest bit of information. Here's hoping that the tech department had found something on his or Stephen's phone, because if there was something Mia was certain of, it was that James Newark had no idea who this new victim was.

***

Ella sat in their office at the precinct. In front of her was a laptop and around a hundred pages of printed paper. Photographs, text messages, email threads, phone numbers, contact names. The entire contents of James Newark's phone were sitting in front of her.

The door opened up and Agent Ripley walked in. She headed straight for her own desk and sat down. She pulled off her glasses, threw them down and rubbed her eyes with her fingertips. Not a good sign.

"Still nothing?" Ella asked. She was hoping maybe Mia had some kind of magic track; a mental hack that could force James Newark to comply. Wishful thinking.

"Still nothing," Mia confirmed. "Quieter than a graveyard. I presented him with the new developments, and he seemed disinterested."

"He didn't even respond?"

"No. Judging by his expressions, he doesn't know anything about Stephen Treen. Either the person or the fact he's dead. So, like I said, we should assume we're dealing with a completely different unsub altogether."

It wasn't what Ella wanted to hear, but the truth was sometimes a bitter pill to swallow. "Well, if it was an accomplice of James's, then we've got our work cut out for us."

Mia reached over and grabbed a few of the pages littering Ella's desk. "This is all from his phone?"

"Yeah. It looks like our suspect was a popular guy."

There were photographs of James arm-in-arm with hundreds of other artist types. There were photos of him at galleries and performances and parties. There were selfies with friends. Guys and girls of every age and race.

"Who'd have thought a shit weasel like him would have friends," said Mia.

"It's a double-edged sword. On the one hand, we have some potential allies to look into. On the other hand, we have a *lot* of people to check out." The idea of investigating and interviewing all of these new people knocked the wind out of her sails. It could take months to get through them all. She could be stuck in Seattle until the summer. And what after that? What if she had to return to D.C. with no answers? With more questions than when they arrived?

"Get all the officers we can checking these people out," Mia said. "Dial every number on his calls list. Run these photos through image-recognition software. Check every text message, every email. "

"We are," Ella said. "We've got five officers going through them right now, but they've barely made a dent in them. They've uncovered a handful of names so far but a lot of them are pulling up zero matches on the police database."

The door opened with a slam and Brooks jumped in. Mia spoke before he could.

"Sheriff, we need as many officers checking out this data as you can spare. Our suspect could have an accomplice out there and if he does, his name is going to be somewhere on this phone. We need to find it."

Brooks held up his hands in defeat. He looked drained. "I've spared every officer I can. I know this is a priority, but we have other cases ongoing too. I can't just give you my whole team."

"At this rate we'll be spending the new year here," Mia said.

"What do you want me to do?" Brooks asked. "I'll have more men available sporadically but that's the best I can do." He left the room and disappeared from view, probably to avoid Mia's questions.

"We're going to drown in all this, aren't we?" Ella asked.

"Maybe we could get some people in D.C. to help out," Mia said. "James could have had galleries all over the country. Or he might have visited other people's performances across state lines."

"Possibly," said Ella.

"So, we might not have any luck searching for them on Seattle databases because they're in other states. We should run some of the images through VICAP and see what they pick up. It'll first pick up on any associates of his with criminal records. That could be a good start."

Mia stopped abruptly and stared at her phone. It was buzzing with an incoming call. Ella saw the name *William Edis* flashing on her screen. Ella saw Mia's face drop.

"Won't be a second," Mia said. She took the call in the hallway outside. Maybe Edis was just checking how the investigation was going, Ella thought. Maybe he was just looking for an update. For whatever reason, Ella couldn't focus. What was so important that Mia had to talk to the FBI director out of earshot? They were in this together, weren't they?

Ella used the moment alone to scour through the photos laid out in front of her. She considered organizing them in some fashion, maybe by height, race, gender, hair color. What that even help? Was it worth it?

She quickly decided it would be a waste of time, instead focusing on one person at a time. She pulled a picture of James arm-in-arm with an older man in front of her. No one she recognized. As she stared his face, her mind began to wander. She found herself thinking not of James, or the photograph stranger, but of Mia outside. Just as she shook the thought off, the office door sounded.

Mia came back, a look of trepidation across her face. Ella rarely saw that look. Even at their most desperate, Ella never saw Mia like that.

Ella couldn't help herself. It wasn't her business, but she needed to know. "What was that about?" she asked.

"Nothing. Don't worry about it. Focus on this."

Ella nodded hesitantly, instantly knowing that something was amiss. "I'll pass some of this along to some of the guys in D.C. to see if they can help," she said.

Mia sat staring at her phone. She scrolled through something then discarded it on the table with force.

"I need some fresh air," Ella continued. She grabbed her phone off the table and stuffed it into her pocket.

What did Edis want? She had to know.

CHAPTER TWENTY FIVE

Ella stood at the main road beside the precinct, phone in hand. It was nice to take a minute for herself and watch the ebb and flow of life, but despite the welcome interval, she was beginning to hate this city. She sat on a bench, the same one where she'd sat with Dax and thought about how wrong she'd been to think he was their culprit. There'd been so many developments since her altercation with him that it felt like months ago that it happened.

She scrolled through her email to find one from the FBI director. Despite the chilly breeze, sweat formed on her hands. She hovered her finger over the director's number and herself shaking with nervousness.

Was she stupid to do this? Was it even any of her business? Could Edis and Ripley be working together on something outside of this case? Something that didn't involve her? It wasn't a stretch to think that the FBI director and an elite field agent would need regular contact.

No, if something was going on, she deserved to know. If she didn't, she'd constantly worry about it and it would affect her performance. Or she could ask Mia if it was safe to call him first?

Better to ask for forgiveness than permission, Ella thought. Besides, every time Ella had asked for permission to do something, Mia usually declined.

Ella clicked his mobile number in his signature. It started to ring.

"Hello?" he said after four rings.

"Hi, Mr. Edis. It's Ella Dark."

"Yes. What is it?" His usual warm tones were nowhere to be found.

"Agent Ripley just spoke to you and she seems... not herself. I was just worried if everything wasn't okay."

"Okay?" Edis said. "No, Miss Dark. Things are not okay."

His voice began to boom. She felt like she'd rattled a cage she should have stayed the hell away from. "What's wrong? Is it something to do with this case?"

"Yes it is," Edis said. "I'm getting crucified over here. People want answers. The superiors, the press. It's a circus. And guess who gets the brunt of it all? Me."

"I'm sorry, sir. We found a very viable suspect but..."

127

"I know, Dark," he interrupted. "I know everything that's taken place. I'm more concerned with how the media got a hold of all this. You have a body that's still cooling, and the papers already know about it. Do you know how this makes us look? The fact we caught someone and now we have to admit he's probably not the killer?"

Ella always found it strange how the FBI were so preoccupied with appearances. What did it matter what the public thought? She decided now wasn't the time to question it. "We're doing everything we can, sir."

"That means nothing. I've already had to tell Ripley that if there are no solid leads in the next two weeks then I want you back here in D.C. while the frenzy dies down. Once that's done, I'll send some other agents to take a look at things."

"But what about the..."

The line went dead. Had the connection cut out?

No, Edis had hung up. He didn't want to talk to her.

It seemed that Mia had been given a tongue lashing from the director too but didn't want to reveal so to Ella. Maybe she was trying not to hurt her feelings.

She'd known failure before, but this one hurt more than anything else. She felt like she'd been punched in the gut. Mia had warned her that the failures far outnumbered the successes, but she didn't really believe it until now. Was this what most cases felt like? Would she have to endure this sensation every time she ventured out in the field? If that were the case, she wasn't sure if she could handle it.

The heavy traffic drowned everything out. She let it, using the white noise to try and alleviate the oncoming stress. Right now, she wanted to disappear for a few days. She wanted to take a break from being herself, to get out of her own head. Maybe that would help kick-start everything and she'd be able to make some headway in this investigation.

She should have predicted it. Catching a serial killer in a matter of days? If history was anything to go by, that wasn't how it happened. Sure, sometimes detectives got lucky and managed to bag a suspect straight away, but in most cases, it took years to hunt offenders down. Did she really think she was something special just because she researched these people? Just because she had beginner's luck last time? She almost felt like a fraud for believing that she could do this full-time. Imposter's syndrome, they called it. She'd felt it in other avenues of her life and of course, she felt it here too. Why wouldn't she?

When she closed her eyes, she saw the limp body of Stephen Treen hanging from a tree. A bloody mess. He was someone's brother, someone's son, and those family members were right to blame her for Stephen's death. Maybe if she hadn't been so adamant that James Newark was their killer, she might have been able to piece together the identity of the true killer. Mia was right. Don't go so fast down one-way roads that you miss the turnings. That's exactly what she did, and now there was more blood on her hands. Who knows if there were more to come today, tomorrow? There could be another murder every week for the next ten years and it would be her fault for being too confident, too cocky.

Her thoughts moved to her dad. The letters from the strange woman. How could she even hope to find out more about him if she couldn't even solve the cases in front of her? How could she dig up the past when she couldn't see the present? If she couldn't make any headway with fresh evidence, what hopes were there of solving a mystery from two decades ago?

Her phone began to flash in her hand. Incoming call. She pressed the green circle.

"Jenna?" Ella said.

"Ell, guess what?" She never gave a greeting. They'd been friends too long for that.

"Not now. Just tell me."

"Do you remember that guy you met at the club? Right before you ran away like a little bitch?"

"Yeah."

"He came round here looking for you. He wanted to know if you were interested in meeting up with him."

A few days ago, she would have loved nothing more than to see this gentleman again. Right now, it was the last thing she wanted. She couldn't bring herself to even think about it. The idea just exhausted her, like she wasn't going to be good enough company for him.

"How does he know our address?" Ella asked.

"Because I've been hooking up with his friend. His better-looking friend at that."

Ella wasn't in the mood for laughing. "Right. Tell him thanks but no thanks."

"Are you insane?" Jenna shrieked. "This never happens to you and you're going to blow him off straight away?"

"I'm probably going to be in Seattle for another two weeks. Tell him I appreciate it, but I'm not interested." She hung up and stared at the concrete beneath her feet. She'd dreamt of being a field agent all her life, but as always, reality never lived up to fantasy.

But if she gave up now, there'd be even more disappointment to come. Every time she'd read about these murders online, she'd be reminded of the grieving families, the widows and childless parents, the people she let down. Those same people were relying on her to get this job done, and if they had the resources she had, they'd probably jump at the chance to extract justice for their loved ones. Ella had those resources at her fingertips. She had the skills and the know-how. She'd already come close to the finish line and that meant she could do it again. Bad things sometimes gave the good things new light, and inside that precinct they had a lot of material to work with. Too much, but that was better than the alternative.

Ella rose to her feet and stormed back inside. The name of their unsub was *somewhere* in their files, and she was going to find it even if it killed her.

CHAPTER TWENTY SIX

Ella returned to their office and found Mia lost in a pile of paperwork. She appeared to have calmed down, so that was a small positive. She shuffled through papers faster than anyone Ella had ever seen do so.

"Feel better?" Mia asked.

"A bit."

"Word of advice, don't ever called Edis in the middle of investigations."

Ella opened her mouth to say something, but nothing came out. How did she know? "Oh. I'm sorry. I just…"

"Don't apologize. I understand. You're worried what the boss is thinking. It's perfectly normal."

She nodded, feeling a little sleazy for going behind Mia's back. "I thought we might be in trouble or something."

"When Edis scolds you, and he will, don't take it personally. He just wants answers. He's hounded by the big chiefs every hour of the day, and when he doesn't have answers, he gets it in the neck. Worst of all, he has to take it. He can't punch people in the nose like we can."

"I get it," Ella said. "You know how much I worry."

"Too fucking much. Forget what people think about you. You'll care a lot less about what people think of you when you realize how seldom they do."

"You think?"

"Yeah. Edis isn't upset with you, he's upset that there's a media shitshow on his ass every second of the day. Sit down and start trawling through this crap. Forget about everything else. I've got one of the boys to bring us a few brews. We're going to catch this asshole, okay?"

Mia's optimism enlivened her a little. She steadied herself and tried not to let the anxiety creep in. Mia was right about everything. Ella just needed to let herself believe it.

"Let's do it," Ella said. "What are we looking for? Where should we start?"

"Let's think about this. Truth be told, I'm having a hard time piecing this together. Whether we're looking for one perp, two perps, more, I don't know. But there a few things I *do* know, so let's start there." Mia stood up and moved over to the whiteboard. She grabbed a marker pen and began to jot down her thoughts.

Ella pushed out all the invasive thoughts and tried to think of the case, only the case. Forget FBI directors and forget guys at her apartment doorstep. This was more important. Lives were at stake.

"The first three murders were definitely committed by the same person," Mia continued. "We have no doubt of that. Absolutely everything matched and there were no inconsistencies in the profile."

"We profiled this killer to be an organized offender, capable of stalking and hunting his victims without them being aware of his presence. He plans his disposal site locations in advance. He brings the necessary equipment in order to display his victims in the intended way. There is nothing impulsive about what he does."

"Yes. So far, modus operandi has been consistent, as has victimology. He sees himself as an artist and these victims are works of art. As much I don't understand why, everything points to the person we already have in custody. So how could this same man kill from behind bars?"

"Because it wasn't him. That's the obvious answer," Ella said with a renewed confidence.

"Now, given that we have evidence against James Newark, I'm inclined to agree. The only other option is that someone framed James by planting the evidence in his house, but given how he refuses to talk, I sincerely doubt that. If I had to put money on it, I'd guess that James Newark killed Janet, Jennifer and Katherine."

"So, who killed Stephen Treen?" Ella asked.

"That's the million-dollar question. Who did this and why?" Mia drew a new column on the board. "What do we know about Stephen? The tech department found that the last call he made was several days ago. They found he most likely used an encrypted messaging service to arrange his meetup last night, which means we have no way of finding out who it was to."

"Shit. But even if that's the case, it's more evidence that Stephen's murder is the work of someone else. Like you said, our killer didn't interact with Janet, Jennifer or Katherine before killing them. They were surprise attacks. This person went to the hassle of arranging a park meetup with the victim? That's not something our original killer would do."

Mia nodded. "Correct. It's like they weren't comfortable enough to blitz attack, manipulate the body and then discard in the woods. He needed this victim at the disposal site while he was alive. That suggests uncertainty. Weakness."

"It sounds more and more like James had someone working with him. It must be a friend, since Jennifer was his lover."

"And he's got a lot of friends, plenty of which are eccentric artist types," Mia added. "So, going off all the available evidence, be it circumstantial or not, we can assume that Stephen's killer is someone different. You know I hate speculation, but given what we know, this absolutely *has* to be the case. There's no doubt about it."

"Yes. A thousand times yes. I can't see it being anything else. We have James dead to rights. The clothes, the weapons, the performance, the connections. Why did we ever doubt it?"

"Then we need to treat this murder as a secondary incident. If it's a different killer, everything else will be different too. The victim will have no connection to James Newark, but might have a connection to…"

There was a knock at the door. Both agents turned around.

"Here's your coffees, agents," a young officer said. He placed them on the table and backed away. "Miss Ripley, I put some whiskey in yours. Put a little Irish on it. We worked together on a case a few years back and I remembered your tastes," he smiled.

Mia laughed. "A man after my own heart. If you don't be careful, you could end up being my next ex-husband."

He chuckled as he left.

But something hit Ella hard, like a light switch had been turned on in her brain.

"What did you say?" she asked.

"It was a joke, Dark. Don't take things so literally."

"No, not that. You mentioned a heart."

"So?"

Ella did what Mia asked. She isolated the two cases in her mind. Suddenly, the answer seemed obvious.

"Oh shit. I think I know how we can find this guy."

Ella took a gulp of her coffee. It burnt her mouth, but it felt good. The caffeine hit her immediately and she used the buzz to enhance her voice.

"When James Newark killed Jennifer Hoskins, he took her heart out. Why?"

133

"Because she broke his heart. It was a symbolic act."

"Right. So why are we overlooking the fact that this new killer removed the heart of Stephen Treen?"

Mia considered it for a moment. "Because he didn't remove it. We don't even know if he tried to. It could have just been stab wounds to the heart to kill him."

"No," Ella said. She picked up the coroner's report between the stack of papers on her desk. It wasn't the official report, but a faxed copy of the basic information. "It says in here the cause of death was via throat laceration. If he was already dead, why would he stab the heart?"

"Could be a lot of reasons, could be none," Mia added.

"I think we're looking at this wrong. I think this killer is starting his own lineage of murders. We've been referring to this possible accomplice as a *he* up until now, but I think we're actually dealing with a woman. A former lover of Stephen Treen, to be exact."

Mia scratched her head. "I don't know, Dark. It's a stretch. And even if it is a former lover of Stephen's, it could still be a man. Let's not jump to conclusions."

"Look at these wounds," Ella said. She thought back to some of the female serial killers who'd stabbed their victims and came up with a very short list. "They're hesitant. Some of them barely penetrated the muscle. How do women prefer to kill?" she asked.

"Poison. Arson. Rarely do they stab or shoot."

"Exactly. The knife work is amateur, meaning it's someone who didn't want to kill but had to. Whoever did this is doing it to throw us off the scent of James being the killer, but at the same time, they needed it to *fit* alongside the other victims."

Mia sat back in her chair and held her pen between two fingers like a cigarette. Maybe she was subconsciously craving a nicotine hit, Ella thought idly. "But if he was trying to throw us off the scent, why wouldn't he – or she – just kill a random stranger? That way we'd never be able to connect them."

"How many female killers over the years have killed strangers?" asked Ella. "Off the top of my head, I can name one. Joanna Dennehy. Literally zero others. And could you really see a woman trying to abduct a guy off the streets? If we're going by the law of averages, most men would be able to fight a woman off. This unsub needed to lure someone she knew to the disposal site and attack him while he was there."

134

Mia tapped her pen against the desk now. "Right. I'm with you on that point. So, you think we need to look into Stephen's ex-girlfriends?"

"That's exactly what I'm saying."

"Well, what the hell are we waiting for? Let's do this."

CHAPTER TWENTY SEVEN

Watching James commit murder was one thing but doing it herself was a thrill like no other.

She'd snuck into James's apartment after the officers had been and gone. They'd taken everything with them. The clothes, the scalpels, James's paintings, even the cat. All that she had left were the memories of this place. The chair she sat when she'd posed for him while he painted her. The sofa they first made love on. The wine glass she'd smashed and then broke down in tears about. How dare those FBI agents come in and here and take everything away? They'd ruined the best thing she'd ever had in her life and she'd never forget that fact.

She thought that coming here would let her relive that high, as though this apartment was intrinsically bonded with her and James's murderous activities. But now that she was here, she just felt the same dread she had when James was first taken away. She had to leave. There was no point in visiting here anymore. It didn't even smell like him anymore and she could always take the memories with her. The window still hadn't been shut properly and this was how she made her exit out into the street. She had a key to his place but knew better than to unlock any doors.

Out into the open, she began to make her way to the main road. By some invisible force, she found herself walking towards the park where it all took place the previous night. The gates came into view and the excitement coursed through her like she was recalling a particularly memorable sex session. In a way, she guessed she was.

The whole thing was still cordoned off. Gates were locked, crime scene tape bordered the area inside. She'd caused that. It was all her. She kept her head down as she walked past the entranceway, noticing a few specks of Stephen's blood on the walkway. Goddamn, just the sight of it made her legs quiver. It was hard to believe that she was the one to create this mess, and not only had she created it, but she'd gotten away with it too. A part of her expected the cops to be hammering her door down within the hour but so far, nothing. She was a murderer hiding in plain sight and it felt like she was living out one of her many deadly fantasies for real. This was what real living felt like.

Two businessmen walked past her and stopped to gawk beyond the park gates at what remained of the crime scene. She eyed them up and down as her thoughts dissolved into a fantasy world filled with mutilation and dismemberment. She imagined doing to them what she'd done to Stephen, hacking at their throats, sawing at their bones, stringing them up like puppets for the world to see. The excitement came back as she realized there was nothing stopping her doing exactly that. Her knowledge and skills were more than adequate, to the point that she didn't need James anymore. Sure, he had the dexterity and the artistic eye, but who cared about that when the killing part was so much fun?

Her partners had always been the bad ones in the relationship. She was drawn to them like a moth to flame. Modernists would call her previous engagements toxic relationships, but to her it was all perfectly normal. She was an enabler of their bad behavior and always had been. When her ex-boyfriend was trying to kick the habit, she'd come home with bags of meth and leave them lying around the apartment. When money was tight, she'd encourage them to burglarize a store, ambush an old woman, steal their belongings. Living vicariously through them gave her the thrills she craved, but she never realized how much better it felt to commit these acts herself.

It was a new high for her. In fact, it was a world of new highs. There was a lot she could do with this newfound power. Who could she target next? A complete stranger? Maybe one of those snot-nosed businessmen behind her?

No. While it would be fun, there was no personal connection there. What she enjoyed most about last night was seeing the look on Stephen's face as he succumbed to death's embrace. How many nights had spent fantasizing about the ways she could kill Stephen, or everyone else who wronged her?

Now it was all a real possibility, and she knew one thing. She needed to do it again.

CHAPTER TWENTY EIGHT

Ella laid out printouts of every text message Stephen Treen had sent in the past year. They'd fast-tracked the job of digging into his phone contents through the tech department and they'd delivered within a matter of hours. Beside her, Mia was trawling through Stephen's social media profiles.

"Let's focus solely on the women in his life," Mia said. "By the looks of it, he doesn't have all that many. That makes things a bit easier."

Ella narrowed her eyes to read the text on the paper. Since it was a rushed job, the formatting of the printouts was quite rough. They were more or less walls of text that Ella had to assign her own conversation breaks to.

"I've got an Abby here," Ella said. "They don't converse a whole lot though."

"That'll be his sister, Abigail. Throw her on the discard pile."

"Of course," Ella tapped herself on the forehead. She rifled through the pages finding male names and strange aliases. She guessed that drug users sometimes wanted to keep a low profile. "Okay, next up is a Kelly. When Stephen talks to her, he puts a small x at the end of his messages. Maybe she's an ex-girlfriend? He talked to her a few days ago about exchanging a gram of angel dust, whatever that is."

"Another street name for coke," Mia said.

"Oh, hold up. They canceled their meeting at the last minute."

"Could still be something there. Put her on the investigation pile."

Ella did. She continued her search. On the next page, a certain block of text stood out to her immediately.

DON'T EVER CONTACT ME AGAIN, it said.

"Woah, hold up. Looks like we could have something here."

"Name?" asked Mia.

"Claire. No last name."

"What are they talking about?"

Ella scanned the conversation from top to bottom. It seemed to start mid-argument, as though Stephen had deleted all of the previous messages to her. Anything that was deleted couldn't be retrieved, not

138

without contacting the phone's service provider, not to mention it could take weeks before they produced their findings.

Sorry, I'm just not feeling it, Stephen had said.

As if you'd ever find someone better than me, Claire had replied.

This seemed to go on for several hours, with Claire responding to all of Stephen's comments with something unnecessarily aggressive. "Looks like Stephen broke things off with this girl, but she didn't take it lightly. She seems to take every opportunity to call him a loser. Ella passed the transcripts to Mia for her insight.

Mia pushed her glasses up and read from a random section. *"They must have circumcised you with a chainsaw."*

"She sounds like a bag of laughs. Here, look at this," Ella said. "She spent about an hour sending him pretty abusive messages but there's an error next to all of them. What's that mean?"

"It means he blocked her, but she carried on hurling abuse at him."

"Damn. You think someone like this could progress to murder?"

"Absolutely they could. When was all this?" Mia asked.

Ella looked around for a date. "Last July. Seven months ago. Maybe she's the type to hold a grudge."

Mia fell silent for a moment while she read the conversation in full. "I've seen a million women lash out when they get dumped, but never one quite like this. Who is this bitch? We need a name."

"If he blocked her phone number, he might have blocked her on social media too. Can you see his blocked list?" Ella asked.

Mia tapped around on her laptop. "I can, and yes, there's a Claire in this list. Claire LaRoux."

Ella moved around to get a closer look at this potential suspect. Mia clicked into her profile and Ella was taken aback by what popped up. Claire LaRoux was an incredibly attractive blonde girl with model-good looks with a figure to die for. "Are you thinking what I'm thinking?" Ella asked.

"Why would Kate Moss over here go for a guy as ugly as Stephen?"

"No. Could you imagine being this girl and getting dumped by someone who looks like Stephen?" Ella tried to phrase it without speaking harsh of the dead. "No wonder she went stir crazy. Something tells me this Claire woman isn't used to being rejected."

Mia scrolled through some of Claire's posts. Almost every day she seemed to post a picture of herself, and days without pictures seemed to have some inspirational quote attached to them. "I know women like this. This is what happens when an overwhelming need for validation meets a hatred for the patriarchy," Mia said. "I could absolutely believe that this woman is capable of violence."

"We've got her full name. Can we check her out on the police database?" Ella said.

"Yes we can. Come with me."

***

The two agents stood beside Sheriff Brooks while he crouched over the desktop computer in his office. Every time Ella saw him he looked more exhausted than before. Ella wondered whether to ask him if he was alright or whether she'd be overstepping a boundary doing so.

"Name?" Brooks asked.

"Claire LaRoux," said Mia. "Lives in the Capitol Hill area."

"That name sounds familiar, actually." Brooks murmured to himself while he typed in the name and scrolled through the results. "Are you sure? There are three women with that name in Seattle but none in Capitol Hill."

"Maybe she's registered in another city," Ella said.

"Could be. What kind of age range are we talking?"

"Mid-twenties. Thirty at most," Mia said.

Brooks shook his head as he clicked around. "Nope. All these ladies are over forty. Are you sure you have the right name?"

Mia rushed back to her office and grabbed her laptop. She showed the screen to Brooks. He clenched his teeth. The look on his face told Ella that he recognized her.

"Err… I think LaRoux is…" he hesitated. "Her stage name."

"Stage name?" Ella asked.

"I recognize her, but I've only seen her through my computer screen. She's a… how to put it. Adult worker," Brooks said.

"Ah, she's a damn porn star," Mia said. "That describes her obsession with her appearance. And maybe her dislike of men."

"Star might be optimistic. And she doesn't do men. She's all-female."

Brooks froze for a second, realizing he'd given the agents an unwilling glimpse into his private life. Silently, all three of them decided not to address it.

"We still need her real name," Ella said.

"A quick Google should do the trick," Brooks replied. He pulled up the internet and typed her name. The images at the top of the page quickly confirmed that Claire LaRoux was indeed an adult actress. Brooks quickly scrolled past them.

"Wait, what did that say? Go back up a second" Mia said. She tapped the screen with her pen, pointing to a news article. "Holy shit."

ADULT ACTRESS CLAIRE LAROUX CHARGED IN DOMESTIC VIOLENCE ATTACK.

"Ahh, of course. That's where I know her from," Brooks said. "She was arrested last year by the East Seattle department. She got done for battering her boyfriend. Total headcase. The boys over there were lining up to take her mugshot."

Ella wasn't sure if the Sheriff was trying to cover for his previous divulgence or whether he was being genuine. "So she's got a capacity for violence and has a link to Stephen Treen. That seems like a pretty good place to start."

"Real name is Claire Jones. I can see why she changed it," Brooks said. He searched her name and location on the database. "Got her. Lawrence Street in Capitol Hill. Are you agents heading there now?"

Mia ignored him and returned her attention to her laptop. She rushed back to their own office and Ella and Brooks followed. "I'm just going to do a quick search and see if this Claire woman has any links to the other victims."

"Ladies? You need me to come with you? Some back-up just in case?"

"No, we'll call you if we need you. We just need to talk to her," Mia said. Ella had to try her hardest to conceal a laugh. Brooks looked like the kid who hadn't been invited to the party.

"Okay. Do," said Brooks, backing out of the room.

"Pervert," Mia said. She slammed her palm on the desk. "No matches. Can't find any mention of a Claire in any of the victims' phones or emails. Nothing on James Newark's phone either."

Ella thought about it. "Why would we?" she asked. "This new killer would have no links to any of the first three victims, only to Stephen. The first three victims were James's kills. Stephen and onward is a completely new lineage."

This was the first time Ella had spoken aloud the fact there could be more murders to come. The thought of it made her feel light-headed.

Mia shut her laptop with force. "Right now, I'll take any lead we have. Grab your things. Let's go meet this woman in person."

CHAPTER TWENTY NINE

Ella tried not to gawk, but she couldn't help herself. They pulled up outside Claire's home and it was like something ripped from a rich wives's reality show. Two wrought iron gates led up to a brick driveway spacious enough to fit a 747. The entrance to the home was a huge glass porch that spanned the entire width of the detached property. She never expected such homes to even exist in this part of the city, let alone find one belonging to someone in Claire's line of work.

"I think we're in the wrong job," Mia said. They approached the glass entranceway and peered inside. "I don't even know where to knock."

Ella banged on the glass. They waited a few seconds. There was no car on the driveway and Ella was really hoping they wouldn't have to break their way in, although she was curious to see the interior.

A buzzing sounded. "Hello?" said a voice through the intercom. Both agents looked around but couldn't see anything that resembled technology.

"The fuck?" Mia said.

"Hello? Who is it?" the voice said again.

Ella decided to just shout. "Miss Jones, we're with the FBI. We'd like to talk to you about a recent homicide in the area."

"A what now?"

Judging by the inflections in her voice, Ella could already sense Claire wasn't the sharpest tool in the box. "A murder," she said. "Someone who we believe was friends with you was killed this last night."

"Who?"

"Miss Jones, it would be much easier if we could talk about this in person."

The intercom cut off, wherever it was. The glass panel in front of them clicked off its hinged and sat slightly ajar, inviting the agents to come inside. The agents walked through. Just as Ella shut it behind her, a figure appeared in the adjacent doorway.

"Sorry for the security measures. I get a lot of weirdos trying to get in."

142

Even in sweatpants and a tank top, Claire Jones pulled off a striking figure, Ella thought. She was enviably attractive, with slender legs and muscle forged from hours in the gym. Ella put in some hours herself, but some people just had those freak genetics that were greatly complimented by daily resistance work.

"Understandable," said Mia. "May we sit down?"

"Sure, come on through. Mind my dogs."

On first impressions, Claire didn't seem like she had a violent bone in her body. She had a calming presence, and a welcoming one at that. But if her work in the field had taught her anything it was that physical appearances were often deceiving.

They headed into the spacious hallway and Ella couldn't help but admire the architecture and design. A spiral staircase with silver handrails led up into the heavens while the wooden pathway beneath her led in three different directions. On a nearby table, Ella spotted pictures of Claire arm-in-arm with a number of celebrities.

Into the lounge, Claire offered them a seat on her white leather sofa. The room was a solid square of luxury with a fish tank taking up the majority of the far wall. A few pieces of artwork were displayed beside it. Ella wondered if she lived in a house like this, would she ever want to leave it?

Claire took a seat in a recliner chair and sat forward. "What's this about?" she asked, flicking her hair off her face. Clearly, she was good at keeping up appearances. She had sex appeal written on her forehead.

"Miss Jones, do you know a gentleman by the name of Stephen Treen?"

Ella scanned Claire's face for any sign of discomfort. There was a slight purse in her lips but nothing more.

"Steve? Yes, I know him." It took her a moment to put two and two together. Her hand smacked to her mouth. "Oh my god. Are you saying...?"

"I'm afraid Stephen was found murdered last night."

"You are kidding, right? I... can't believe that. Stephen is a wonderful man."

"Miss Jones, please drop the act. We know about your history with Stephen."

Ella saw something change in Claire's demeanor. Her hand dropped from her face and the look of sadness she'd adopted vanished in a heartbeat.

"Yeah, Steve was a dick sometimes, but I don't want him dead!" she yelled. "Oh Jesus, and you think it was me that did it?"

"We never said that," Mia said, adjusting her legs. "We just want to talk to you about him. Care to tell us about your relationship with the victim?"

Claire took a deep breath. She took a clump of her blonde hair in one hand and squeezed. A stress relief mechanism, Ella thought. She sometimes did the same thing herself.

"Steve was a fan of mine. We ran into each other a few times in the bars and clubs around here. We struck up a friendship and one thing led to another."

Mia went quiet, prompting Ella to take over. She was getting used to this give-and-take style of interviewing. It was good to share the burden. Plus, showing the suspect that there were two competent agents in their presence would put them under more pressure. "Don't think of this as offensive, Miss Jones, but what would someone like you have with someone as... unconventional looking as Stephen? Let's not pretend like you're not leagues apart."

"It's not always about looks, honey. Your husband is a model, is he?"

The question took her off guard. She'd never been asked about her mythical husband before, at least not by a suspect. She suddenly thought back to the guy from the bar and had images of him shacking up with someone new.

"No, he's not."

"Well then. Sometimes, people connect on levels outside of looks."

"You mean he gave you drugs," Mia jumped in. Claire went quiet for a second, probably considering her answer wisely. Few people wanted to admit doing drugs in front of FBI agents. "Don't worry, we don't care about that," Mia said.

Claire arched herself forward and nodded. She clasped her hands together. "Yes, he did."

"You slept with him in exchange for narcotics," Mia said, pretty much putting the words right in Claire's mouth.

"More or less. But I liked him too. He was different than the others. In my line of work, I hook up with shredded muscle men every day of the week. Sometimes it's nice to bag a normie."

Ella couldn't read this woman. A part of her seemed genuine, but there was something not quite right about her. Maybe because they were from completely different worlds, Ella thought. It was normal to

144

have a subconscious distrust of people you didn't share a worldview with.

"What happened? Why did your relationship break down?"

"Did it?" Claire asked.

"We've seen your texts," Mia said. "You were very harsh on Stephen. Unnecessarily so."

"Look, back then, I wasn't the person I am now. I was on a lot of gear at the time. It drove me to the edge. Steve realized that I was using him for his stash, and he ended things with me. I'm not used to being dumped so I went a little overboard. That's all there is to it."

The two agents swapped a look. Ella could tell that Mia wasn't buying it. Herself, she didn't quite know what to think. If Claire was an actress, and she guessed she was in a sense, then she was a good one.

"And what about your recent trouble with the law, Miss Jones?" asked Mia.

Claire fell back in her chair and sighed, like she'd been asked this question a million times already. "You ever been in a relationship you couldn't get out of?" she asked. "Ever been with a guy who tells you you're worthless to the point that you start to believe it?"

"No, but I know it happens," Mia said.

"My ex was a monster. I was his toy to do what he wanted with. He used to tell me that if I left him, he'd tell everyone in the industry I was diseased. That's the kiss of death for someone in my world. One night I decided I'd had enough and packed my bags. He tried to stop me, and I beat the shit out of him. If that's a crime then lock me up."

Ella began to think she had this all wrong. She even felt a little sorry for this woman. If everything she was saying was true, then she deserved all the sympathy in the world. She turned to Mia who still sported a look of hesitation. Beyond her, Ella noticed a few more pieces of artwork adorning the walls. Some landscapes, some classic pieces, Van Gogh's Starry Night.

And an abstract piece.

A flood of memories rushed through her head. Something looked very familiar. She squinted to see the full details of the piece, the broad strokes and the strange color theory. In the bottom right-hand corner, she saw the same mark she saw in Jennifer Hoskins's bedroom.

What the hell is that doing here?

Mia was asking something else, but Ella interrupted. She couldn't help herself. "Miss Jones, do you know someone named James

Newark?" She watched her reaction closely. Her eyes were trained on her like a sniper's scope.

Claire shook her head with a look of obliviousness. "No idea who that is."

"Then why do you have one of his paintings in your house?"

It was undoubtedly a piece of James Newark's work. It was a portrait of a very nondescript face; almost a color-for-color rework of the portrait he did of Jennifer. Mia scanned the room, landing on the same painting Ella had. She was awash with a look of surprise. Finally, there was a crack that they could dig into.

Claire shrugged. "I dunno the artists' names. What am I looking at? The portrait thing?"

"Yes. The one with JEN in the corner."

"A friend got me that. I don't remember who. It was a house-warming present."

"And you're not familiar with someone named James Newark? A local artist," Mia said.

"That's not my scene at all. I couldn't even pick a Picasso out of a line-up and you're asking me about some no-name local guy. No, I don't know anyone with that name."

Mia stood up and moved over to the piece. Ella went silent. She wasn't quite sure where to go next. Was this all an act by Claire? Was this too much of a coincidence to ignore? She was glad Mia was around this time. This wasn't a decision she could make on her own.

"I'm sorry, Miss Jones, but I don't buy your story at all." Mia crossed the room in seconds and stood beside Claire. She reached into her back pocket and pulled out of a pair of handcuffs. "We're arresting you on suspicion of murdering Stephen Treen."

Claire protested, jumping out of her chair and backing herself against the wall. Ella had already familiarized herself with the exits and there was no way Claire was getting out of this room freely.

"Arrested? Are you fucking serious?"

"Yes, I'm serious. Don't make this harder than it needs to be."

Claire backed away but Mia jumped forward and grabbed her arm. As soon as Mia connected with the suspect, she submitted and let Mia attach the cuffs to her wrist. Claire's anger turned to tears as she wiped her face with shoulder. Mia led Claire out of the lounge, through the hallway and out onto the driveway. Behind them, two tiny dogs started yapping at them. Ella shut the door, making a note to send officers to check on the animals in a few hours.

Ella watched Mia load Claire into the back of their cruiser. Claire buried her face in her hands, looking ashamed to be stuck in such a place. Ella was unsure exactly what was going on here. There was something very strange about Claire, something she couldn't quite figure out. What was going on with her? And what was her connection to James Newark?

At some point today, she was determined to find out the truth.

CHAPTER THIRTY

Claire Jones looked like a fish out of water in the Seattle Police Department interrogation room. Tears soaked her eyes while she suffered full body tremors every few seconds. Ella, Mia, and Brooks watched her from behind the two-way mirror. Ella turned around to find a sea of police officers gawking through the window.

"Got nothing better to do?" Ella shouted, surprising even herself. She was struggling to contain her frustration. A few of the officers mumbled something before dispersing.

"What's the deal with LaRoux?" Brooks asked. "Sorry. Jones."

"She has a history of violence and she has a painting by James Newark in her home. She insists it was a gift but I'm too old to believe in coincidences. There's something she's not telling us," said Mia.

"Should I get some officers to interview Newark to see if he's willing to spill anything?"

"No point. He hasn't talked so fa,r and he won't. Even if we're right about this, he'll just carry on giving us the silent treatment to throw us off."

"Understood."

"But you can get some officers to Jones's house in Capitol Hill. Find her phone and get it to the tech department. Fast-track a warrant if you can."

"On it," Brooks said and disappeared.

"Rookie, get in there and find out where she was last night."

Ella had a feeling this was going to be the case. Still, it was better that she interrogated her and not Mia. Ella guessed she and Claire were roughly about the same age which meant she had a better chance of building a rapport. "Alright. Anything in particular I should know?"

Mia didn't take her eyes off the suspect. "Remember that she's an actress. She can be whoever she wants to be. Just because she turns on the waterworks or tries to come across like an innocent sweetheart doesn't she mean she isn't capable of murder. Don't fall for her shit."

Ella heeded the advice and made her way into the interrogation room. Claire Jones looked a sorry sight; frail and downtrodden, but whether it was genuine or not was another question. The low temperature of the room caused goosebumps to form on Claire's bare arms.

"Here, take my jacket," Ella said, passing Claire a black hoodie. She placed it around her shoulders and took a seat opposite her.

"Thanks," Claire said through sobs. "I don't know what you want from me, but I haven't done a thing. I swear to God."

"We're not charging you with anything yet, Claire. We just want to understand a few things."

"I don't know who got me the painting, okay? I swear on my life. I had a house-warming party about six months ago and I received a thousand gifts from a thousand people. That was one of them. That's all there is to it."

There was desperation in her voice. Could an adult performer be this good of an actress? Least of all a lesser known one?

"And where you between midnight and 2am this morning?"

Claire's eyes rolled around the room then rested on the table between them. "In bed. Alone."

It wasn't what Ella wanted to hear.

"There's no one to vouch for your whereabouts?"

Claire shook her head forcefully, realizing the implications of her statement. "I did nothing last night. I watched some videos on my phone then fell asleep about 1am. My phone will show that, right? All the data will be on there to prove I'm telling the truth?"

"Possibly, but it wouldn't prove you didn't meet up with Stephen at some point."

"I don't know Stephen anymore. We're not friends. After we went our separate ways, we never spoke again. Check my texts. Check my emails. Whatever. If I met up with him, wouldn't there be some contact between us?"

Claire was right, Ella thought. But there was always the chance that Claire had thought this scenario through and prepared for it. A burner phone, an encrypted message through some chat software. There were plenty of ways they could have communicated without the standard text message or email format.

"I'm telling you. I swore off men after my breakup with my ex. I have nothing to do with them and I definitely don't have any reason to kill Stephen."

"I wish I could believe you, Claire, but I've got a seasoned FBI agent who thinks differently. If you want my honest opinion, then I'm almost convinced you're innocent. But you have a painting in your

149

house by someone we have in…" Ella stopped herself mid-sentence. Only now did she realize something, something she could use to her advantage. "Excuse me for a second."

Ella exited the room, leaving Claire alone. Mia met her outside.

"Rookie, what's wrong?"

"I know a pretty easy way we can determine whether or not James and Claire are working together."

The look on Mia's face told Ella that she was now realizing the same thing. "Got your wits about your rookie? You're gonna need a good eye for this."

"I'm ready."

"Stick her in cuffs again and bring her out here. This should give us an answer pretty quickly."

***

Ella and Mia escorted Claire Jones from the interrogation room, out through the precinct and into the adjoining building. She caught the eye of everyone she passed on the way there.

The idea came to Ella from an incident in France during the eighties. A string of homicides were thought to be the work of a killer duo, but eventually, one man confessed to being the sole perpetrator. Several years later, authorities discovered a number of other potential suspects involved in the case, and after isolating each one, they took . them on a tour of the prison grounds where the first murderer was incarcerated. Naturally, when the imprisoned murderer saw his accomplice passing by, he couldn't help but acknowledge her. This was how they found the killer duo.

If James Newark wasn't expecting it, there'd be no way he could hide his surprise from seeing his accomplice in front of him.

Ella led Claire through the row of holding cells while Mia stood back to observe. There were a couple of new folks in there, drunkards and petty criminals, Ella assumed. When they saw the two ladies passing by, everyone stopped and stared. But there was only one reaction they were concerned about.

"What am I doing down here?" Claire asked. Her voice echoed through the grimy hallways, drawing the attention of everyone in the row. Well, everyone except one person. They passed James Newark's cell and Ella saw him sitting on the end of his bed fondling with a

Rubix cube. He was dressed in his new standard-issue prison jumpsuit, making him look even scrawnier than she remembered him.

When their footsteps drew his attention, he looked up. Ella laser-focused herself on his reactions, looking for the slightest sign of any recognition in his eyes, nose, lips, cheeks, forehead, anything.

But James dropped his head again and sat back against the wall. There was nothing there. Just another passer-by. Ella struggled to contain her disappointment.

"Miss Jones, recognize that person in there?"

Claire kept a good distance away from the cell bars but peered her head forward, gawking at James like he was an animal in a zoo. "No, I've never seen him in my life."

Something about Claire's delivery led Ella to believe she was telling the truth. Usually, when people lied, they gave very brief answers. Either a *yes* or a *no,* rarely full sentences. But every time Ella had asked her something, she'd given solid, undeniable statements. *No, I've never seen him in my life.*

It was no use. Another dead end. There was no spark on either James or Claire's face. Judging by what she could see on the surface, neither had seen each other before. Back to square one, Ella thought.

Ella led her back through the cells the way they came, no doubt confusing Claire regarding their intentions with her. They met Mia at the door. "Anything?" Ella asked her.

"His micro-signals gave nothing away. As far as I'm concerned, these two don't know each other. If they did, one of them would have shown subconscious signs of it. I don't care how good of actors they are, they couldn't fake that."

"I'm telling you now, I don't know who that is. If you're thinking I slept with him then there's no chance of that. He's not my type at all."

It was a long walk back to the main precinct, so Ella decided to fill the gaps with conversation. The more Claire talked, the more they could glean from her.

"So, what is your type?" Ella asked.

"Women. But back when I was in the straight scene, I used to go for burlier guys. A scrawny little thing like that," she motioned her head towards the holding cells behind them. "I could make him do whatever I wanted. That does nothing for me. Then again, I guess some women like being in control."

Ella almost stopped where she stood. Something connected. Something suddenly made sense. "Say that again," she said to Claire.

"What? I'm just saying. Weedy little thing like that. Probably falls in love with any girl who shows him attention."

"Holy shit," Ella said. "Oh my god. Why didn't we see it before?" She stopped herself from revealing too much in front of the suspect. "Ripley, we need to get back to the precinct, quick. I think I know how all this connects."

CHAPTER THIRTY ONE

Back in their war room, Ella summoned in Brooks as she presented her thoughts. It all made sense now. She thought of history's most famous killer couples; Ian Brady and Myra Hindley, Fred and Rose West, Paul Bernardo and Karla Holmolka. There was a stigma around killer couples that still persisted to this day despite the growing evidence to the contrary. That belief was that the male half of the relationship was the one in charge and that the female was simply coerced into doing his bidding.

But the reality was that in most cases, the female was in charge. Myra Hindley encouraged Ian Brady to murder children.

Rose West was the driving force being torturing and killing multiple men, women, and children.

Karla Holmolka was responsible for just as many brutal rapes and murders as her husband, possibly more so.

They said the female of the species was deadlier than the male, and history's killer couples proved it.

"I think we're looking for a hybristophile," Ella said.

"Come again?" asked Brooks.

"Someone sexually attracted to people who commit violent acts," Mia added. "Dark, why?"

"Look at everything we know so far. James was wronged by his victims months ago, and he suddenly kills three people within the span of two weeks. Why would he do that? Why wouldn't he kill them sooner?"

"Because he was waiting for the opportune moment to strike?" Mia said.

"Possibly, or it's because someone else put him up to it. Someone else was pulling the strings during these murders, someone who James was totally devoted to. We've given James multiple opportunities to protest his innocence and he hasn't taken a single one. It's because he's not the one in charge. He knows that if he starts talking, there's a chance we'll capture his controller. But James is happy to spend his life in prison if it means this other person goes free. The same way Ian

Brady tried to take responsibility so that Myra wasn't charged, the same way Fred West tried to put the blame solely on himself."

"Okay," said Mia. "And? Assuming this hybristophile is a woman, how does this help us catch her?"

"Because we know how hybristophiles work. James's accomplice is not only sexually aroused by his acts of violence but judging by the murder of Stephen Treen, is devoted to avenging his capture."

"How do you mean?" Brooks asked.

"The first three victims were killed by James, probably while his partner watched or directed him. The fourth victim was killed solely by his partner to make it look like James was innocent. She was trying to mimic James's style as best she could but got it incredibly wrong. That's why there were so many inconsistencies. But this partner could have simply moved on and found another guy to manipulate. She could have left James to take the blame and she'd be off the hook, safe in the knowledge that James would never snitch on her. But she didn't."

Mia scratched her cheek and dropped back into her chair. "That's true. She didn't have to kill Stephen at all. It was an act of love. That means their bond goes beyond just sexual fulfillment. This partner loves James and he loves her back."

Brooks looked lost, like he was just waiting for the big answer. "Right, but doesn't that just mean we're still in the dark? We still have to search through all of James's phone records, don't we?"

Ella thought about it, hoping that her revelation might give Mia an idea or two.

"You're right, Sheriff. We'll still have to do a thorough search of his life, but this little tid-bit could..."

"No," Ella interrupted, suddenly realizing something new. "We don't have do any searching at all."

"What, Dark? Do you really think this partner would..." now Mia stopped mid-sentence. "Oh, hold up. I see what you mean. Well, it could work, but it's a bad idea."

"These kills were all very personal," Ella added. "This woman was systematically going through James's life and encouraging James to murder anyone who'd wronged him, no matter how long ago it was. Agent Ripley, you said something to me a few days ago. Something that stuck with me."

"Did I? I say a lot of things."

"I'm paraphrasing, but you said that unsubs who target the source of their issues are some of the most dangerous suspects to hunt. You said their psychopathology is complex and volatile, and they don't stop until the person they're targeting is dead or unobtainable."

"Yes, and what are you trying to say?"

"You then said that this sometimes stretches to the people hunting them. You said that if this suspect knows who we are, or learns our names, then there's a chance they'd come after us."

Mia's eyes widened in disbelief, as if Ella was crazy to suggest such a thing. "No, absolutely not. Never in a million years. That's not how you do this."

Ella expected resistance, but she knew that this was the quickest and most accurate way of unearthing this mysterious accomplice. "Why not? Do you know a better way?"

"Yes, I know a better way. We go through James's life until we find this woman. It's as simple as that. Rookie, you never, *ever* dangle the bait and hope a shark bites. Not in this game. I've done it before and every single time it's been a disaster."

"Ladies, mind explaining what the hell you're going on about?"

Mia jumped in before Ella could. "Agent Dark wants to make ourselves known to the public. If we present our names and faces to this accomplice, then chances are she'll come for us. We'll be the target of her rage."

"She'd do that?"

"Almost certainly," said Mia. "She'd do anything to exact vengeance on the people who took her lover from her. I'm not saying it wouldn't work, but there's a much higher chance of her killing you first. We saw what she did to Stephen. It doesn't matter how good at martial arts you are; you can't stop someone slitting your throat while you sleep."

"What would this entail, actually?" Brooks asked. "Not that I'm for it, I'm just curious."

"It doesn't matter what it would entail because it's not happening," Mia yelled. "Dark, I've lost a lot of partners in my time and I won't lose another one. Least of all one with as much promise as you, understood? Now get this idea out of your head before I slap it out."

Ella understood Mia's reluctance, but surely this was the best option they had? It could save months of leg work, perhaps even years. "So, you're saying we just have to trawl through James's stuff day and night until we find something? What if his partner's name isn't even on his phone or emails? What if they were careful?"

"Then there's nothing we can do about that. What happens if you go out there, make your face known and then nothing happens for a week, a month, a year? Every time you go to sleep, the last thing you'll think of is whether or not you'll be alive by morning. Then three years down the line, you wake up dead, all because of a stupid idea you once provoked a mentally unstable killer?"

Ella conceded. "Fine."

The atmosphere changed. There was confrontation in the air. Ella decided to let it settle.

But in her mind, she was already making plans.

***

Ella went and got some air outside the precinct. It was nearing 4pm and the distant traffic was in full swing. Up above, the light grey sky gradually faded to black.

She leaned against the wall and thought things through. Mia was undoubtedly right about all this. It was a bad idea to try and lure the killer to them, but the idea of heading back to D.C. with more questions than when they started was even worse. That feeling she'd got when she thought the case was solved was unlike anything else, so she was determined to chase that high again, no matter what it took.

Besides, it wasn't like Mia was always right about everything. Just because she was an expert in one field, didn't make her an expert in everything. Ella thought back to the last case when Mia was desperately opposed to her theories from day one, only to eventually conclude that she'd been right all along. Back then, if it hadn't been for Ella constantly pushing to get her ideas heard, they'd still be chasing the Mimicker in the Louisiana backwoods.

But because of her determination, they weren't. Sometimes, you had to stick to your guns no matter who it upset. Was Ripley even her boss in the formal sense? No, they were partners, and partners didn't always have to agree with each other. Edis needed this case solved pronto, and she was going to give it her best damn shot at making it happen.

The precinct door opened, and Sheriff Brooks walked out. He pulled a cigarette from his coat and lit up.

"I didn't think you smoked," Ella said.

"I don't. It's the only excuse they accept for leaving my office." He took a deep drag and exhaled. Ella didn't know whether he was joking or not. "You know, I think it's a good idea."

She didn't need to ask what he was referring to. "Really?"

"Absolutely. It's risky business, don't get me wrong, but this whole job's a risk. What's another one to the pile?"

"True. I just don't want to go behind Ripley's back. She's made her thoughts pretty damn clear."

"Yeah and imagine how she'd react if your plan actually worked. She wouldn't be so outspoken then, would she?"

Ella imagined the scenario. She didn't know exactly how this accomplice might reach out to her, but she struggled to imagine a scenario where she couldn't defend herself even for a second. It wasn't like she could break into her motel room, or her top-floor apartment in D.C.

"You don't like her?" Ella asked.

"She's alright, I just think she's mad at herself for not thinking of your idea first. You see it all the time in law enforcement. Veterans don't like newbies with their new ideas and aversion to tradition. It's the way it's always been."

Ella wafted away the second-hand smoke. "I guess. But anyway, I have no idea how to arrange a press conference. I don't exactly have those kinds of contacts."

"Dark, just ask."

"Huh?"

"We do press conferences every week. If you want, I can get you in front of a camera within the hour. You'll probably even make the 6pm news."

"Seriously? You could do that?"

"Sure, it's just a guy with a camera. It's not a whole host of reporters like the TV shows make it out to be. It gets sent to the news outlets after it's been recorded."

Ella knew what Mia's reaction would be, but she wasn't going to let this opportunity slide. She had to strike now while the iron was hot. If they left it any longer, there was a chance this accomplice might realize she had a golden ticket to freedom and flee the state.

"Do it," Ella said. "I'll be ready in ten minutes."

CHAPTER THIRTY TWO

The office was empty now. Mia told Ella she was going for a drive to pick up some lunch and coffees. Apparently, they had a lot of work to do when she returned.

Not if Ella could help it.

For the past hour, news channels around Seattle (and possibly the world, Ella didn't know) had been reporting that a major breakthrough regarding the recent murders would be announced at 6pm.

Brooks banged on the office door. "They're here. Out front. You sure you want to do this?"

"Out front? Can't we do it in a private room?"

"No. No TV cameras allowed inside a police station. Security risk."

Ella didn't like that. She wanted to keep this as discreet as possible, ideally fully completed without Mia's knowledge or involvement at all. Only when the killer reached out to her would she reveal how it all went down.

Ella quickly checked her appearance to ensure she was camera-ready. Sure, she was doing this for the case, but she still wanted to look half-decent. Was there a chance that guy from D.C. might see it?

No. She scolded herself for being ridiculous. That didn't matter right now. Time to focus. She grabbed a cluster of papers from her desk and headed out the front of the precinct. It was beginning to get fully dark, but the floodlights gave off adequate illumination for what she had planned.

But there was a problem. Standing outside were about fifteen people, not a single one she recognized.

"Miss Dark?" a man said, reaching out his hand. "Are you Miss Dark?"

"Yes, that's me. Are you...?"

"I'm with WBC Seattle News. These are the only reporters I could gather in such a short time. Are you ready to go right away?"

She suddenly felt a rush of anxiety. She was only expecting one person and a camera. "I didn't think there'd be any reporters here," she said.

"You're joking, right?" the man said as he set up a tripod. "Breaking news in a case like this? These guys will be all over it like a cheap suit. Ready to get going? Right here is fine."

"Aren't these things pre-recorded? The Sheriff told me they were."

The cameraman laughed. "Sure they are... when we do pieces about wildlife conservation and lottery winners. But a murder case? Then we're as live as the Superbowl."

The panic came. The crowd amassed around her, some with their own cameras pointed at her. She'd never done anything like this in her life and suddenly found everything a bit overwhelming. She composed herself, scanned her papers and put herself in the position of this unknown accomplice, hopefully watching somewhere from her couch. She'd prepared herself for a simple video in front of one person, now she was going live to the whole state.

"Give me the signal, Agent Dark, and we'll get rolling."

Ella checked her surroundings. Not a soul in sight and relatively quiet, despite the distant traffic. It made for welcome white noise, a good distraction from her own voice, maybe. Brooks guarded the precinct door so no one would interrupt. She quickly ran through the structure of the speech in her head and was happy with it. "Start rolling," she said.

The cameraman held a thumbs up to let her know they were live. No countdown like they did in the TV shows.

Ella recalled her old drama class days. Speak to the audience, not the camera. "Good evening everyone. Thank you for coming. My name is Agent Ella Dark and I'm an FBI agent working alongside West Seattle Police Department. We're here today to announce a breaking development regarding the case of the Seattle Park Murders. In the past two weeks, four victims have been discovered, all of which we have confidently attributed to the work of two perpetrators. As reported, we made an arrest yesterday, only for one half of the duo to attack again." She took a deep breath and scanned the crowd. Everything seemed to be on point. She'd all the right notes so far.

"Today, we can confirm that we've made a second arrest, and we now have both major suspects in custody. We have sufficient evidence to charge both suspects with all four of the recent murders. We were able to catch the second culprit so quickly due to a series of mistakes which he or she made. If anyone out there has any further information about these killings, you can find me or my team either here or at the

White Night Motel in downtown Seattle. That's everything for now. Thank you for…"

"Dark!" a voice screamed from beside her. It disoriented her. She lost her placing mid-sentence. "What the fuck are you doing?"

Mia rushed in front of her and held up her palm to the camera. "Are you out of your mind?" She moved in closer to her, their shoulders touching. "Why the hell would you do this? Didn't I tell you?"

Ella looked out at the audience. They still had their cameras pointed at them, no doubt enjoying the altercation. It probably made for great live TV. Ella didn't want Mia to ruin what she'd done, so she turned away from her and ran back into the precinct. Mia's thunderous footsteps followed. She slammed the door with a resounding clang.

"Ella, don't tell me that you've just announced to the world we've caught this killer."

It felt strange, going right from a press conference to an argument. "That's exactly what I did, Ripley. And now it's done, so there's no point getting mad about it."

Mia threw the coffees in her hand to the floor. The lids popped off and the contents flooded the foyer. "You've really fucked us here. You know that? Why would you do this without telling me?"

"Is this another of your hang-ups?" Ella yelled. "Did you try this yourself once and fail, and that's why you're so dead against it? Just like you did with my copycat theories on the last case? Because, newsflash, I was dead right all along about that, and I'm dead right about this too."

Mia stormed around the room, holding her head in her hands. "Dark, just because you solved one case doesn't make you a genius. Yes, I've tried this before and it failed. Do you know why it failed? My partner was shot dead right in front of me. FBI agents that do stupid shit end up dead, and you've pretty much just signed your own death warrant."

This was news to her. She had no idea. But maybe it was on Mia to inform her of these things beforehand? It wasn't on Ella to read Mia's mind. If Mia didn't communicate her feelings properly, that wasn't Ella's fault.

"I can handle it. And I didn't mention your name, so you don't have to worry about anything."

"Dark, if you'd have spent longer than a few minutes thinking this plan up, you'd realize that that's the thing you should be least concerned about. If anything, you should *only* have used my name."

"Huh?"

"I'd rather this guy come after me than you. If you cut out the dumb shit like this, you have a career ahead of you. I don't. I'm coming to the end anyway. If you'd have explained things to me, we could have done it that way."

"I tried!" Ella said. "You just dismissed it straight away. What was I supposed to do?"

Mia clenched her hands together and dropped them on her head. She turned around and looked at the reporters outside, now scrambling to get away. "Was it live?" she asked.

"Yes. It was on the 6 o'clock news."

"And you gave out your name and location?"

"Yes."

Rather forgiveness than permission, she told herself again. Ella knew this was for the best. Maybe if Mia had been honest with her reasoning, she might have considered not doing it. But she was convinced this plan was going to work. It had to.

Mia sighed again. "Fine. Here, take this." She pulled her pistol out and handed it to Ella. She took it reluctantly.

"I'm not licensed to carry one," said Ella.

"I don't give a shit. License or no license, sleep with that in your hand and for God's sake keep the safety on. You're too smart to get killed by your own stupidity, so don't let it be the case."

Ella looked the pistol over. She knew her way around a firearm but hadn't got the credentials to use one in the field. "Alright. Thank you."

"Go back to the motel. Stay there. There's nothing more we can do now. I'm gonna finish up some stuff here and head back too. I need a drink."

Ella nodded and did as Mia asked.

It would be the first of many nights sleeping with one eye open.

CHAPTER THIRTY THREE

The assistance of the minibar would calm her down and help her through this night. Mia Ripley sat in the lone chair in her motel room, gun in one hand and whiskey in the other. She'd given her Glock 22 to Ella, so she'd had to borrow an inferior Glock 17 from the police armory, but like her old man used to say, a bullet was a bullet. Any caliber could kill a man so long as it was aimed at the right spot.

It was still hard to grasp exactly what Ella had done. She'd put herself right in the firing line of an unhinged, homicidal maniac and didn't see it as a problem. Or maybe she was fully aware of the risks and willing to embrace to them? Mia found that there were usually two types of field agent, ones who jumped in headfirst and ones who assessed every single move they made. One type lived a lot longer than the other.

There were times when Ella reminded her of herself. At least, back when she was a new recruit. The determination, the passion, the willingness to do whatever it took to achieve victory. Maybe it was because Mia's passion had long since vanished and Ella was a reminder of what she once was. Maybe she didn't like it because Ella had everything she used to have, or maybe it was because Mia knew that being a reckless chancer awarded you an early funeral.

Edis told her it was her job to guide the rookie to being the best she could be, not be her boss. Ella was her own agent and, despite what their relationship looked like on the surface, was equally as authoritative on this case as she was.

Mia jerked the curtain and peered out the window at the few passing cars below. It was close to midnight and there'd been no signs of intrusion yet, but if someone was going to come for them, they'd come around now. One of the consistencies of this whole case was that all of the victims were attacked between midnight and the morning hours. Mia did not expect that to change, even given the specialist circumstances. In fact, it was even more likely if the suspect knew they'd be up against a competent foe.

She necked her whiskey and placed the empty glass bottle on the window ledge. If any intruder came in via that route, then the toppling glass would wake her up. Although given how she felt, she very much doubted sleep would come. She managed five hours on a good night, and tonight wasn't one of those. She decided she'd give it until 6am. If there was no sign of an intruder, then she'd get back to the precinct and get some work done. Hell, she could even catch a few winks in her office if it came down to it.

The lights would remain low, but she had to do something. Sitting in the dark with your own thoughts was a surefire way to make a woman question her life choices, so she grabbed the remote and turned on the TV. She skipped through the channels, finding mostly late-night panel shows and adult cartoons. She landed on the news. Not ideal, but better than the alternative.

Ella's face appeared on the screen, standing outside the police precinct. If Mia didn't know any better, she'd assume she was a seasoned detective given her delivery. Most people slipped up at least once during their first TV appearance, but Mia couldn't see anything worth commenting on.

The more she thought about it, the more she thought that once upon a time, she would have done the exact same thing as Ella did tonight. There was a fine line between bravery and foolishness, and it was difficult to categorize Ella fully in either one. It took a reckless mind to do it, but it took a bold one too. If anything, such a combination made for an ideal field agent.

There was no use being mad at Ella. While Mia would be the one to explain this decision to the higher-ups, she was confident she could spin it into something they *had* to do, not something they just wanted to do. First thing in the morning, she'd go to her room and apologize for her outburst. She just hoped that Ella had forgiven her too.

Mia sat back in her chair and closed her eyes. She gripped her pistol tightly, praying that at some point tonight, she'd have to use it.

***

Ella blinked herself awake, not even being fully sure if she'd slept or not. She remembered the clock saying 05:37. Now it was 06:00. Worst possible scenario is she'd been unconscious for twenty minutes, but in those twenty minutes, she'd saw herself tied to a tree, her raven hair blowing in the wind while a team of forensic offers took swabs from her lifeless corpse.

163

Worse than her brief hallucination was that there'd been no intruders on this night; she'd simply spent eight hours staring at a rigid door with nothing behind it. No signs of a break in. Nothing. Beyond the drawn curtains, daybreak was on the horizon and life was continuing on its merry way. Another day had arrived without any murders, at least that she knew of.

She took a gulp of water and washed away the sour taste in her mouth. Now that dawn was here and nothing had changed, she felt a surge of panic. Was this how every night would be for the remainder of time here? Is this how things would be back in D.C. too? Was she naïve for thinking that their suspect would target her on the first night? What would happen if she had to sleep somewhere unsecure, away from the security of bolts or locks or guard dogs? Would she be haunted by the constant fear that somewhere out there sat a murderous lunatic waiting for an opportune moment to kill her?

Ella rubbed the tiredness from her eyes and shook the numbness away. She tried to stand up but couldn't summon the energy. Exhaustion kept her planted in her motel chair.

Then something instantly quenched her fatigue. A bolt of adrenaline jumped from her feet to her fingertips.

Knock, knock.

Barely audible. For a second, she thought maybe she imagined it. She looked out of the window, seeing a couple of new cars in the parking lot. Cars which weren't there the night before. Two of them were rentals, meaning the owners could stay anonymous if they were savvy enough.

Knock, knock.

There it was again.

Ella clutched her pistol, pulled off the safety and slowly moved to the door. She peered through the spyglass.

No one there.

She grabbed the door handle and quickly planned her route. A potential attacker would keep themselves in the area with the most space. First left, then right.

She pulled the door open and stepped outside in less than a second, assuming the Weaver shooting stance and pointing her Glock down the corridor into the stairwell. No one.

Then to the right. A figure stood there, breaking up the motel's all-red interior with her black jumper.

"Didn't sleep either?" Mia asked.

Ella sighed and sheathed her weapon. "Not a wink, I don't think."

For someone who'd been up all night, Mia certainly didn't look it. Maybe she was used to running on no sleep.

"Look, I'm sorry I kicked off yesterday. I didn't want to admit it, but you did a good thing. It might not feel like it right now, but you did."

Of all the things Ella expected, an apology wasn't one of them. "Thank you. I'm sorry for not consulting you. Are we heading to the office?"

"No. Take the day off if you like. Catch up on your sleep. I'll get an officer to keep an eye on things."

She wasn't sure if taking a day off was a good idea but if she was playing the waiting game, was there much else to do? "Alright. Are you doing the same?"

"I might. First point of call is coffee, and not the shit from here. Do you want me to bring you one?"

"Please. Decaf so it doesn't keep me awake any longer."

"On it. Back in ten minutes. Wait here."

Ella watched Mia disappear down the hallway. Suddenly, the whole place felt a lot more claustrophobic than before. There were rows of doors either side of the corridor, yet almost no signs of life in the hotel beside her and Ripley. On her way back to her room, she listened through the doors for any movement, any early risers preparing for business meetings.

Nothing. Only the sound of her footsteps on the old carpet.

She returned to her door, grabbed her keycard and swiped. She welcomed the click to break the silence.

But when she stepped inside, she heard a sound from down the hallway. Like something had been dropped. She jumped up to the spyglass and peered out. There was no one there, and the dim lights made it hard to identify anything anyway.

But even so, something didn't feel right. Was it Mia's absence? Was it a sudden noise from another room, despite not hearing anything from the other rooms all night?

Ella clutched her pistol, moved away from the door and sat down on the bed. She kept her wits about her. There was every chance the killer could still come for her.

CHAPTER THIRTY FOUR

Of course, there'd be CCTV at the motel. Even a shit-hole like this would have the bare minimum of security. That's why she needed the disguise.

The idea of stalking the White Night Motel wasn't a decision she made lightly. In fact, there was still one side of her that wanted to leave it a few months, maybe a few years, until the attention around the murders had died down. Then she could emerge from the shadows, take the agent's life and the connection wouldn't be obvious.

But whenever she thought of her love sitting in a jail cell, the urge to kill the people responsible was unappeasable. And if she did this, then it would help dislodge the coffin lid cementing James's guilt. The press seemed to love the second-killer angle, and if that's what they wanted then they were going to get more of it. And with every new body, James would be one step closer to freedom.

All it took was some lifts in her shoes, some temporary hair dye and enough make-up to blur the details of her face. As she spotted her glassy reflection in the motel window, she realized she could easily pass as a sex worker. Even better. Few people had the marbles to question a hooker's late-night activities.

She'd walked the whole way here, not running the risk of having cameras recognize her license plate. She entered the motel foyer expecting to find a bored clerk behind the desk, but to her surprise, it was entirely vacant. A sign beside a bell declared *PUSH FOR SERVICE*.

That was the last thing she was going to do. She stood still and listened for any signs of life in the little room that said *OFFICE* beside them but could make out nothing. Maybe someone was asleep in there?

She pulled the bell off the table and stuffed it into her pocket. If anyone asked, there was no bell here when she arrived, giving her ample excuse to be in an area where she shouldn't if caught. Just looking for a member of staff, she could say.

Keeping her footsteps light, she skulked around the other side of the desk and peered into the office. Empty. Just a small desk and a flashing computer screen and a door leading to the outside rear. Beside the

166

screen was a leather-bound notepad. Huge. Too thick to steal and conceal. She scanned the first page.

Dates and check-in times. Every single occupant. Exactly what she needed. Fortunately, it didn't seem that many people had checked in here over the past few days, so she only had to flip back a few pages until she found the name she needed.

ROOM #334 - MISS ELLA DARK. NOTES: INDEFINITE STAY.

This was her. The bitch off the TV.

Room 334.

She hurried back around the desk into the foyer and discreetly returned the bell. She had everything she needed, but if there was CCTV recording her every move, she needed to brush off any suspicion. She put on her best exasperated face and scanned the room. She threw up her arms in a *where the hell is everybody* kind of look. To the untrained eye, she was simply a punter looking for a room.

"Hey," a voice said. She turned around, startled. A man in a suit looked her up and down. Short, balding, the wrong side of middle-aged.

"Hello, sir," she said.

"Everything okay? You look lost." His gaze seemed to be locked on her legs.

"Oh, I was supposed to be meeting someone but they've canceled. Typical," she laughed.

"That's a shame, a girl like you. I'd offer to keep you entertained myself, but something tells me you have other plans."

"Thank you for the offer, but..." she stopped herself. There was an opportunity here. She had to seize it. "Well, actually. Got any drinks in your room? I'm dying for a quick pick-me-up."

She watched the look on his face go from mild animation to feverous excitement. Pathetic. "Sure. Absolutely I do. You want to come up for a while? Sorry if this is all very forward. I'm here on business and I don't know the area very well."

"I'll be your tour guide," she laughed, *although I don't think we'll be leaving your room*. "What's your room number?"

"Uhm..." he checked his keycard. "Room 330."

"Perfect," she said, and followed the man upstairs. Luckily for her, he hadn't seen the blade, or the piece of rope concealed in her jacket pocket.

***

167

It was an easy death. A mercy killing. Clean and bloodless. She hadn't even needed to use the blade. After poor old Jasper had drunk himself silly and made a pitiful attempt at seduction, she'd used the opportunity to strangle the frail old man to death on the bed. He barely even put up a fight. That was five hours ago, and the stench of death was beginning to make her light-headed.

From this room, she could keep a watchful eye on room 334 next door. Whenever she heard a noise in the corridor she could be at the spyglass, ready to pounce within seconds. Between midnight and now, she'd heard a whole lot of nothing. No coming or going. Now morning was rising, and footfall would increase. Surely, the FBI woman would be coming or going eventually.

Tch, tch.

A trickle of life, somewhere on this floor.

She rushed to the door and peered through but couldn't see anyone. She pressed her ear to the wall and heard a commotion from one of the rooms on her row. At last, someone was here.

She opened up the door and peered down the hallway. She eyeballed the handle to room 334 as it began to shake. Someone was exiting.

She retreated back into the room and watched a figure come into view. Was it her? She could only see the back of her head. Hair tied back, around the same height and weight, undoubtedly a woman. It had to be. The agent wouldn't be sharing a room with another woman, would she?

Then a voice

She recognized it.

The bitch off the TV. Talking about coffee and sleep or some stupid shit. She couldn't see anyone else in the hallway. Was she talking to herself?

The figure headed down the corridor and out of sight. Everything went quiet again.

Time to follow. Slowly. Stay out of sight. Killing someone in a motel hallway was asking to be caught, and that wasn't going to happen. Once the bitch was dead, she'd come back and clean up here. Pack the old man's corpse into a suitcase and dump him in Thornton Creek.

She readied the blade and stepped out of the room.

CHAPTER THIRTY FIVE

Mia exited the motel into the crisp morning air, daybreak on the horizon. The front parking lot was mostly empty save for two or three vehicles, probably belonging to the motel staff. She'd parked hers in the overflow area behind the building, if only for privacy's sake.

She fiddled for her car keys, unable to find them in their usual right-hand pocket location. She felt that irrational surge of panic that always came such a thing happened. After digging around, she found them in her jacket pocket instead. Relief.

Mia pressed the fob and unlocked the car door. She told herself to relax. Maybe it was the lack of sleep. Even at her worst she got around five hours a night, and there'd been similar times when she'd stayed awake for 24-hour periods. What was different now?

Age. The stress of the case. The paranoia of someone tailing her. Lack of rest. Mental exhaustion.

Together, it all made for a hell of a cocktail.

She didn't know exactly what today would bring, but she didn't want Ella to leave that hotel room at all. It was way too risky. If someone did try and find her, being in a secure location would give Ella the advantage. Once the day was over, they could review the motel's CCTV footage from the past few days and look into any suspicious persons around the area. If they found anyone, they could then match them up with the pictures from James Newark's phone.

Maybe Ella was right. It had been a pretty good idea.

As Mia's hand reached the car door, she heard the sound of something scraping along the ground behind her. It came out of nowhere.

Mia instinctively clutched her weapon and spun around, pointing it at the source of the sound. There was nothing but empty space and a few cars. A soda can rolled along the floor, clinking against the gravel.

She went to sheathe her weapon but decided against it. It might be the exhaustion talking, but something felt off. A special agent always trusted her gut, and her gut told her that she wasn't alone. She could feel the warmth of another person nearby; a skill that Mia believed couldn't be taught. It was just something you either had or you didn't.

Then another sound. A thud this time, like someone had slapped the hood of a car.

It could have been a morning commuter. It could have been anything, but now wasn't the time to take chances. Mia hurried back around the front parking lot with her weapon drawn and searched every inch. She peered into the vehicle's windows and checked every seat. There was still no one.

To be safe, she pulled out her phone and snapped pictures of the licence plates. She'd check them out when she got to the office later.

Assured, Mia put her pistol in its holster and went back to her car.

She was two feet away when everything turned black.

***

Following the FBI woman was easy. Staying hidden was even easier. It was the attack that needed to be executed perfectly.

Down the hallway, she'd kept her steps silent on top of the dirty old carpet. The FBI woman had gone to the service desk and shouted out for a clerk. No one answered her request.

She watched from the staircase, using the small walkway to stay concealed among the shadows. Finally, the FBI woman had given up and moved out into the parking lot.

Peering through the motel window, she watched the FBI woman head towards her vehicle at the rear. Noticing that the entire area seemed deserted, she decided now would be as opportune time as any to make the move.

But she couldn't just attack in plain sight. The FBI woman looked sturdy, muscular, like she could definitely put up a fight. Chances are she'd have a gun hidden somewhere on her person. It was too big a risk to take. She had to strike and kill in the same motion. Don't give her time to react. That's how it had been for the others and that's how it had to be now.

At the motel door, she needed to distract the FBI woman. A Coke can lay at her feet. With her heeled boots, she kicked it across the rough ground towards her.

Distraction. Misdirection.

Back in the lobby, she peered out the door and saw the woman retracing her steps. Moving back, pistol in hand.

Perfect.

Remembering the previous night when she'd invaded the staff office, she did the same again. She pushed open the office door, praying that no one would be in. If there was, she'd just lie about her reasons for being there.

Empty.

Out the back door and into the rear parking lot now. She heard the footsteps of the FBI woman up ahead, searching the car park. From what she could see, she looked like shit. Her eyes were glazed red ,and she was slumped forward when she walked. That meant she wasn't in pristine condition. She didn't look anything like she had when she'd stormed James's performance the other night.

A row of bushes concealed her movement. She edged her way along, arriving at the passenger side of the FBI woman's vehicle. She crouched down low enough to see underneath, ensuring she was able to see the woman's feet.

And then she came back. The car beeped alive.

She moved to a crouching position and readied her rope. If she could knock the wind out of her straight away, the whole thing would be much less messy. That meant less DNA evidence left behind and more chance of escape. The blade was a last resort.

The footsteps came heavier now.

The agent was on the other side of the car.

Round the back of the vehicle, still crouching, she peered up and saw the FBI woman no longer had her gun drawn.

One last survey of the area. No one around, just the distant hum of traffic beyond the parking lot. None of the passing cars could see them.

And she struck. There was a moment they locked eyes, she was sure of it. But it all happened so fast. A few milliseconds later, they were locked together. She launched herself at the FBI woman, wrapped the rope around her neck and pulled so hard her the rope burnt her palms. Spit escaped her mouth and covered the car windshield. She gargled loudly and fought back, kicking and desperately trying to gain leverage over her defender.

But the life was draining from her. She felt a kick against her knee, almost toppling her off balance. A reaction kicked in, forcing her to slam the FBI woman's head into the car door. Glass cracked, coating the agent's forehead with crystal shards.

The agent's grip against her neck loosened. Her face washed of all color. Her eyes shut.

Dead.

171

If only James could see her now.

CHAPTER THIRTY SIX

Despite her best wishes, Ella knew that sleep would be a struggle. She knew that she'd just wake up every hour in a state of confusion until her subconscious had come to terms with recent developments. Maybe she could get some work done from the hotel room today. She liked the idea of spending the day alone somewhere safe and secure. After the past few days, she needed it.

Ella dropped onto the bed and let the exhaustion root her to the mattress. Her eyes closed and brief dreams began immediately. First, there was a car alarm.

Then the sound of smashing glass.

A scream.

Two voices.

Her eyes jolted open as she realized she wasn't imagining the sounds. They were very real.

Ella shot up and pulled open the curtains. She looked down on the rear parking lot and saw Agent Ripley leaning against her rented car. All that remained in the driver's side window was fragments of jagged glass. The rest lay at Mia's feet.

"What the hell?" Ella shouted. Confusion forced her to continue watching to make sense of this situation. Ella grabbed her pistol from the bedside table and hurled herself out of the room. She passed the corridor and staircase in a matter of seconds and found herself outside the motel. The sounds of struggling came louder now, a woman's voice, definitely not Mia's. Ella approached to find a young woman, bright red hair, petite but muscular, pulling a rope taught around Mia's neck. Mia's face was pale white but there were still signs of life there. Was it too late? Her eyes were glazed over, like she'd suffered a severe head wound. Concussed. She was out of it. How had this woman managed to subdue Agent Ripley? She must have blitz-attacked from the shadows. There was no way she could take her down in a fair fight. The sight of Mia in such a perilous state was almost unbelievable to her. She'd never seen her struggle in a fight, never seen her be anything but dominant. But here she was, reduced to her knees. If this woman could topple Ripley, what chance did a rookie have?

She trained her pistol on the pair.

"Freeze. Let her go, *now*" Ella screamed.

Mia's body fell limp in the woman's arms. They both fell back against her car. "It's you," the woman yelled. "You're the bitch off the TV."

Ella's priority was to get the woman away from Mia. She peered around for any onlookers who could perhaps help Mia if a chase ensued. There was no one. The parking lot was deserted except for the three women and two vehicles.

"Yes, I am," Ella said. "It's me you want, not her."

"It's this bitch, too. She was the one who stormed James's performance."

Ella's scope was trained on the woman, but her frantic movements made it almost impossible to get a clean shot. There was the risk she'd take Mia down with her.

Would Mia want her to take the shot anyway?

No. She couldn't live with herself if anything happened. Ella wondered if she could talk this woman down, but by now, she must know that her game was over.

"If you let her go, you can have me," Ella said, doing her best to keep her still somehow. If she stopped shaking, maybe she could take the shot.

But the woman laughed. "Don't talk to me like I'm stupid. I know it's over for me, but if I'm going down then I'm taking one of you with me."

There it was. The briefest of moments. The suspect held her back when she laughed, and Ella knew she had to go for it.

In her line of sight, she aimed for the suspect's shoulder; the only part of her visible that wouldn't result in fatality. The recoil jolted her wrists as a deafening shot rang out through the Seattle streets.

The suspect screamed loud enough to rival the gunshot blast, but still maintained the grip around Mia's throat.

Ella locked her sights in again, preparing for a second shot. Screw it, she'd have to go for a killing blow.

Suddenly, Mia fell loose, toppling to the floor. Not moving, unconscious.

Ella panicked. Was the best agent in the FBI dead because of her actions? The thoughts rushed in, crushing her head to the point of agony. It took a lot of effort to shake off the invading things, and when she did, the suspect was a few feet in front of her.

Ella fired at her, but the suspect strayed. A gleaming silver blade glistened in the sunlight, catching Ella's wrist and thrusting the pistol out of her hands. It dropped to the floor and rolled into the bushes.

More blade strikes came at her, hitting her shoulder and forearm. The attacks sent a shooting pain through her chest, realizing it was her body's response to sudden blood loss.

Adrenaline came surging. Ella dodged the incoming blade attacks, managing to grab the suspect's wrist and keep her hand locked in place. Ella dropped her forehead onto the suspect's nose, crushing the bone and cartilage within. Blood sprayed out, disorienting her for a moment. Ella tried to use the opportunity to ground her, but the suspect managed to bend her wrist, digging the blade into Ella's forearm. The pain shook her from head to toe, weakening her grip.

The suspect broke free and rushed to where Mia lay on the ground. She began to search her body.

"Where the fuck is that gun?" she shouted.

By the time Ella had composed herself, the suspect was clutched down and desperately trying to unhook the gun from Mia's holster. Ella saw Mia's body move of its own accord as the suspect violated her, meaning there was still blood pumping through her. It wasn't over for her yet. Ella hurled herself in their direction, not concerning herself with form or technique. She just needed to stop her from grabbing that pistol.

She dived, connecting her knee with the suspect's head. They crashed together against the side of Mia's vehicle, denting it and shattering one of the rear windows. Glass rained down on them both as Ella held the suspect down and wrung her arm behind her back. The suspect reached her other arm behind her, clawing at Ella's eyes with her fingernails. She kicked back with her heels, thrusting one into Ella's thigh. The suspect slipped out of Ella's grip, turned around and elbowed her in the side of the face. The blow sent Ella reeling backward but she managed to hold herself still on the car.

The suspect came for her again, blade readied. Ella felt disoriented. Her vision blurred. She tasted blood on her lips and felt pulsing lacerations along her arms and chest. She had to think fast.

A silver knife was pointed towards her. Her fingers gripped the car door handle, and in her desperation, she pulled it open with as much force as she could. The door swung, smashing the suspect in the ribs with a sickening crack. The suspect hunched over, spitting out a thick globule of blood. A sound of clanging metal rang out. The suspect had dropped her weapon to the concrete and fell to her knees.

Ella ran over and kicked the blade out of reach. She gripped the suspect in a rear chokehold submission so that her arms were incapacitated. She forced her down to the floor and held her face against the stone-cold gravel. Ella topped her, kicking Mia in the process to try and wake her up.

This time, she didn't move.

Ella felt the rage build. If Mia was gone, had it been her fault?

No, it wasn't. It was this woman's. Ella thought of the victims, Jennifer's childless parents, Janet and Katherine's widowers. She slammed her elbow into the back of suspect's head, ensuring that she'd be in no state to fight back. She resumed the submission, straining the suspect's joints until her bones were at breaking point. The girl screamed, pleaded for Ella to stop. Blood leaked from her mouth. The side of her face was grazed. A bullet wound decorated her shoulder.

"Stop," a voice said. "You got her, Dark."

"Thank God," Ella said, collapsing her grip. The suspect remained still. "Thank God you're still here."

Mia scrambled to her feet, unsteady. "Gonna need more than that to kill me," she said.

"You okay?" Ella asked.

"Keep your lock on this bitch. I'm still woozy."

The suspect began to cry. Her shoulder-length red hair blew in the wind. A cheap dye job. Recently done, judging by the leaks on her forehead. A disguise, Ella realized.

This was James's controller, there was no doubt.

Behind them, Mia clambered around. Ella couldn't quite see what she was doing and she didn't dare turn around.

"Bring her up," Mia said.

Ella did, raising her to her knees. Mia had the gun pointed towards her. Ella relieved herself, moving slightly back so Mia had a clean shot if anything went wrong.

The suspect clutched her hand to her face, smearing it with blood from her injuries. She reminded Ella of a child who covers their eyes believing it makes them invisible.

"Don't kill me," she pleaded. "Please don't kill me."

"Why not?" Mia asked.

Ella knew there was no chance Mia would shoot an unarmed suspect, especially fatally. But the threat of execution was a solid way to elicit a confession.

"Because I never meant things to come this far." Her words barely audible behind her clenched hands.

"Are you James Newark's accomplice?" Ella asked.

"Accomplice?" she screamed. "Accomplice? I was the love of his life. I was everything to him."

Ella and Mia exchanged a glance. That was all the confirmation they needed.

"Why did you do it?" asked Ella.

The suspect's hands fell down. "If I tell you, you promise not to kill me?" She struggled into a sitting position and raised her hands in the air.

"Promise," Mia said.

"I just like to see people get hurt," she said.

"And you want someone else to do it for you?" Ella moved closer now, realizing that this woman had all but given up hope. Mia did the same.

The woman nodded. "I can't do this. I don't want this anymore. It was meant to be just a game."

The agents were within touching distance. Mia pulled some handcuffs from her pocket and snapped them on. She quickly searched her pockets for weapons or valuables. All Mia uncovered was a piece of rope.

"What's your name?" Mia asked.

"Becca."

"And you admit to playing a part in the four recent murders?"

She nodded heavily. "There's another one in the hotel. A man. I killed him last night."

The victory was soured by this new revelation, but right now, Ella didn't have time to address it. All that mattered was this woman was locked away from the public. Mia unlocked her vehicle and shoved Becca inside.

"Keep her here," Mia said, handing Ella her gun. "I'll call Brooks in to take her away."

"Will I be in the same prison as James?" Becca asked from the backseat.

Ella sighed. "No. You'll be kept far away from him. You're never going to see him again," she said.

177

She looked a sorry sight, this Becca woman. Ella had to pinch herself to make sure this wasn't all just a sleep-deprived hallucination.

It wasn't.

She'd never felt so alive than she did right now. She'd done it. Made good on her promises. Nothing else in life could ever match this feeling, and despite her wounds, she was going to enjoy it. The world seemed different. The sky looked brighter, like she'd entered a new dimension had opened up to her. She knew right then and there that this was the life she wanted.

Five bodies and even more suspects later, the game was finally over.

CHAPTER THIRTY SEVEN

Ella had never looked forward to a plane ride as much as she had this one. The smog-infested air of D.C. was still six hours away, but for the first time in a long time, she looked forward to seeing all those familiar sights she suddenly felt she took for granted. On her way back to her apartment, she might even make contact with that Abe Lincoln statue that always gave her the creeps.

Mia was reading something on her phone. She clicked it off and threw it on the table. "We've got all the evidence we need," she said.

"What did they find?"

The agents had left the rest of the work to Sheriff Brooks and his team. They'd taken Becca Marsh, elicited a confession and searched her home.

"They found the organs in jars in Becca's house."

Finally. It felt like a weight had been lifted. Undeniable evidence that would cement her guilt without question. "Trophies. James must have given them to her."

"I'd say so. She confessed to being the one who put him up to everything. If James hadn't met her, he'd be a free man now. She committed Stephen's murder alone as a way to throw us off the scent. There's also a fifth victim. A 60-year-old man she met in the hotel. She used his room to watch us."

Ella's face dropped. Mia held up her palm to her. "I know what you're thinking, rookie and you need to drop it. You didn't cause that murder. You can't blame yourself for every single victim that falls in our laps. There's no rhyme or reason to serial killings. They just happen."

She didn't know quite what to say. She felt like the fifth murder could have been avoided, but if she hadn't done the press conference, how many other victims might there have been before they caught her?

"It looks we have them dead to rights. There's no way out of this for them."

"Thank God. I'm happy to go a long time without seeing Seattle again. I mean, it's a lovely city, but…"

The stewardess brought them a coffee each and placed them in their cup holders. Ella found comfort in the aroma. "No miniatures?" she asked her partner.

"Making a change. I'm trying to avoid the silent killers. You made me question some of my choices."

"Me? What did I do?" Ella was a little shocked. To think she could have any influence on Mia Ripley's life choices was unbelievable, and it made her feel amazing.

"Well, to put it one way, I don't want you to think that this is how it all ends. Just because I'm a twice-divorced witch with a drinking problem doesn't mean you have to be. There are plenty of agents out there just like me too, so there's definitely something in this job that drives people to the edge."

"And you're worried it might happen to me too?" Ella had been on the receiving end of Mia's well-wishes a few times before, but even so, she enjoyed hearing that her partner cared about her outside of the job. Not many people could say that about their colleagues.

"Pretty much. If I saw you in twenty years and you'd turned out like me, I'd feel like I failed. I've never been partnered with a newbie before, so this is all a learning curve for me too. If I sometimes get hot-headed, it's because I care. That's one of the worst things about being an expert in human psychology. You can see your own flaws but it's still hard to change them."

Out of the window, the Seattle buildings disappeared below the clouds.

"I totally get it. Looking back, doing that press conference was a little reckless. You had every right to be upset about it."

Mia took the lid off her coffee and took a small sip. She pulled her laptop out of her bag and set it down. "Back when I first started, I would have done the exact same thing, Dark. No question about it. You do a lot of things that remind me of my younger self, except you look a lot better doing it. Somewhere along the way I got tired and cynical, and I don't want that to rub off on a young upstart."

Ella smiled and sat back. "Seems fair. But right now, I just want to get home and forget about murder for a day or two."

"Agreed. I'm off tomorrow so you should take the day off too. We'll reconvene on Monday. Edis will want our verbal reports first thing Monday morning."

"Deal," Ella said. She waited a few seconds before indulging her curiosity. "What are you up to tomorrow?"

"Tomorrow's my birthday," Mia said. "Fifty-six years young. Two more years and I'll be the oldest field agent in FBI history."

For some reason, it didn't seem normal for Mia Ripley to even have a birthday. In Ella's head, she was born in her fifties and had stayed there ever since, despite everything she knew about her life story.

"Oh, wow. Happy almost birthday. What are you doing?"

"Nothing, and that's another reason for me to stay in this job. I don't want anyone else to be alone on their fifty-sixth birthday, least of all someone like you."

So, tomorrow, Mia would be alone. What would Ella be doing? She didn't know yet, but there were a few options. There was still the matter of the letters playing on her mind, and there was also an apology she had to make. She didn't know about the former, but maybe she could do the latter over a few drinks.

*****

Ella arrived in D.C. in the afternoon and was sitting the Milestone bar by 6pm. It was the local pub favoured by FBI agents and law enforcement. The kind of place that gave you free shots or a bigger glass if you showed the bartender your badge. Better yet, it was a quiet place, ideal for getting to know someone without the intrusion of music.

Ella sat alone with her phone in her hand, in awe of the abilities of the FBI graphology expert. She'd sent him a sample of the woman's signature from her dad's letters, and within a few minutes she had the information she needed.

SAMANTHA HAWKINS.
AGE: 54.
OCCUPATION: SELF-EMPLOYED.
LOCATION: RICHMOND, VIRGINIA.

All this from a single signature. The graphology software had found the same signature on a number of tax returns and legal bills within the past year, meaning this strange woman was still local.

Would she still remember her father? Would this woman think Ella was crazy for tracking her down? What if this woman had moved on, happily married and living in harmony with the love of her life? Maybe she didn't even want to be reminded of her old friend Ken.

But if there was a chance someone else out there knew her dad, she was going to take the risk. As she found out the night before, risks sometimes paid off.

The bartender dropped two drinks on the table. A Hibiki whiskey to take the nerves off and a Diet Coke. If she remembered rightly, he said he was tee-total. *One of those annoying types*, he'd said.

"Hey. Ella?" a voice said. "I know your name now."

Even though she'd only met him once, she recognized the voice straight away. How did people greet each other on dates anymore? Hug? Kiss? Shake hands? Fortunately for her, Ben took the lead. She stood up to greet him and he leant over and kissed her cheek. He took a seat opposite her, not too close and not too far away. He wasn't wearing double-blue this time. He'd gone for a nice long-sleeved sweater and jeans.

"Hey, thank you for coming. Sorry I took so long to reply."

"It's cool," Ben said. "I like a woman who doesn't spend her life on her phone," he laughed.

She scrambled to stuff her phone into her pocket. "That's good. I'd happily throw this thing in a woodchipper if I could."

"Love it, and thanks for the drink" Ben said. "So, what have you been up to?"

"Oh, not much. What about you?"

It was just a drink, Ella thought to herself. Nothing too serious. But then again, wasn't this how all the best love stories started?

She didn't really know, but for the first time in a long time, she was happy to find out.

EPILOGUE

Friday was meant to be her day to recover but Ella had been awoken by a message from FBI director William Edis. Something about its tone unsettled her, so she had arrived at the FBI offices just after 7am.

Ella ascended the spiral walkways to the top floor, finding the whole building eerily deserted. Most staff arrived at 8, but she always thought there'd be more people on duty at this hour. Through the frosted glass in Edis's office door, she could see the blurry outlines of two people. She knocked and entered.

Edis sat behind his desk. Mia Ripley sat on a chair to the right and offered nothing in a way of greeting. Beside Mia was a cardboard box.

"Miss Dark, please sit down," Edis said. He pointed to the chair next to Ripley.

"Okay. Is everything alright?"

"Not quite, Miss Dark. We have a development."

"God no. Please don't say…" Ella was half-expecting Edis to say there'd been another murder in Seattle.

"Dark," Mia interrupted. "Do you remember what I told you in Seattle? About the time I had to see the psychiatrist?"

Ella scanned her memory bank. "I think so."

Mia pulled the box onto her lap and opened it up. Inside was a pair of shoes.

"Oh my god," Ella said. "Tobias Campbell."

Mia nodded hesitantly. "Every year on my birthday. Without fail."

Ella cursed herself. She'd forgotten it was Mia's birthday, and given the atmosphere, she didn't feel comfortable wishing her many happy returns.

"But there's something different," Mia added. "This wasn't sent to my address. It was sent here."

"Right," Ella said, struggling to see where this was going. "Is that all?"

"No." Mia pulled out the shoes. Black Jimmy Choo suede designer heels. Probably close to a thousand dollars, Ella thought. "He knows I'm a size 7, but this year he sent a size 6."

183

Ella admired the footwear. She'd kill for a pair like that. As she thought about it, she didn't think she'd ever worn a shoe that cost more than fifty bucks. "Maybe he got it wrong."

"No, he didn't," Edis said. "Miss Dark, these shoes weren't meant for Agent Ripley. They were meant for you."

Ella had to stop and digest the information for a second. Something didn't seem quite right about it. "Excuse me? I do wear a size six but how the hell would Tobias Campbell know who I am? He's been in prison since I was a kid."

Edis and Mia exchanged a look that said they were withholding a secret. They both looked worried, even ashamed.

"Not quite," Edis said. "The FBI have had regular contact with Tobias Campbell since Agent Ripley apprehended him eighteen years ago. He's been a continuous source of information for us. He has contact with various networks around the country. Terrorist organizations, trafficking rings, underground heist networks, even other serial killers. In his free life, Tobias was a career criminal. A spider at the center of many webs. And even during his incarceration, he continues to be a kind of criminal architect. To tell you the truth, we don't know how he does it. He has informants in high profile organizations, including the police, the prison system and even the FBI."

Edis's words chilled her to the bone. This was all new information to her. How could someone behind bars have contacts in the FBI? "And he suddenly knows who I am? But how? I'm not exactly on TV every..." She cut herself off. "Oh. Shit."

"Yes, it's possible that's how he's become aware of you. Alternatively, it's possible he became aware of you through your work on the previous case. We have no way of knowing without speaking to him."

"Hold up," Ella held up her palms. "Are we just assuming all this? Ripley? Aren't we just jumping to conclusions here?"

Mia shook her head. Ella didn't like her unusual silence.

"He sent a note along with the shoes."

"A note? Saying what?"

Mia motioned to Edis who picked up a thin sheet of paper off his desk.

"Dear Miss Dark, I hope this gift finds you well. I would like to have sent this to your home address, but I know how bad the postal service can be in apartment blocks. I have something I'd like to talk to

you about. Something I think you'll find interesting. I'm sure your partner knows exactly what I'm talking about. Please come and see me at your earliest convenience. Tobias."

Ella's lips seemed to be stuck together. A million thoughts ran through her head. One of the most prolific serial killers of all time? The Executioner, as they called him. The thought of sitting opposite him was as terrifying as it was exhilarating. She'd be lying if she had she hadn't dreamt of talking to someone of his notoriety.

"I mean. I have to do it, right?" she asked. "How does he know I live in an apartment?"

"Dark, you don't have to do anything. I can't stop you, and I know you're going to think I have an ulterior motive, but you really shouldn't do this. Tobias Campbell might be stuck behind bars literally, but he has eyes everywhere. He has accomplices all over. If he wants you dead, you will be. You understand?"

Ella took a moment to consider things. Was this Mia being stubborn again? Jealous, even? "Then why aren't *you* dead?" she asked, her comment sounding more spiteful than was intended.

"Because Tobias doesn't want me dead. He wants me to live with the idea that he killed a lot more than we're led to believe. I told you, he gave me a punishment worse than death."

"Miss Dark, I have to agree with Agent Ripley. We considered keeping this information from you, but we thought it would be worse if something from Tobias appeared at your doorstep. And we don't know how he knows your living situation. It could be a good guess, or it could be a testament to his awareness outside the prison system."

Mia returned the shoes to the box and closed it. "Once you meet Tobias Campbell, he'll get inside your head and never get out. I can't say for sure, but I think he wants to talk to you about what took place between me and him. He's teased the FBI about it for years now, always hinting that he'll reveal something new and then never does."

Ella tried to imagine how their meeting would play out. Would she have to speak to him in the conjugal visit section or would she have to sit near his cell? The thought of being in the middle of a row of inmates, least of all one who'd killed five women, sent ice up her spine.

"I can't deny that it could be useful," added Mia. "But like I said yesterday, I'd rather you stay alive than solve a decades-old case."

"Let me think about it," Ella said.

But deep down, she knew this was an opportunity she couldn't miss.

185

NOW AVAILABLE!

GIRL, HUNTED
(An Ella Dark FBI Suspense Thriller—Book 3)

"A MASTERPIECE OF THRILLER AND MYSTERY. Blake Pierce did a magnificent job developing characters with a psychological side so well described that we feel inside their minds, follow their fears and cheer for their success. Full of twists, this book will keep you awake until the turn of the last page."
--Books and Movie Reviews, Roberto Mattos (re Once Gone)

GIRL, HUNTED (An Ella Dark FBI Suspense Thriller) is book #3 in a long-anticipated new series by #1 bestseller and USA Today bestselling author Blake Pierce, whose bestseller Once Gone (a free download) has received over 1,000 five star reviews.

FBI Agent Ella Dark, 29, is given her big chance to achieve her life's dream: to join the Behavorial Crimes Unit. Ella has a hidden obsession: she has studied serial killers from the time she could read, devastated by the murder of her own sister. With her photographic memory, she has obtained an encyclopedic knowledge of every serial killer, every victim and every case. Singled out for her brilliant mind, Ella is invited to join the big leagues.

After a woman barely escapes from the car of a serial killer, Ella recalls unique details from prior cases just like it.

But this serial killer recalls them, too—and he is determined to do the one thing Ella never anticipates: to stray from his predecessors.

The deadly game of cat and mouse that follows leaves Ella wondering: do her talents have a limit?

Has she finally met her match?

A page-turning and harrowing crime thriller featuring a brilliant and tortured FBI agent, the ELLA DARK series is a riveting mystery, packed with suspense, twists and turns, revelations, and driven by a breakneck pace that will keep you flipping pages late into the night.

Book #4 in the series—GIRL, SILENCED—is available now.

Blake Pierce

Blake Pierce is the USA Today bestselling author of the RILEY PAGE mystery series, which includes seventeen books. Blake Pierce is also the author of the MACKENZIE WHITE mystery series, comprising fourteen books; of the AVERY BLACK mystery series, comprising six books; of the KERI LOCKE mystery series, comprising five books; of the MAKING OF RILEY PAIGE mystery series, comprising six books; of the KATE WISE mystery series, comprising seven books; of the CHLOE FINE psychological suspense mystery, comprising six books; of the JESSE HUNT psychological suspense thriller series, comprising nineteen books; of the AU PAIR psychological suspense thriller series, comprising three books; of the ZOE PRIME mystery series, comprising six books; of the ADELE SHARP mystery series, comprising thirteen books; of the EUROPEAN VOYAGE cozy mystery series, comprising six books (and counting); of the new LAURA FROST FBI suspense thriller, comprising four books (and counting); of the new ELLA DARK FBI suspense thriller, comprising six books (and counting); of the A YEAR IN EUROPE cozy mystery series, comprising nine books); of the AVA GOLD mystery series, comprising three books (and counting); and of the RACHEL GIFT mystery series, comprising three books (and counting).

An avid reader and lifelong fan of the mystery and thriller genres, Blake loves to hear from you, so please feel free to visit www.blakepierceauthor.com to learn more and stay in touch.

BOOKS BY BLAKE PIERCE

RACHEL GIFT MYSTERY SERIES
HER LAST WISH (Book #1)
HER LAST CHANCE (Book #2)
HER LAST HOPE (Book #3)

AVA GOLD MYSTERY SERIES
CITY OF PREY (Book #1)
CITY OF FEAR (Book #2)
CITY OF BONES (Book #3)

A YEAR IN EUROPE
A MURDER IN PARIS (Book #1)
DEATH IN FLORENCE (Book #2)
VENGEANCE IN VIENNA (Book #3)
A FATALITY IN SPAIN (Book #4)
SCANDAL IN LONDON (Book #5)
AN IMPOSTOR IN DUBLIN (Book #6)
SEDUCTION IN BORDEAUX (Book #7)
JEALOUSY IN SWITZERLAND (Book #8)
A DEBACLE IN PRAGUE (Book #9)

ELLA DARK FBI SUSPENSE THRILLER
GIRL, ALONE (Book #1)
GIRL, TAKEN (Book #2)
GIRL, HUNTED (Book #3)
GIRL, SILENCED (Book #4)
GIRL, VANISHED (Book 5)
GIRL ERASED (Book #6)

LAURA FROST FBI SUSPENSE THRILLER
ALREADY GONE (Book #1)
ALREADY SEEN (Book #2)
ALREADY TRAPPED (Book #3)
ALREADY MISSING (Book #4)

EUROPEAN VOYAGE COZY MYSTERY SERIES

MURDER (AND BAKLAVA) (Book #1)
DEATH (AND APPLE STRUDEL) (Book #2)
CRIME (AND LAGER) (Book #3)
MISFORTUNE (AND GOUDA) (Book #4)
CALAMITY (AND A DANISH) (Book #5)
MAYHEM (AND HERRING) (Book #6)

ADELE SHARP MYSTERY SERIES
LEFT TO DIE (Book #1)
LEFT TO RUN (Book #2)
LEFT TO HIDE (Book #3)
LEFT TO KILL (Book #4)
LEFT TO MURDER (Book #5)
LEFT TO ENVY (Book #6)
LEFT TO LAPSE (Book #7)
LEFT TO VANISH (Book #8)
LEFT TO HUNT (Book #9)
LEFT TO FEAR (Book #10)
LEFT TO PREY (Book #11)
LEFT TO LURE (Book #12)
LEFT TO CRAVE (Book #13)

THE AU PAIR SERIES
ALMOST GONE (Book#1)
ALMOST LOST (Book #2)
ALMOST DEAD (Book #3)

ZOE PRIME MYSTERY SERIES
FACE OF DEATH (Book#1)
FACE OF MURDER (Book #2)
FACE OF FEAR (Book #3)
FACE OF MADNESS (Book #4)
FACE OF FURY (Book #5)
FACE OF DARKNESS (Book #6)

A JESSIE HUNT PSYCHOLOGICAL SUSPENSE SERIES
THE PERFECT WIFE (Book #1)
THE PERFECT BLOCK (Book #2)
THE PERFECT HOUSE (Book #3)
THE PERFECT SMILE (Book #4)

Made in United States
North Haven, CT
30 March 2024

50673570R10125